Love in the Time of Taffeta

By Eugénie Olson

Love in the Time of Taffeta
The Pajama Game
Babe in Toyland

Love in the Time of Taffeta

Eugénie Olson

An Imprint of HarperCollins*Publishers*

HarperCollins books may be purchased for educational, business, or sales promotional use. For information please write: Special Markets Department, HarperCollins Publishers Inc., 10 East 53rd Street, New York, NY 10022.

FIRST EDITION

Interior text designed by Elizabeth M. Glover

Library of Congress Cataloging-in-Publication Data

Olson, Eugénie Seifer.
Love in the time of taffeta / by Eugénie Olson.—1st ed.
p. cm.
ISBN-13: 978-0-06-081544-8
ISBN-10: 0-06-081544-2 (acid-free paper)
1. Women photographers—Fiction. 2. Proms—Fiction. I. Title.

PS3615.L74L68 2006
813'.6—dc22 2005019401

06 07 08 09 10 JTC/RRD 10 9 8 7 6 5 4 3 2 1

For Betty
1931–2005

Acknowledgments

Stacey Glick, Lucia Macro, Les and Amy Seifer, Ben Seifer, John and Julie Cargill, the Olsons, the Allisons, Meredith Obst. Special thanks to my editor, Kelly Harms, whose passion for Iley was exhilarating; and, as always, to my husband, David, whose love and encouragement keep me going.

sisu (*sih*-shoo)—n. Finnish word that describes a combination of special strength, courage, and determination that is held in reserve for moments of adversity or hard times.

One

There are few things more annoying than hanging up frame samples at the end of the day. Well, I suppose I can come up with some: listening to a friend complain about how her new diet causes breath like a camel's; filling a Laundromat washing machine with clothes and detergent, only to learn that it's broken; dropping blush on a tiled bathroom floor and watching it crack into a dozen pieces. But at six o'clock on a Tuesday, I am having a difficult time imagining any of these fates, because I am singularly focused on placing every one of these samples on tiny, spindly pegs. Chrome samples to the left, brass ones to the right. Wood ones on the opposite side, from stark and spare to ostentatious and ornate, marching from left to right across the seafoam green wall.

"Hey, those don't look very tidy," brays Andrew, my manager. He is on his way out the door and is sporting a lumpy, Members Only-style jacket the color of desiccated dog shit.

"*You* don't look very tidy," I mutter under my breath as I accidentally drop a gray-speckled sample to the floor.

"What?" he asks sharply, folding his arms in front of his chest and squishing his vinyl lunch sack under his left armpit. I pick up the sample, reach over the counter, and haphazardly hook it over an empty peg, so it sits between a glossy, gray sample and a matte, green-speckled sample. "That one doesn't go there," he says, shaking his head and looking at me with mild disgust. "God, Iley, take some pride in what you're doing here." He reaches over and straightens a few of the more crooked samples that I've been hurriedly throwing on the wall during the last fifteen minutes. One of them, a pale yellow number with fake gold engraved curlicues, falls off the wall the moment he touches it and lands silently on the tan carpet. "This one wasn't even hung properly," he complains. In the time it takes him to bend at the waist, groan as though he's giving birth, and pick up the sample, I've decided that I've finally had enough of this place.

"You know what?" I ask loudly, slamming down a metal frame in an eye-popping shade of tangerine. The tinny, hollow sound of metal hitting the countertop sends a little shiver up my spine and makes Andrew shake his head quickly and involuntarily, not unlike a retriever fresh from the swimming pool. "I don't like this job. And I don't need this job!" I holler.

"Oh, yeah?" he asks, snickering.

"Yeah!" I spit, feeling the heat rise in my face. "I quit!" I storm out from behind the counter, miraculously sidestep a pile of framed prints leaning against the wall, and stand face-to-face with him. "Effective right now." I falter for a minute, then yank from the wall a thin, nut-brown wood sample that features inlaid, primitive-looking line drawings. Since I began working here six months ago, I've always thought the sample bore a striking resemblance to a boomerang and repeatedly had to resist the temptation to throw it across the store to see if it would come back to me. I hold it in my hands for a second as Andrew studies me with lips pursed, then hurl it as hard as I can. It does not return.

In the twenty minutes it takes me to ride my bike from the frame shop to my apartment, I morph cleanly and effortlessly from hero to goat. Those first few pumps of the pedals were infused with the kind of surging power that can only come from telling off an incompetent boss and striding out with one's head held high. But soon my legs grew tired, my feet weary, as reality sunk in and I was faced with the prospect of finding another job that might tether me oh-so-tenuously to my life's calling once again.

I'm panting hard as I lock my bike and make my way up the sagging porch steps to my apartment, which is really the first floor of a two-family house. Here in Brighton, home to noisy immigrant families, Boston University students slumming in off-campus digs, and single people in their late twenties and early thirties who have not yet found their way, the multi-family house is the prevalent style of architecture. From the exterior, these places are reminiscent enough of homes that immigrants, Boston University students, and single people may have spent some formative years in and left behind. But the interiors, all diced up into apartments via hasty retrofitting with cheap appliances, cabinetry lacking in ninety-degree angles, and plumbing of questionable quality, are a bittersweet reminder that you're definitely not home.

I pause with my hand on the doorknob. I can hear Gary moving inside the apartment and I know that he's hovering. Waiting with ears pricked, taking fast but measured breaths as I turn the key. I open the door and he greets me with reproachful eyes; he can't have intuited that I've quit The Framery, can he?

"Well, well, look who's here," I say as I set my bag down on a low table that's buckling under the weight of magazines and newspapers. Gary lunges forward and nuzzles my crotch, nearly knocking me into the doorjamb. For an Airedale terrier, he's especially outsized in body shape and personality, and the small apartment frequently fails to restrain either one. "OK, OK, we're going out," I say, and his eyes instantly light up. He sits still just long enough for me to clip on his red, twill collar printed with glow-in-the-dark bones, and we begin walking around the block. By the time we reach the deli, he's peed six times and hasn't offered any compelling arguments about why I should have stayed on at the frame shop.

"You see," I say, resting my hand on my hip as Gary sniffs an overstuffed garbage can with interest, "it's not like I was going to be making any contacts there or anything. It was a nowhere road." He gives the garbage can a nudge so firm that the precarious pile of rubbish on top starts to quiver and ejects a mini soda can and a piece of bologna onto the ground. Gary is on the bologna so fast that it disappears between his gums before I can even grab his muzzle. His interest in the Red Bull is minimal, which is probably best for all involved. "Besides, this will free me up to find something that suits me better. Something where I can use my *camera* at the very least, right?" I ask as we begin heading back to the apartment. Gary wisely chooses not to answer.

When we arrive home, Erin is crouched on the porch steps with a cigarette in one hand and the *Boston Herald* splayed out in front of her. It's mid-April, still just a bit too brisk to dally outdoors in the New England night, but obviously she couldn't wait to read the police blotter. Erin claims to hate the *Herald* lately, and I don't blame her. Its new format features the brand of screaming, insane headlines and blunt graphic design employed by papers like the *Weekly World News*. Exclamations like BETTER RED THAN TED (in reference to a conservative Southern senator who claimed that one of Ted Kennedy's bills was a thinly veiled Commie plot) and ONE IF BY LAND, TWO IF BY FLEA (a sensitive lead-in to a story about a mysterious flea infestation at a posh, downtown hotel) routinely march across the front page, making me twitter and feel depressed all at once. But Erin doesn't worry about such things; she steals the paper from her workplace for one feature and one feature only.

" 'Officer Hit in Face with Carrot,' " she begins, enunciating every syllable as though she's reading news to a national audience. She stops reading and turns to face me. "You want?" she asks, shaking her pack of Marlboros.

"Oh, God, yes," I say hungrily as I unclip Gary from his leash and send him inside with an affectionate pat on his fuzzy rear end. I can hear him sloppily lapping up water from his dish in the kitchen as I light the cigarette and inhale deeply. Ride my bike some, smoke some. People often express shock at how someone could do both, i.e., treating one's heart and lungs like the miracle they are and caring for them with lots of cycling, while simultaneously treating one's heart and lungs like a huge filthy ashtray to be blackened and weakened with chemicals. I tell these people that it's simple: I like to bike and I like to smoke. If that doesn't work, explaining that it's none of their damn business tends to set things straight.

" 'Officer John Banton of Watertown was crossing the intersection of Galen and Main Streets when something struck him on the left side of the face,"' Erin continues. " 'It appeared that a carrot had been thrown from a passing school bus en route to a Watertown elementary school. Banton suffered no injuries from the vegetable, which hit his left cheek and then fell to the ground. No one was apprehended, and the event was later logged as *Attack with Foodstuffs* at the Watertown police station.' Ahhh," she says, satisfied with today's entry. "Attack with foodstuffs; it sounds like such wholesome fun, doesn't it?" She stretches her arms out wide, shakes her wavy red hair, and stubs her cigarette out on the step. "I notice that Gary looks troubled today. What's on his mind?"

This is code, of course. Erin is well aware that I converse with Gary on a regular basis, but as skilled a listener as he appears to be, we both acknowledge that a creature who once ate so many unguarded Snausages that he needed to be hospitalized isn't capable of too much introspection. I sigh and bite my thumbnail for a few seconds, then take a quick drag before answering. "Gary learned on our walk that I quit The Framery today."

"No kidding?" she asks, her eyebrows disappearing behind her bangs. "Well, you hated that gig. All those horrible frame samples." She looks hopeful as she scans my face for some sort of reaction. Suddenly I'm exhausted, and I put my head in my hands for a long minute.

"Yeah. That place wasn't for me," I finally say. *So what place is?* I ask myself silently, trying to ignore the thick, nervous feeling in my stomach, as though heavy cogs are grinding together and pulverizing my innards. "Anyway, one good thing did happen," I add. "Remember the boomerang sample?"

Erin's eyes grow wide. "No. Don't tell me that this whole time it was really a boomerang."

I shake my head and laugh aloud at the memory of Andrew staring at me as the wood sample hit the back wall with a resounding *click* before landing on the carpet. It even left a small mark on the paint, which I found rather impressive. "No, it's not a boomerang. But I threw it like one, just in case."

Erin bursts out laughing and reaches over to give me a quick embrace. "Good for you, Iley," she says emphatically, squeezing my shoulders. At just that moment, an SUV with four baseball cap-wearing halfwits skids around the corner, and one yells out, "Dykes!" at the top of his lungs. The other three snort and hoot as though they've never heard such sidesplitting comedy. Erin and I stand up and she rolls her eyes as we walk into the apartment. "This neighborhood, I swear. Where are some foodstuffs when you really need them?" she asks.

* * *

Although Erin and I are certainly not dykes or lovers, we aren't exactly just roommates or friends either. Our relationship falls into a different area, one marked by a level of comfort and understanding achieved through years of cohabitation. We met nearly seven years ago, when we both answered the same ad in *Boston* magazine. *Seeking roommate,* it read. *Easygoing male musician with one cat looking to share giant Fenway-area apartment. No gender preference, smokers OK.*

Robin, the easygoing male musician, set up back-to-back appointments for Erin and me, but I was running so late that he ended up showing us the apartment at the same time. For this she and I were both grateful. Robin was not the sexy bass player that we had each separately envisioned and planned to bed shortly after setting up the CD player and framed photos. Instead, he was a balding folk singer who wore his remaining fringe of hair long and ponytailed, twirling it as he spoke about the basement laundry room. He asked if we would like to hear some of his music, and before either of us could respond, the embroidered guitar strap was firmly around his neck and he was crooning a low, mournful tune about a lost love. The cat referenced in the ad was a piebald, scrawny thing that nearly caused me to wet my pants when it leaped from a chair and onto Robin's shoulder as he sang to us.

The last straw came when we toured the bathroom, which contained a large, wooden platform where the toilet seat should have been. Using a strangely reverential tone, Robin explained that squatting was actually much healthier than sitting upright, and that in most non-Western cultures, this in fact was the preferred way of relieving oneself. In the cracked vanity mirror, I watched Erin's mouth fall open, and it took all of my power to keep a straight face and tell Robin that although I just *adored* the apartment, I'd need to think about it. Erin wordlessly followed me out of the apartment and into the elevator, and once the squeaky door shut, we became hysterical with laughter.

After walking together for a few blocks, we became composed enough to begin asking one another questions about favorite neighborhoods and ideal price ranges for rent. I don't remember who suggested to whom that we become roommates, to forge ahead on our own and leave Robin and his squatting toilet out of the picture entirely, but it proved to be an excellent idea. Over the years, we've lived in Robin's neighborhood, in Harvard Square in Cambridge, and now in our little hovel in Brighton. Every few years, I prod myself into thinking I should move, perhaps find a little place to call my own. But in the end, I am made too nervous by the idea of paying all that rent, and more importantly, I don't see any reason *not* to continue living with Erin. Sure, if asked to leave, I certainly would—and for a time two summers ago, when Erin thought she'd be shacking up with her then-boyfriend who turned out to be hooked on Vicodin, I *was* leaving. But things fell through with Jake, the way they so often do when narcotics are involved. And so I stayed, our calm roommate rhythm continuing, like a low-key but content marriage, to this day.

The next morning finds me working in my rented darkroom space at the New England School of Photography and banging on the wall as I hear Rithy enter on the other side. "Yo, Rithy!" I shout, pausing as I grip my photograph between the rubber tongs, leaving it hovering between the developer and stop bath. "Is that you?"

"Yeah, it's me," he says in a gruff voice. "*Joey*." This is the name he chose for himself seven years ago, when he arrived from Thailand with his father, his uncle, and a few cheap, floral-print suitcases. They had come to join some entrepreneurial cousins who had launched a successful restaurant in Boston three years earlier and sent to their homeland for reinforcements when it came time to open a second restaurant. Twelve-year-old Rithy didn't know much about American culture, but he knew that if he ever hoped to fit in, he'd need a more suitable name. He selected Joey because whenever he sat in his family's tiny apartment and watched *Friends*, everyone always seemed to laugh and smile a lot whenever that character was onscreen. It wasn't until he gained a command of English that he realized with horror that Joey was a moron and that the cast and studio audience were laughing *at* Joey, but by then it was too late. I delight in calling him Rithy, partly because it annoys him, partly because I think it is a beautiful name, and partly because I can't stand Matt LeBlanc. "How's it going?" he asks.

"It's good," I say uncertainly as I peer at the black-and-white photo lying gently in the tray of fixer. Staring back at me is a silvery print of a sweet-cheeked cherub, who I discovered above an ornate Beacon Hill doorway quite by accident and shot in early-morning light last weekend. The mouth is parted just so, but there is a tiny glint of pure white plaster showing through the paint on the top lip, too bright and causing a distraction from the rest of the image. "You staying long?"

"No. Just bought some paper and wanted to drop it off. I need to go to the restaurant, so Yankees can have enough pad thai to eat at dinner," he yells bitterly. Although poor Rithy is enrolled part-time at Wentworth Institute of Technology, it is implicitly understood that the bulk of his waking hours are to be spent washing vegetables, chopping peanuts, and boiling soft noodles. His family's restaurant has won Best Pad Thai four years running, and now he is a prisoner of peanut sauce. Photography is his only outlet, and he spends virtually all of his money on film, paper, and darkroom rental fees. His photographs are elaborately staged and lit affairs, mostly still lifes of objects found in nature. His images of irises in particular capture a clean, spare beauty that bodes very well for his artistic future. He once shyly showed me a collection of prints, shots of small, smooth stones he arranged in concentric circles on the grass, and it was so exquisite that I momentarily turned as green as the grass with envy. "Your fan working?" he asks.

"No," I say, squinting in the red light at the dust-coated vent on the far wall. Photo chemicals stink and require adequate ventilation, but because the New England School of Photography is one of the very few places left that rents darkroom space, beggars can't be choosy. Since the advent of digital photography, darkrooms have been quietly shuttering one by one as sales of Photoshop rise. I'm no Luddite, but no mouse and scanner can give me the feeling that standing silently in a darkroom does, breathlessly watching and waiting as the image appears like magic. I appreciate what digital photography can do, but digital photographs aren't mysterious, and they aren't romantic. Uploading pictures will never give me the fizzy tingle in my chest that this does. "Well, I guess no fan just means more brain cells down the drain," I add cheerily as I drop the cherub into the water bath for a little soak. Rithy doesn't reply, and a moment later, I hear him leave his darkroom space, muttering in Thai.

Laptop? Check. Cigarettes? Check. Scrap paper and pen? Check, check. Unmistakable feeling of weight on chest, the kind that accompanies a fruitless job search? Check. I give a dramatic sigh as I start up Erin's gleaming white iBook, by far the cleanest thing in our cluttered living room. Gary responds with a little sigh of his own, resting his head on his front paws and making me momentarily jealous of the simple life of a dog.

Search jobs by keyword: photography, photo, studio. A whole lot of nothing appears on the screen—retail positions at the Walgreen's photo counter, a project management job at Polaroid, a dozen zippily worded ads for Photoshop wonks. I read each one anyway, which is to say I rest my gaze on the screen and use my index finger to scroll while my mind wanders.

Can I really keep doing this, I wonder, as the list of benefits for the Polaroid job slides by. *Do* I really want to keep doing this? After graduating from Emerson College nearly nine years ago with a degree in photography and a portfolio bursting with arresting, black-and-white pictures, I was more than dismayed to learn that the world had not been impatiently waiting for me to arrive with my Nikon. Humbled, I took a job at the Brookline *TAB*, a free newspaper produced by a large chain that churns out identical weeklies for Boston-area cities and towns. It didn't take long for me to get my fill of photographing lame local events: gap-toothed Girl Scouts accepting awards, a dedication of shiny, new park benches in front of the library, the grand opening of a sub shop that was subsequently closed for spreading hepatitis B. Even as I was focusing my lens and yelling at the Girl Scouts to scrunch in tighter, I was plotting my escape.

It came in the form of a job in a swanky, Newbury Street photography gallery, where I was essentially a glorified salesgirl who was able to speak with some authority about photographic technique. It was dreadfully dull, with pompous customers who looked past their trendy eyewear and down their noses at me. I wasn't making enough money to buy the matte black wardrobe I needed to look the part, and my feet screamed by the end of each day. The job's only selling point was that I got to spend time with local photographers, some of whom were charming, rakishly handsome, and eccentric. One was so charming, rakishly handsome, and eccentric that he and I found ourselves in the back office during his show's opening, in a sloppy, grabby make-out session fueled by too much champagne. Although sales didn't suffer that night, the owner decided that this was not behavior befitting a gallery employee and let me go. It hardly mattered to me; when the photographer hit it big in a New York show the following year, I recalled with fondness that his lips tasted of Clark's Teaberry gum but couldn't bring to mind one memorable detail of my stint at the gallery.

Next came the freelance jobs, which are too tiresome to describe, then a period at a small camera shop in Harvard Square. This job suited me, despite the fact that no one who knows me well would ever use the words "Iley Gilbert" and "customer service" together in the same sentence. Still, I liked the clientele and relished the challenge of trying to talk men out of bigger and bigger telephoto lenses, explaining with a wink that just as with some other things, size isn't everything. It was a relaxed, run-down store, with a homespun atmosphere and no opportunities for make-out sessions to get me in trouble. It closed when the owner's wife had a stroke, and he sold the store for a tidy sum to help pay for her home health care. Eventually I found myself at the frame shop, with its attendant frame samples and boneheaded manager. The job made me feel as though I had been marooned on an island as I watched my aspirations slowly but surely drift away from me, the stiff current taking any hope of making it in the photography business and tossing it about, before swallowing it up.

I close the laptop with a snap and light a cigarette, watching the smoke curlicue into the air. Gary gives a little snuffle that makes me feel guilty. He turned six last month and got high marks at his trip to the vet's, except for his seasonal allergies and asthma. Erin and I dutifully dose him with doggie antihistamines when his breathing becomes too labored, but we both know that he might not need the pet pharmaceuticals if the air around here were less polluted. "Well, nothing here, friend," I tell him before leaning back in the chair and staring at the ceiling, as though the ideal job posting might be up there, in between the cracks and water stains. Tomorrow I'll call the temp agency; they're always glad to hear from me because I'm too smart for the jobs they send me on. Then I realize that I can't tell whether or not I'm relieved that there were no photography jobs. This thought haunts me well into the evening and keeps me awake for the better part of the night.

Two

It starts with a barely audible *whoosh* sound, not unlike the tiny hiss that comes from a seashell held to your ear on a day at the beach, and quickly gains momentum as it slides past my cheek and lands on the scuffed hardwood floor of the living room. "Damn it!" I yell as I pick up the tortoise-shell clip and indelicately jam it back into my head. I've got what I've come to call Houdini hair: it's so fine that it consistently escapes any kind of hair accessory, throwing off clips, barrettes, and ponytail holders like so many locks, chains, and shackles. Erin looks up from her English muffin and takes a sip of coffee before asking, "Do you want a hair cut? Maybe some layers."

"Nah," I say, feeling impatient. "I have to go for my interview at the temp agency in an hour." I realize that my pants are covered in wiry dog fur, and I begin sifting through piles of junk in search of the lint roller. When I finally locate it, wedged behind a boxed set of hideous mugs gifted to Erin at Christmas by one of her clients, it's out of sticky sheets and only the cardboard tube remains. I resignedly toss it on the floor.

"Well, that works out OK, because I don't actually have my good scissors here," she admits. "But we'll do something with it yet."

"Yeah, whatever," I say, giving the hair clip a tentative touch, knowing full well that I'll lose it somewhere in the downtown streets of Boston before the morning is out. I do bitch about the texture, but at least I can't complain about the color—I was born with an artist-ready hue, a rich jet-black that virtually all of the painters and photographers I know are forced to create in their bathrooms using a box of Féria No. 21. Mine comes courtesy of my mother's side, the Ruttila family with the Finnish bloodlines. Whenever I tell people that my background contains a heavy dose of Finn, they become confused and immediately arch their eyebrows at me, because they mistakenly think that I should be blond and blue-eyed and cheery, much like the ladies from ABBA or the Swedish Bikini Team. But Finland isn't *like* the rest of Scandinavia, I patiently explain to them as their eyes glaze over. It's like Russia. The people aren't delightful and bubbly, and their hair often isn't blond. They are dark and frequently difficult and unyielding. Just like my hair, and sometimes, just like me.

The visit to the temp agency goes predictably: sit in stiff-backed chair and act elated at the prospect of answering phones at law office or venture capital firm, give hearty handshake complete with pasted-on smile for good measure, ride elevator down while resisting the urge to scream, light up cigarette the moment I hit the street. A prissy-looking woman with a well-tailored, navy blue suit and a glossy helmet of dark brown hair crisply informs me that I'm not allowed to smoke in front of the building. I consider giving her the finger, but then realize that it's entirely possible I may be assigned to work at a business located in this enormous, sterile office building, and think better of it. I walk to the corner instead, feign interest in a window full of hulking photocopy machines at the Xerox office, stub my cigarette butt out on the sidewalk, and toss it into a nearby trash can. I may smoke, but I don't litter.

When I arrive home, Gary is sitting in front of the TV looking especially cranky, and I immediately know why: he doesn't like soaps, and especially not ones with steamy love scenes. Because he's a purebred, he can be a little old-fashioned that way. Erin must have been in a hurry this morning—normally she remembers to switch the set to Animal Planet after her daily dose of insipid morning shows, and Gary spends delightful afternoons watching warbling birds and mating hippos.

"Well, this sucks for you!" I exclaim despairingly as I switch the channel from a close-up of a wide-eyed, wet-lipped, busty actress to one with majestic giraffes gliding across the plains. I drop down on the sagging couch and fidget for a minute or two before my stomach growls, and then head to the kitchen. But I don't even make it as far as the decrepit, round-edged refrigerator, because something catches my eye. Clearly, it's meant to, as Erin's taken a giant piece of pink paper and in a huge scrawl in black Sharpie, written this disjointed directive:

ILEY, CHECK IT OUT. WEIRD, RIGHT! CALL! —E.

Beneath the piece of pink paper is the *Boston Herald*, and I give an annoyed snort as I bypass the table and open the refrigerator door, because I realize it's probably just one of her police blotter entries. But as I yank the tenacious little foil cover off my strawberry Dannon, I think, why on earth would she want me to call one of these yahoos in the police blotter, the ones who hold up stores and then dally outside to eat a candy bar pocketed during the transaction, or carjack vehicles with manual transitions and find themselves stalling during an attempted getaway that never goes beyond first gear? So I move the paper, and beneath it there is a circled ad that reads:

PHOTOGRAPHER'S ASSISTANT WANTED

I pause for a minute, then clear some catalogs off the chair and sit down with my yogurt. Pottery Barn slips to the floor and hits my ankle as I read:

> *Very unusual opportunity for energetic person with photography background and excellent sense of humor. MUST be able to work Friday and Saturday nights. Please call (617) 555-2368 and leave message for William.*

Well, Erin was certainly correct in her assessment of this ad: WEIRD, RIGHT! indeed. I can't say that I've ever yearned to work weekend nights, but then again, I'm not exactly going to be so fulfilled and busy that I'll need that time to kick back and unwind from a grueling, forty-hour workweek. Nor am I burdened by a boyfriend, a lucky guy for whom Friday and Saturday nights would be reserved without question—Matt and I have been broken up for nearly eight months now. A stormy, four-year relationship marked by periods of intense passion and unspeakable cruelty ended last summer. A moody printmaker whose family portrait featured deeply unhappy parents and disturbed siblings, Matt always swore he would never marry or have a family of his own. Like most women, I naturally and naively assumed that would change somewhere down the line.

When I developed conjunctivitis after swimming in a mucky public pool and dutifully dripped antibiotic drops into my eyes for ten days last summer, I had no idea that they could wreak such havoc on the power of the Pill. And when I found myself pregnant at the end of August, I imagined that after all this time, Matt might undergo a miraculous reversal of opinion about wives and babies. He didn't. For a long time after, the abortion and our breakup remained in a dead heat in terms of which one caused me the most anguish. In the end, it was the abortion that did the most damage, by affecting my already tentative grasp on my creativity. It was a surprise, as much of a surprise as the pregnancy itself had been. Every time I would look at a negative in the darkroom, it would call to mind those black and white ultrasounds of fetuses, the kind that pregnant friends and former co-workers would proudly wave around while chirping about their babies' tiny arm buds. Time passed and eventually I grew able to look at my negatives. But my photography was slow in recovering—

probably still is, if I'm honest with myself—and I have since vowed that never again will I allow someone or something to wrest my creativity from me like that.

Well, William, I think as I toss my yogurt container in the trash and reach for the cordless phone, let's give this a try.

"Come on, come on!" I plead, pulling my camera from my face and squinting up at the sky. The sun has slid behind a cloud for the second time in as many minutes, stripping my subject of all its brights and darks. A vine has wound its way around the back half of an old bicycle that's leaning against an ornate railing, and the sight of the leaves curling around the spokes of the decrepit wheel nearly threw me right off my own bike as I sailed by. Now my shiny, red Cannondale is leaning against the railing a few feet away, and I'm crouched on the sidewalk of this chic block of Commonwealth Avenue trying to ignore the splintering pain in my calves as I command the sun to return.

"Hey, hey, there you are," I say approvingly at the sky as a matronly woman descends the majestic staircase in front of the building. She gives me a wide berth, walking behind me and leaving a lingering scent of old Brahmin money, something like lavender and cedar and crisp Madras fabric. I know the scent well; it clings to Erin sometimes, and she can't even smell it herself. After the woman is out of sight, I get down to business with the camera and take my shots from several angles, using different apertures: 4, 5.6, 8, 11; oh, hell, let's do some 16 for good measure. The light and shadow playing off the old, dull metal and the glossy, shiny leaves are making my heart skip a beat, and just as I look through the viewfinder for one last shot, who wanders in but a plump little ladybug. It's lazily walking over one of the leaves, effortlessly imbuing the scene with a darling quality that has no place in my portfolio. I nudge my index finger under it and lift it up, saying, "OK, here we go. It's like they tell you in the bars at closing time: I don't care where you go, but you can't stay here." I gently deposit it on a yellow tulip in the immaculately maintained flowerbed next to the base of the steps, take a last shot, and get on my bike.

As I'm riding up the gradual, steeping slope of Commonwealth Avenue, gasping hard and sweating around my hairline, I remember that seeing a ladybug is supposed to be good luck. I think I may need it for my interview with the photographer tomorrow. He left a message on our answering machine, using a tone and tempo that could charitably be called languid and laid-back, but would more accurately be called nearly comatose. He didn't offer any details about the job, just told me in a gravelly voice the location of the studio and said I could come by anytime in the next few days. No appointment necessary, no "looking forward to meeting you," no "call me if you need directions." It sounded as though he didn't care if I came or not, and when I replayed the message for Erin by way of explaining why I'd decided not to pursue this job lead, she insisted that I go. I relented, mainly because I don't have much else to do this week. And if nothing more, I'm sure whoever this William is will provide a great story for me to tell later.

I give two sharp knocks, the door swings open, and I look up and think, *Well, hel-lo, who's this?* Standing in front of me is quite simply one of the most breathtaking men I've ever seen, with black, shaggy, chin-length hair that's pushed off his face and bright blue eyes that tip at the corners like those on a sly cat. "Look at that," he says, pointing to my feet. "Fluevogs."

"Yup," I say, nodding and wiggling my left foot, which is shod in an olive green and hot pink John Fluevog shoe with a pudgy, heart-shaped heel.

"Fluevogs," he says again, pointing to his right foot. He's wearing a pair that I remember from the Newbury Street store's window display last fall, in black leather with red whipstitching. I decide immediately that should I get this job, I will ask to work alongside this guy, no matter how odious the photo shoot. And although I could stand here and talk to him all day about footwear, I realize it's time to get down to business.

"I'm Iley, and I'm here to see William," I say confidently, following him into a small room that features a metal desk, a few beat-up chairs, and an enormous old fan leaning precariously in the far corner. On the desk sits an open bag of Mint Milanos, a blue plastic ashtray, and a neatly stacked pyramid of film canisters; the wall behind has a giant piece of white paper with Massachusetts towns and dates written in block lettering. Milton, 5/15. Natick, 5/16. Hingham, 5/22. Brockton, 5/23. And so on.

"I'm William," he says, gesturing to one of the chairs and giving me a slow smile as my jaw drops. "Were you expecting someone different?" He hoists himself up onto the desk and lets his legs dangle off the edge. He's wearing dark denim jeans and a zip-up black sweater with brown stripes running down the sleeves, and he shoves them up to expose the bright white skin on his arms.

"Um," I say as I sit down, "I suppose so. I thought you'd be . . . you know, a little less lively." He cocks his head to the side and fixes me with a quirky expression, with one eyebrow shooting halfway up his forehead. "You sounded sort of . . . older, or tired, when leaving your message, I suppose," I offer diplomatically.

"Oh!" he says, leaning back and setting his hand squarely in the center of the film canister pyramid, toppling it and sending everything falling to the desk with a clatter. Several film canisters roll off the desk and hit the floor, and I bend over in my chair to collect them. "I took too much Sudafed that day, and it felt like my tongue was no longer attached to my mouth," he explains. "My apologies. I'm usually more with it. Hey, thanks for grabbing those," he says kindly as I stand up, reach over, and drop the canisters on the desk. Out of the corner of my eye, I can see him looking at me, his gaze lingering a little bit too long on areas between my neck and my knees.

And who could blame him? I'm wearing a black ensemble today, my all-purpose, interviewing-for-artsy-job uniform that consists of a tight turtleneck and snug-fitting jeans. My body isn't perfectly proportioned by any means: between a rack that has been known to overspill a C/D cup when I have PMS, a comically short waist, and legs that have been toned by a decade of bike riding, my physique looks not a lot unlike a pair of big marshmallows perched atop two well-formed carrots. Still, I know how to play to my strengths, and I'm more than pleased that William is noticing.

"So, I guess it's time to talk about the job," he says, absently feeling the faint shadow of stubble on his face with his left hand. "I take photos at proms in the area. You know, at high school gyms and catering halls. I need someone to help me get the kids rounded up, keep them organized as they wait in line for their photos, help them pose, that sort of thing. It's Friday and Saturday nights, starting at around five o'clock or so. We're all done by midnight, usually. It pays twelve an hour. Let's see, is there anything I forgot?" he asks himself, looking at the ceiling. "Oh, also—"

"They still *do* that?" I interrupt in a dumbfounded voice. "They still have proms and take pictures and all that?" I ask, thinking back to my prom photo, with my laughable asymmetrical haircut and candy pink, dyed-to-match shoes.

"Oh, yes, they do!" he laughs. "Nothing has changed, trust me. I mean, the clothes and music have changed, but not too much else." He pats his chest with both hands for a second, then frowns and reaches behind him, opening a desk drawer and procuring a pack of Camels. "Do you mind if I smoke?" he asks, standing and pulling a lighter out of his front pocket.

"No," I say warmly. "I don't mind at all." So that's why I'm liking this place so much, I think, as I suddenly realize that the air is redolent with two of my favorite odors: cigarette smoke and photo chemicals. William holds the pack out to me and arches his eyebrow again. I nod eagerly and take a cigarette, and he leans over and lights it before lighting his own. "So this job, it's like being in so many John Hughes movies, night after night?" I ask, crossing my legs and exhaling a stream of smoke into the air.

"Yeah, more or less. Only don't be looking for Duckie, or you'll be very disappointed," he warns, moving the ashtray to the edge of the desk. "I mean, some of the trappings are there, but no one's got that same goofiness anymore," he says a bit sadly. "Some of them might dress OK, but they're all nervous and tense, waiting for their acceptance letters to Amherst College."

"Ew," I say, wrinkling my nose, and we both laugh. There is a long pause that I don't mind at all, because it affords me the chance to sit quietly and take note of the gently curved cupid's bow above William's top lip. He doesn't seem terribly bothered by this lull in the interview either; he's spending a few seconds looking directly at me. As part of the standard interview uniform, I've left my black bangs shaggy and pulled the rest of my hair back in a low, messy ponytail. My lips are coated with a deep red, matte lipstick, and my heart beats fast as I involuntarily lick them, tasting the waxy pigment.

"So," he says, snapping to and setting his cigarette in the ashtray, "the first prom is in a few weeks, in Milton." He gestures to the list on the wall. "All of the proms are in May and June. Some schools start earlier, and some do it later, which is good for us."

Us? Does this mean I have the job?

"I can tell you where the school is and give you directions," he continues. "Or we can go together, whichever is easier."

"Well, I only have a bike," I say, shrugging. "So I guess I'd need a lift." I pause for a second as I watch him bring the cigarette to his lips. "I live over in Brighton."

"Oh, that's not far. So we can work something out," he says, standing up and sticking out his hand. "It was great to meet you, Iley. Why don't you call sometime next week, and we'll work out the details then."

"OK," I nod, shaking his hand and then demurely pulling mine back, in a move that surprises me. "That sounds good." I walk out into the bright sunlight with my back stiff and my chest tight, excited and slightly jittery, as though I'm readying for my very own prom.

Three

"Hey," comes a muffled voice from the other side of the wall, "you got filters?"

"Yes, Rithy," I shout wearily, in the same tone of voice a teacher might use when a student comes to class unprepared and begs for a pencil or protractor. "I'm using the red one right now, though. Which one do you need?"

"Yellow. I'm coming over, OK?" I hear him leave his darkroom space, and a few seconds later he's pushing past the heavy fabric curtain and knocking into the wall of the twisting entrance, despite the fact that the entryway to my darkroom area is identical to his. He peers at the image floating in the water bath as he plays with the drawstring on the hood of his Wentworth College sweatshirt. "That's nice," he says unconvincingly.

"No, it's shitty," I correct him. "I mean, the composition is good, I like that. But I should have done something differently. The sun played some weird tricks on me." The spokes on the bicycle wheel are much too dull, and the leaves winding around it are coming up gray and flat, with none of the beautiful silvers that normally spring to life from my black and whites. "So I'm going to try some filters and see what happens. Here, I think it's in this box," I say, handing Rithy the small, square cardboard container that holds the filters.

"Thanks," he says, yanking a tissue from his jeans pocket and sending tiny cotton fibers floating into the air, dancing in the low light. He blows his nose loudly, gives a few dry coughs, and shoves the tissue back. I pull a piece of photo paper from a thick, black plastic envelope and set it beneath the enlarger as Rithy looks over my shoulder. I can hear him wheezing quietly during the ten-second silence as the enlarger clicks on and off, bathing the paper in white light. I gently slide the photo into the developer, set the timer, and lean against the wall.

"They got you working in the restaurant with a cold like that?" I ask critically. "You shouldn't be doing that."

"I know. I wash my hands a lot."

"Still. You should be resting. Or coming here instead," I say as I grip the photo with the tongs and drop it into the stop bath. It looks better than my first three attempts, but still not up to my standards, which makes me stamp my foot hard against the cement floor.

Rithy snorts loudly at the notion that anyone would let him spend extra time in the darkroom, even if he's a vector for a virus that can be spread via an order of crispy Golden Triangles. "Fat chance," he spits, pulling the yellow filter from the cardboard box. This is one of Rithy's favorite colloquial expressions, along with "get out!" and "batting a thousand." He says that peppering his conversations with these types of phrases prevents people from paying too much mind when he makes mistakes with other, more mundane words. Like when he recently mixed up "interrupt" and "intercourse" and told a girl in class that he was sorry to intercourse her while she had been speaking, for example.

"Well, try to take it easy. Oh, and I may not be here on the weekends for a little while—I got a job. Helping to take prom photos," I say, trying out the sound of it.

"What? That sounds strange," Rithy says bluntly. Well, yes, it may be strange, I think to myself as he leaves the darkroom with the filter, but have you seen the guy I'll be working for? I know I have; I've seen him plenty in my mind's eye as I'm lying in bed at night lately.

It's only eleven-thirty, and I've already answered the phone no less than one hundred times. My ear is burning, and I can just feel the pimples on my jaw line waiting to spring up as punishment for holding this slimy receiver to my face all morning long. The receiver also has Bad Phone Smell, that rank odor that emanates from the mouthpiece, the lingering sour breath of a million temps before me. I can't figure out for the life of me why this law office can't have voice mail; but then, I am at one of Boston's largest and most venerable firms, where I suppose the sound of a human voice does confer a certain amount of respectability and old-worldliness.

The place is fairly frantic today, with lawyers running every which way, but only one of them has treated me as anything more than a piece of furniture. It was a young, pretty woman who was immensely pregnant, her conservative, navy-blue maternity dress stretched over her protruding belly as though it concealed a beach ball. She leaned wearily against my desk and whimpered that she hoped her case didn't go to trial later this afternoon, because she didn't know if she could stand for more than a few minutes at a time. Her swollen feet oozed from the tops of her low-heeled, navy blue pumps, and I suggested she try some peppermint foot cream. She said that she could no longer reach her feet and that it wouldn't really be within the confines of the law to ask her paralegal to do it, and we had a little laugh about that. But once she righted herself and waddled to the elevator, there were no others who would deign to speak to me.

So in between calls, I'm counting pairs of suspenders and keeping track using hash marks on the little cream-colored notepad that sits next to the mouse pad on the desk. So far there seems to be no shortage of these horrible things—I even spotted a pair in pink paisley!—but I figure that when I've exhausted the suspender quotient, I'll switch to wing-tips with tassels or women's frilly-front shirts. Maybe in a few minutes, I'll try to sneak onto the Web and do some searches for the high schools that were written on William's giant piece of paper. I hear that many high schools have their own Web sites now, which at age thirty-one makes me feel old—not just because *we* didn't have a site in high school, but because it makes me scratch my head and wonder why a high school would need one. But I want to know what I'm dealing with here—and not according to stiffly written articles about American teens that I skim in the conservative magazines that arrive for Erin, magazines she didn't ask for and doesn't want. I need to go to the source directly, so I feel prepared for this adventure. If only the switchboard didn't keep glowing and blinking like some litigation light show.

Gary is taking his sweet time this evening, stopping to piss on more bushes, lampposts, and fire hydrants than I can count. "The world is not your urinal, buddy," I say irritably and give a little tug on his leash. He turns and looks at me nonchalantly. That's because he and I both know that he's right and I'm wrong: the world is in fact his urinal. But I've got a hair appointment to get to, so I decide to cut the pee party short and drag him back to the apartment. When I let him off his leash, he bounds inside without looking back, which is the canine version of getting out of a car and slamming the door without saying good-bye.

I walk into the living room and Erin is sitting on the floor, the *Herald* in front of her and an open can of iced tea at her side. She's reading and holding her left arm aloft; in her hand is a shiny pair of shears, and she's opening and closing them slowly, making a slick *sssssssshk* sound each time the metal pieces slide against one another. "Ready?" she asks, giving the shears a few quick snipping motions.

"Sure," I say eagerly. "No police blotter today?"

"Uh," she says, twisting her lips around and flipping through the paper, "there was nothing that really leaped out at me." She puts her index finger on a small headline that reads "Hyde Park" and smiles. "No, I take that back. This one is OK. 'Police were called to the home of a thirty-six-year-old Hyde Park resident who claimed that his wife refused a request to do laundry. She then threw the laundry from the window of their fourth-floor apartment, followed by a sixty-four-ounce bottle of detergent. The event was later logged as *Defenestration: Household Items*, and the woman was released without incident.' They don't show scenarios like that on Downy commercials, do they?" she chuckles as she stands up and pushes up her sleeves. Today she's wearing a purple and magenta striped top and jeans with a little tear in the ass, right beneath the right cheek. "Let's do it."

Ten minutes later I'm wet-haired and seated in a chair in Erin's bedroom, on top of a white plastic tarp. Actually, I think it may be a large piece of leftover Tyvek that Erin swiped from a nearby construction site, but the purpose is the same. I've got a gray, threadbare salon cape around my shoulders, and the snap pinches my neck if I move my head too fast. Erin is standing behind me, touching my hair and frowning, looking at me in the full-length mirror that faces us.

"All right. Here is what I think. Medium-length layers, but nothing too seventies. OK?"

"I dunno," I shrug. "Whatever you think is best, Erin." A police siren blares by outside, making both of us jump slightly and sending the shears to the floor and Gary to the window. Erin picks up the shears and studies the tips for a second.

"Well, I just like to be cautious. I don't want to give you something that you don't like," she says.

"Yeah, but I always end up liking what you do, so come on and share your gift, woman!" I command her.

She begins tentatively, working in silence. Gary's quiet growling is the only sound, as he remains vigilant, anxiously awaiting another police car. I close my eyes and wonder what it must be like to have not only found one's calling by accident, but to have to keep it a secret as well.

Erin was raised exceedingly preppy by a Connecticut family of significant social standing and enjoyed a childhood complete with sailing lessons, a horse farm, a madras-rich wardrobe, and the expectation that she would grow to become a woman of grace and understated elegance. All was going according to plan until one night at boarding school, when there was a weekend prank involving impromptu haircuts. Well, according to the story, calling them haircuts would be like calling scalping a head massage. After passing out at a party, three unpopular girls had their hair positively butchered by a clique of famously mean bitches. All three woke up humiliated the next day, but one became so hysterical that she refused to leave her room. This girl's roommate was Erin, who was at once so pained by seeing the girl in such a state and terrified that she'd never have her room to herself again, that she impulsively grabbed a pair of scissors and tried to do her best with her roommate's hair. And when she finished and stepped back, it looked . . . great. It looked so great that the other two girls had their hair cut by Erin as well. Word got out, and Erin was soon trying different styles on her classmates, honing her craft in between field hockey practice and writing essays for her application to Brown University.

Eventually all of these girls would go back to the page-boy or shapeless, pony-tailed style that generations of preppy women adopted before them, but not Erin. Her appetite had been whetted, and while studying at Brown, she practiced cutting hair on her friends and dorm mates. She read books and watched training videos when she should have been cheering on the crew team. She started to cruise Sally Beauty Supply instead of Lilly Pulitzer. She thought of it as a type of Rumspringa, the Amish tradition that encourages teenagers to take a year-long break from their laced-up lives and sample the things that the outside world has to offer—only in her case, she was distancing herself from a world of gin and tonics, not horse-drawn buggies and home-churned butter. She figured it would get out of her system eventually; Hotchkiss girls don't cut hair for a living, do they?

Well, they do. Or this one wanted to, in any case. But Erin was a good and respectful daughter, and she knew that this career would never, ever fly with her family, who quietly made their money in finance and law and regarded haircuts as a necessary nuisance at best. She knew that if she worked in a salon, doing what she loved, her mother would have to lie at the country club, and she could picture Bitsy thrusting out her locked jaw and trying to maintain a believable expression as she detailed Erin's imaginary, high-profile position at a respected company.

Then Erin got a brilliant idea: why not cut out the middleman and lie to her parents herself? They were semi-retired anyway by the time she graduated, traveling to Bermuda and Colorado and nurturing their various leisure pursuits. It's not as though they'd be dropping by or asking too many questions about where she worked, she reasoned. So in one short afternoon, she became Erin Brooks, Assistant Director of Alumni Development at Harvard University. Aping Jim Rockford, she had ersatz business cards printed, with neat lettering in Harvard crimson. She instructed her then-roommate never to tell any callers where she was at any time, and she landed her first job in a salon. She quickly moved through the ranks and ended up commanding the most desired chair at an elite Newbury Street salon. It wasn't just her innate cutting skills and fine eye that made her such a treasured stylist, it was the way she could purr and coo over the richest, most entitled clients, taking their attitude in stride and making them feel as though they were the most important women in the world. Of course she could; she had spent her entire life preparing for this, traveling among the leisure class and knowing intuitively how to behave around them.

"So what happened on your interview?" she asks. "Was he one of those fat, sweaty photographers you see at weddings, yelling for Grandpa to move in closer?" A slick lock of black hair falls onto my lap and I pick it up, rolling it between my fingers.

"Not exactly. He's actually hot as hell, Erin!" I exclaim, jerking my head around and causing Erin to *tsk* and reposition me so I'm facing straight ahead again. "Sorry," I say meekly. "Anyway, he's around our age; maybe thirty-eight, tops. He has black hair and incredible blue eyes. He's very funny. He seems *really* cool."

Erin smiles skeptically as she runs a fine-toothed, plastic comb through the back of my hair. "How cool can he be? Didn't you say he takes prom pictures?"

"Well, yeah, that is true," I admit. "But I'm sure he must do his own work on the side or something. I mean, *I* worked in a frame shop." She doesn't respond, as she's now concentrating deeply, creating the non-seventies layers that will transform me into a glamour girl for my new job. We sit in silence for a few more minutes and she works her way around to my bangs, the tips of which fall to my lips with a tickle as she gives them a few quick snips.

"Well, it sounds good, either way," she says, running her fingers though my new layers and letting the hair flop down next to my face. "At the very least, you've got a job. If he's that hot, maybe there'll be some extra benefits, if you catch my drift," she says, laughing. There's a pause, and she asks, "What?"

"What what?" I ask, confused.

"Hey, you look weird," she says.

"No, I don't."

"I can see your face in the mirror, remember?" she asks, bending down and putting her head next to mine. Our reflections stare back at us, and behind her left shoulder I can see Gary walking into the room, sniffing the air and turning up his nose at the smelly styling cream.

"It's nothing," I shrug, looking away from the mirror, as though Erin might not see me in the reflection if I don't see myself. "I don't know why I look weird. *Looked* weird. See, now I'm fine," I say gamely, giving her a wide, toothy grin.

"Whatever you say." She plugs in her candy apple red, salon-quality hair dryer, turns it on, and begins running her fingers though the hair on the left side of my head. The 1,875-watt blast is accompanied by a noise that could wake the dead, in a high, whiny pitch and volume that effectively kill any opportunity for further conversation.

My kneecap feels cool, and then a bit warm, as the blood trickles down my knee, undoubtedly staining the lining of my pale blue twill pants. When I tripped and fell thirty minutes ago, my portfolio went flying one way, I went the other, and I was left sputtering and cursing about the uneven, cracked pavement that they call a sidewalk in this part of Cambridge. A kindly college student in a yellow ski jacket handed me my portfolio as I stood up, and I took it from him gruffly before sitting on the curb and lighting a cigarette. Then I looked down at my knee, noticed the tear in the fabric and felt the sting of skinned flesh, and knew that this meeting was going to suck.

I wasn't disappointed. Claire, the co-owner of the store, is now sniffing and turning the pages of my portfolio disinterestedly as I tightly cross my right leg over my left, trying to hide the hole and the blood, dreaming of Neosporin and Band-Aids. She pauses over a photo taken in the North End, a shop window filled with old-fashioned scales whose metal gleams in the sunlight. My favorite feature is the shop owner's reflection in the largest scale, warped and beaming at me as I took the picture. "This one is nice," she says evenly, running her index finger absently over her lips.

"Yes, my favorite thing is the owner's reflection," I say, starting to point. She flips the page and nods as though she couldn't agree more, but I know she didn't see it. "I have other ones taken in the North End," I add. "Toward the back." She hurriedly flips some more pages, and I watch several months' worth of hard work slide by in a mere matter of seconds: the cherub from the Beacon Hill doorway, a supermarket shopping cart filled with yellow peppers, a child's old-fashioned wooden desk with the words GO SOX carved into the surface.

"They're good," she decides, closing the portfolio. "I'm not sure it's the right time of year for photos, though. We're coming into graduation season, so we'll be carrying a lot of jewelry and gifts." I look around the store, at the rough-hewn pottery and chunky kaleidoscopes and lumpy textiles, and want to scream.

"But you do sell photos; I've seen them against that back wall before," I say, pointing to a cream-colored wall that is covered with paintings of oily-looking fruit.

"Oh, we do," she says, nodding. She pauses for a second and runs her hand through her frizzy, blond hair. "The truth is that my sister—she owns the shop with me—she thought it might be good to see your work. And I like it well enough, but I don't think it's the right time for us." She pushes the portfolio at me across the table and gives me a tight little raised-eyebrow smile, to make absolutely sure I understand that this interview wasn't her idea. I scoop up the portfolio, thank her for her time in the most disingenuous way possible, and hobble out of the store. On the way out, I am sure to push my leg against some pastel-colored scarves that trail to the ground from a hanging display in an effort to get some blood on them. It doesn't work.

Four

I am sitting on the front steps of our house, twirling my fingers through my long layers and watching two small children fight over a semi-deflated soccer ball that they found in the street, when I swear I can hear The Pixies playing. It's "There Goes My Gun," and it makes me smile broadly, if in a confounded way, because no one in my immediate neighborhood would know from The Pixies. Then I realize it's getting closer and closer, and before long, an old, maroon Volkswagen station wagon pulls up in front of me, the song blaring from the open window. Inside is William, who gives a friendly wave and turns down the music. I take a deep breath and open the passenger-side door. Prom one, here we come.

"I love The Pixies," I say as I settle into the front seat. My nose immediately hones in on that familiar, comforting scent of cigarette smoke and photo chemicals, just as it did the day of my interview. Mixed in with the smell is a note of something delicately spicy, cologne that William must be wearing. I steal sidelong glances at him, studying the arch of his right eyebrow, the collar of his red shirt, the way his lips are slightly parted. The type of details that I notice from years of looking through a camera lens; the type of details that I have a feeling will fuel some memorable sessions with a vibrator.

"Yup," he replies, turning the music back up. "Of course." He looks over and gives me a warm smile as we get onto the Mass Pike. "You got a hair cut."

"Uh-huh," I say, suddenly feeling shy and squirmy again, the way I did when William shook my hand after my interview. Pull it together, Iley. "So, where do you live?"

"In Somerville," he replies, tossing a tollbooth receipt onto the dashboard and adjusting the mirror. "Near Davis Square. Too many Tufts students, but otherwise, it's all right. Although I might not be—" he says, stopping abruptly. "So let's talk about the prom. When we get there, we'll set up the backdrop and the lights together, and then you'll help check the kids in. Oh, I just called them 'kids'—do I feel old."

I laugh mirthlessly. "You're not so old. And then what?"

"So you basically make sure that they've filled out their cards, so we know whose photos belong to who, and that they are in the right order in line. Then you help them get ready—the girls usually need more help than the boys." He looks over at me. "Not to sound sexist or anything," he adds.

"Doesn't sound sexist at all," I say as I peer down at the

detritus in the footwell. My olive green and pink John Fluevogs are surrounded by empty film canisters, scratchy, white napkins emblazoned with a bright red Dairy Queen logo, and crumpled Mapquest printouts.

"After we shoot the posed photos, most schools ask us to take candids during the prom. I think Milton did; I can't remember. I'll have to look it up when we get there." We pull off the highway and William guides the car down the off-ramp as I peer around at the suburban landscape.

"Where is 'there'?" I ask. "Are we going to a school?" I try to picture it, and immediately default to every movie prom scene I've ever seen, with crepe-paper streamers and a giant punch bowl full of sherbet-flavored slime.

"No, they've got some money in this town, so they have it at a catering hall called The Regency. You'll see," he says with a wink. A few moments later we turn off onto a smaller street that features a low-slung, lavender, stucco building with few windows. Save for the loopy, gold letters spelling out THE REGENCY over the front door, the building could easily pass for a warehouse-sized porn shop, such is its stark, nondescript architecture.

"Very glamorous," I say as we park and begin to unload the lights, cameras, tripod, and backdrops.

"Well, for some of these kids, it is, I guess," he says evenly. "Are you ready?" I nod and we head inside, past a uniformed valet who is busily combing his hair in the reflection of the gilded glass and chrome doors.

Ninety minutes later, the circular drive in front of The Regency is filled with limousines, all honking as they try to glide past one another after dropping off their fares. Girls with shimmery gowns, elaborate updos that resemble croissants, and makeup you could chip with a quick tap of a chisel squeal and coo over one another's dresses, nails, shoes. I notice that most of the boys have taken a decidedly lower maintenance route. Although virtually all are wearing identical rented tuxedos, many look scruffy from the neck up, with a bit of stubble or rumpled hair. It gives them a raffish look that I would have been hopelessly drawn to in high school. Alas, when I was in high school, many boys opted for perms, so times have changed, to be sure.

A browbeaten, older teacher who must have been roped into chaperoning is herding the kids toward the photo area. The din is incredible here in the lobby, and Mrs. Carey is yelling to make herself heard, with little success. Some of the meeker-looking kids are wandering toward William's lights and backdrop, but most of them are still shouting and preening, their chemically whitened teeth gleaming as they throw their heads back to laugh. William seems unfazed by the chaos, but I feel a primordial urge for order starting to swell in my chest, and before I stop to think, I put my fingers in my mouth and give an ear-splitting whistle. Suddenly everyone is paying attention, and Mrs. Carey gives me a wide, respectful stare before announcing that it's time to line up for photos.

"Who are you?" I ask the first couple in line, a bored-looking guy with a skinny neck and big eyebrows, and his date, a bird-thin girl with red tresses styled like giant, hanging kielbasas. Her iridescent pink dress is too big in the bust, and she is clenching her armpits in a futile effort to hold it up.

"Katie!" she replies excitedly. "Katie Mitchell and Zack Tomassoni!" She grins at me, and I immediately understand why William said the girls need more help than the boys: her top teeth are coated with lipstick.

"OK; well, first, go like this," I order, rubbing the side of my index finger across my front teeth in a brusha-brusha-brusha motion. Both Katie and Zack do this, making a few couples in line look on with an air of slight consternation. She hands me their card and I review it: it tells William who they are, what size photos they want (wallet size is awfully popular, I'm told), where to mail the proofs, how much of the fee they are to pay tonight, and how much they will owe upon delivery. "Give this card to that guy over there," I say, handing it back to Katie and gesturing over to William, who is testing the flash. "Have fun."

Next up is a goth girl, all bluster and defiance as she spits the words, "Laura Blake. And I'm only here to show these assholes how it's done." She uses both thumbs to point to her black dress, which closely resembles torn-up garbage bags and is distinctly reminiscent of the Derelicte couture clothing line featured in the movie *Zoolander*. I ask her with forced cheeriness if that's where she got the idea, and she fixes me with a disdainful scowl before handing me a check imprinted with her parents' names in the upper left-hand corner and a Bible verse in the upper right. She pushes past me with a snort, and her boyfriend, who looks at least twenty-five, rolls his kohl-rimmed eyes at the ceiling.

I check in a wholesome-looking blond couple sporting matching lavender ensembles and stiff, polite smiles, the combination of which makes me wonder giddily if they are in a cult; a couple whose primary topic of conversation is how soon they can get to the Cape after the prom and start "the real partying" with a generous stash of ecstasy; and a couple whose roles are clearly defined as primper and makeshift vanity. The girl has positioned her date's hands in such a way that one of his palms is supporting a small mirror, and the other, a collection of tiny eye shadows, brushes, and lip glosses. She leans in toward him and applies a generous dab of pink lip gloss, puckering in the mirror and opening her shiny mouth to order him to keep still after he turns away to greet a kid coming into The Regency.

I'm about to turn my attention to a cute, slouchy guy and his bespectacled, bookish girlfriend when I hear William call my name. As I walk over, I hear one of the kids laugh and bray, "What the hell kind of name is Iley?" Just like being in high school all over again.

"What's up?" I ask as I reach the photo area. He's got the backdrop set up, an outdoorsy, flowery scene that just borders on tasteful. The lights are trained on a chubby, freckly guy with wide eyes and a gap-toothed smile, and his date, who is sporting a hat better suited to the Kentucky Derby.

"Nothing, I just wanted to see how you were doing over there," he replies as he reloads the camera with film. "It'll be just a second, OK?" he says to the couple. The girl throws her lank brown hair behind her shoulder with a dramatic flourish, causing her date to sputter for a second as he's hit in the face with a wall of hair and the hat's peach-colored satin ribbon. "Is everything all right? You enjoying yourself?"

"Yeah, it's fine," I say encouragingly. "No problems yet." I survey the camera on the tripod, the lights, and the couple once more. "So this is where the magic happens, huh?"

"Oh, yeah," he says sarcastically beneath his breath, and we trade a quick conspiratorial grin. I walk back to the line of impatient promgoers and snatch a card from a tanned, toned girl sporting what I'm sure is a surgically augmented rack and faux blond-streaked hair. I can smell the faintest whiff of booze on her breath as she and her friend coo over William, their boyfriends standing a few feet away and absorbed in Red Sox talk.

"Check out that hottie, Monique," purrs the busty blonde, her yellow dress rustling as she bends to her left to get a better look. "Mmmm." William is gesturing with both hands to his current subjects in an effort to convince the girl to remove her hat, and she's having none of it.

"Hot," her slender friend, who is swathed in a beautiful gown made of cream-colored silk, concurs as she licks her lips and then immediately reaches in her tiny satin handbag for more lipstick. "Too bad he's wearing a wedding ring, hon. So put it out of your mind right now. Although that never stopped you with that cop from Dedham," she teases. Her friend swats her on the arm and hisses a theatrical *shhhh* before holding her finger to her lips and giggling.

After all of the photographs have been taken, the partygoers sit at polyester tablecloth-covered tables and are served dinner, which appears to consist of a chicken breast-shaped piece of glop, a messy pyramid of electric orange cooked carrot medallions, and some entirely questionable mashed potatoes. Although William told me that he and I are entitled to free dinners at each of these events, he wisely suggested I eat beforehand when we spoke last week. The boys dine with gusto and the girls barely touch their food, preferring instead to chat at the tables and jump up in groups of two or three to run to the bathroom approximately every fifteen seconds. William and I wander the room with our cameras, taking candid shots of the tables. This is harder than it sounds, because I'm finding that I invariably click the shutter when some fat kid is shoving food in his mouth or doing something similarly unflattering. But hey, I rationalize, I'm new at this. My subjects don't normally move, or eat, or brush their hair at the table.

I'm looking around the room and studying the mauve fabric-covered walls and bizarre looping swags of satin over the doors when William appears at my side. "Want some chicken?" he asks, pointing to a picked-over plate on the table nearest to us.

"Want some cigarette," I reply hungrily.

"You can go outside for a minute; it's no problem," he says warmly, waving me away. "Really. This is a good time." He points his chin in the direction of the door.

I slip outside The Regency, making the valet leap up from his vinyl-upholstered chair until he realizes that I'm not a guest. I light a cigarette and walk to the side of the building, winding my way through the line of limos and nosily peering in the windows. One limo driver is sprawled in the backseat and watching a re-run of "Who's The Boss?" while he eats an overstuffed grinder. As I round the corner, I bump into Mrs. Carey, who is hurriedly puffing away.

"Hello," she says, smoothing her floral-print dress. "Thank you for helping to restore some order in there."

"It's no problem," I shrug. "This is my first prom. Some wild stuff in there."

"Not to me," she says quickly. "I've been to a lot of them over the years, and they're all pretty much the same," she adds, sounding tired.

"That's what the guy I'm working for said," I say, nodding. "I've got about six more weeks of these, through the end of June."

"Good luck," she scoffs as she stubs out her cigarette, pressing the toe of her bone-colored Easy Spirit pump against the filter. "You're going to need it."

Same shit, different day, to quote one of the attorneys at the law firm where I temped, a steely-eyed guy with neatly parted, gleaming black hair and even shinier wing-tip shoes. I'd heard that the starting salary at that firm is about $125,000 a year, which really does stretch the definition of what type of work constitutes "shit" in one's mind. I'm sure the firm's cleaning lady, a heavyset, older woman who lumbered cowed and bowed around the firm's employees at the end of the day, would be grateful for the same shit every day if it paid not even a quarter as well.

To be accurate, it isn't *quite* the same shit. This evening we are just north of the city, in Revere, or as the hyper kids keep calling it, "Reh-*vee*-ah." By the time we finished taking all of the photos, collecting the money, and fending off kids begging for just one more shot of their friends pressed together in a sweaty huddle on the dance floor at The Regency last night, it was after midnight. Next came the breaking down of the stunning backdrop, the lights, and the tripod, and the indelicate hurling of said items into the back of William's wagon. We climbed into the car and got into a lively discussion about the music at the prom, which as far as I could tell, heavily featured lyrics that described violent things the singer wanted to do to his baby's mama, or conversely, romantic or erotic things that he wanted to do to or with his ho.

By the time we'd pulled up in front of my house at one-thirty, we were convulsing with laughter and had decided that we liked the passive-aggressive lyrics in the songs of our youth much better. There was a long pause before I got out of the car, and William asked, "Same time, tomorrow night?" in a mock-formal way that called to mind a date, and I laughed uneasily as I slammed the door behind me and walked up the steps to my apartment. I hugged my arms to my chest and watched him as he drove away, thinking firmly, *Iley, listen to the girl in the cream-colored silk gown: Too bad he's wearing a wedding ring, hon. So put it out of your mind right now.*

Now it's less than twenty-four hours later, and things are in full swing at the Revere High gym. Even though it's only May, it's stuffy and overheated and my camera strap sticks uncomfortably to my neck, which is pasty with sweat. The girls' hairdos have gone limp, and I watch a tall redhead wrap her hair around her index finger, trying to coax a curl from the flyaway strands. Luckily, William and I have already taken the posed photos, but the dancing is going on for another few hours yet and the melting mascara and open tuxedo shirts don't do much to flatter this crowd.

"Ovah hee-ya! Lady!" a kid with a thick neck and ripply front teeth yells to me, beckoning me with his beefy hand. He's holding a skinny, ruddy-cheeked girl in a shapeless purple dress close to him, pressing his fingers into the small of her back as her head lolls on his shoulder. For a moment I think he needs help, that perhaps she is ill, then I see her eyes and realize that she's just drunk or drugged.

"My name is Iley," I reply. "Not 'lady.' You want your picture taken?"

"Yeah, yeah. Come on, honey," he says, nudging his date. "Grace, baby, come on," he pleads. They both turn to face me as I focus the lens and try to find an angle that might play down this kid's massive neck and Grace's droopy posture.

"OK, ready? Everybody say, 'Ortiz,' " I shout, invoking a line I overheard William use last night at The Regency. I hadn't gotten too far with "cheese"; only got those sickly, weird smiles that you see in so many photos. I noticed William was getting kids hysterical with glee and bursting into wide, open-mouthed grins when he would command them to say "Ortiz," "Manny," or "Johnny." Some Internet research this morning with Erin's laptop quickly showed these to be David Ortiz, Manny Ramirez, and Johnny Damon of the Red Sox, and even though I don't give one whit about these guys, I'll gladly use their names to elicit some smiles. Ortiz works wonders on this couple, who light up and don't even blink when the flash pops on and off as I take multiple shots in succession.

"Ortiz always does it," I hear William say behind me. "I

wouldn't really have reason to read the sports pages if it weren't for this gig. But don't tell anyone here," he whispers, leaning in close to me and smiling. His temples are shining with sweat, and he's unbuttoned the second button on his shirt, a slouchy, vintage-looking striped number that he's left untucked and hanging over the waist of his jeans. "I think I'm going to need a drink when this is through," he adds, and I nod, unsure of whether he is speaking in that general way about stressful situations that make one thirst for booze, or whether a drink will be part of this prom night.

A sudden scream catches our attention, and we snap our heads up to catch two wild-eyed girls clawing at one another and screeching as they fall onto the well-worn hardwood floor of the gym. A dyed-to-match teal shoe flies into the air and lands perilously close to the punch bowl. Chaperones yank the girls apart, and the more aggressive of the two promgoers breaks free for a split second and lunges at her opponent once more before being tackled from behind by a very tall girl in a strapless sheath dress.

"Ho ho!" William chortles. "Your first catfight, Iley! I shot these proms for almost two seasons before I witnessed one of these. You should feel very honored." We look over again, and order seems to have been restored to the dance floor, although all hairdos are hopelessly lost: one girl's croissant-style updo has come unwound and now resembles more of a spindly baguette, and another's weave has been yanked out of place on the left side of her head.

Everyone slowly drifts back to the dance floor, the deejay wisely chooses to wrap up the block of songs about the singers' babies' mamas, and then announces in a syrupy voice that he's going to slow it down for all the lovers in the house. The couples grip one another as they shamble around the dance floor, barely lifting their feet. Some kiss so languidly that it looks as though they've lapsed into a coma; others get touchy, and I count at least four egregious ass-grabs right in my field of vision. I know that I'm supposed to be capturing these enchanted Kodak moments, but right now I'm just spacing out, watching the kids with a weird mixture of wistfulness and pity. When I peer at William out of the corner of my eye, he's wearing an expression that suggests the same. He snaps to, shakes his head, and looks at me. "If you want to step outside for a minute, go ahead," he says.

"Do I look like I need a smoke that bad?" I tease.

"Well," he says, stepping back and looking at me through the viewfinder of his camera, "yes." It looks like he's starting to focus the lens, so I stand taller, stick out my chest, and give a quirky, closed-mouth smile, and there's a long pause, but no shutter click.

A moment later I step into the cool night air, quickly walk around to the back of the school, and let out a gasp when I see a couple for whom dancing doesn't quite cut it in terms of expressing themselves physically, evidently. The girl, a wispy, pale thing with limp, dishwater-blond hair and an ill-fitting mint green satin gown is busily sucking on the neck of her date, who has hiked up her dress and is jamming his hand between her legs as though he's trying to retrieve a candy bar from a vending machine. There is lots of lip-smacking and low moaning, and I'm transfixed for a second before I hear the unmistakable sound of a zipper coming down, and I hurry back to the gym.

"Have a good break?" William asks as I walk over to the photo area to get more film for my camera.

"There's a couple about to have sex outside," I say, mildly stunned. "I'm sorry, I'm no prude, but . . ." I drift off, shaking my head. "Well, you know. Besides, I didn't think they were allowed outside." This fact had been explicitly stated to all party guests no fewer than six times at the start of the night. Once you're in, you're here for the evening, the Spanish teacher with the glass eye explained. There will be chaperones posted at every school exit, and if you go out, you can't come back in, Señora Remba trilled, dramatically rolling the *r* in "chaperones" and "every." These rules apply to everyone, the vice-principal finished, casting a stern glance around the place.

"Here's the thing, Iley: they *always* find a way outside," William says, drawing out the word always. "I don't know if they go through a window or a vent or what they do, but they get outside. Always."

"Well, yeah, I guess if a person is looking to have some illicit fun, they'll find a way to make it happen," I reply. After the words have left my mouth, I consider what I've just said and bite my lip.

He takes a long look at me and blows a lock of hair off his forehead; now that the gym is full of sweaty, dancing kids, the air is even sultrier in here than it was earlier in the evening. "I think we should hold off on that drink," he decides aloud. "Between the fight and the lovers outside, I think you've had it for one evening, no?" I nod and shrug in a way that I hope looks nonchalant, but I'm a bit disappointed. No matter, I decide later as I study William's pretty hands while he collapses the tripod. They're not too delicate but not too meaty either, and his nails are stained that unmistakable yellow from years of touching noxious chemicals. Next Friday is another school, another prom, another night.

Five

I'm coming out of a recurring nightmare, the one in which I've taken the best photographs of my entire life, and an unidentified villain yanks open my camera and exposes the film to the light, unwinds it from the spool, and sends it cascading in ruined loops to the ground. Only this time, my camera starts to emit a high-pitched sound that I don't recognize, and as I slowly wake up, I realize it's not my camera at all, but the phone. I lunge across the nightstand, knock a glass of water to the floor, and groan inwardly when I hear Erin's mother's voice on the other end.

"Hey! How lovely to catch you at home at ten-thirty on a weekday," she says evenly, and I can picture her rolling her eyes as she uses her index finger to trace the flawless string of pearls around her neck. Although Bitsy Brooks generally treats me with that sort of pinched-face congeniality common to her type, I know that "photographer" is most certainly not on the list of Respectable Career Choices, and this opinion often comes through loud and clear. God knows where "hairstylist" would fall on the list.

"Erin's not here," I mumble, hopelessly groggy from the two Tylenol PMs I took last night to help quiet my menstrual cramps. One of the little blue and white suckers never seems to do the trick, but two seems too many, and I'm seeing double Gary snouts as he pokes his head over the edge of the bed. I close my eyes for a few seconds and reopen them slowly. "She's at the sal—she's not here right now," I say, my chest tightening through the numbness of the Tylenol PM that covers me like an analgesic blanket. Over the years, I have come up with some quick but not especially believable saves when I begin to say the first syllable of "salon" by accident, making Erin an unwitting frequent visitor to salad bars, salsa classes, and, in one memorable instance, the Salty Dog Seafood Bar and Grille in Faneuil Hall. This one seemed the least plausible because, just like today, the call from Bitsy had been placed well before noon, when even the most ardent lover of oysters on the half shell would have a hard time stomaching such a meal. But Bitsy seemed to buy it, the way she always does, hardly acknowledging my excuses and ending with an airy, "Well, just tell the dear I called."

I hang up the phone and look at the open bag of potato chips on the floor next to my bed—I never can resist the siren song of salt when I've got my period, but I feel so bloated and cotton-mouthed that the thought of the chemical zest of a sour cream and onion chip turns my stomach.

I get up, shake the nightmare and conversation from my head, take a long, hot shower, and wash my hair using an inspired combination of the half-dozen creamy shampoos and beautifully fragranced conditioners lined up on the ledge of the tub. The sun is shining brightly outside, my hair smells like an overripe fruit salad, and it's time to take photographs of things more aesthetically pleasing than air-brushed acrylic fingernails, too-tight cummerbunds, and Mylar balloons.

I'm flying down Commonwealth Avenue on my bike and enjoying the cool wind in my damp hair, when I take a sharp turn onto Clarendon Street and decide on a whim to visit Erin. I lock my bike to a pole that has a white sticker bearing a blurry photo of Andre the Giant, and open the brushed aluminum door to George, the eponymous salon of one of Boston's most revered stylists. I trudge up the narrow staircase and am greeted by Monique, who, no matter how many times she sees me here, refuses to remember who I am. Her shiny, chocolate-brown curls bounce around her adorable face as she snaps her head up and takes in my half-dried windblown mop.

"Do you have an appointment?" she asks, pursing her lips, which have been expertly matte-ified with a deep, creamy taupe. I learned this word just four days ago, when I overheard two girls in the bathroom at Revere High talking about the importance of matte-ifying their lipstick. Silly me, I thought behind the stall door as I fished in my bag for a tampon, spending my time in high school worrying about the War of 1812 and cosines.

"No, I'm here to see Erin," I snap as I sail past her without another word. Erin is busy cutting the hair of a bone-thin woman with high cheekbones and a cell phone pressed to her ear. By some miracle, Erin is able to move the customer's head and take snips of her hair without disturbing the woman's conversation. When she slides behind the woman and pulls a lock of hair down in front of each ear to measure the evenness, I walk over.

"Hey!" she says, surprised. She looks around the entire room without having to turn her head once, thanks to the rows of massive mirrors lining every wall. "Furious George is here today," she warns, invoking her nickname for her easily enraged boss. She walks over to the low cabinet beneath the mirror and grabs an orange tube from an open drawer. She squishes something pearly white and viscous into the palm of her hand, a runny blob that definitely calls to mind something else. "Yeah, I know," she says quietly as she hears me snicker, then looks at her palm and suppresses a laugh. "It's gross." She rubs her hands together and runs her fingers through the woman's hair, saying to her in a voice normally reserved for a developmentally disabled child, "I'll need to dry your hair next, so I'll give you a minute to finish your conversation." The woman doesn't acknowledge Erin, so she shrugs and turns to me. "I've got a few minutes between her and my next appointment. Meet you outside for a smoke after I dry her hair?" I nod and walk back past Monique with my head held high, despite the fact that my hair has now dried into a shapeless, black mass that clearly has no place within the walls of George.

Two minutes later, Erin pops out of the salon with her

cat's-eye sunglasses on and a cigarette already between her lips. "I got one of the assistants to dry her hair," she says a bit haughtily as she sits down on the steps next to me.

"Bitsy called this morning. I almost slipped because I was hung over from Tylenol PM, but I think I did OK," I confess.

"She did?" she asks quickly, her shaky, suddenly girlish voice in sharp contrast to her cool shades and black T-shirt. "What did you say? What happened?"

"It's all right," I assure her. "I covered fine. Don't worry." We silently watch an attractive twenty-something couple saunter down the street with matching Emporio Armani shopping bags and an immaculately groomed Yorkshire terrier on a leather leash.

"She needs a better haircut," Erin pronounces as she studies the woman, who has an aquiline nose and perfect, pouty lips. "She could get away with a center part so easily, I don't know what she's doing with that weird side part and ponytail thing," she points, using the two fingers holding the cigarette. The woman glowers at Erin, who doesn't back down and handily wins the staring contest. After the couple is out of sight, she turns to me, ready to talk. "I hate lying to Bitsy, Iley. And I hate that I ask you to lie to her too, you know that," she says in a low voice. I nod knowingly; it's an earnest speech I've heard at least two dozen times. "It's just . . . it's my family. It would kill my mother. I really would hate to disappoint them." She frowns and turns around to glance at George, her biggest pride, her secret shame.

"No problem," I say, leaning back and resting my elbows on the step. I lean forward after a second or two; even through my cotton sweater, the pebbly, painted surface makes the skin on my forearms smart. "Aren't you going home to see your parents sometime?" I ask as we watch a guy in a powder blue Jaguar repeatedly attempting to maneuver into a space in front of the salon. Parallel parking clearly isn't his strong suit, as he's got loads of room and can't seem to cut the wheel at the right time. "Look at this; I think Stevie Wonder could park this car better," I snort as an angry symphony of car horns fills the street.

She rolls her eyes and laughs. "Iley, you're so bad. Yeah, I'm going to see them . . . um, not this weekend but the next one," she says. "This weekend is Cara's party—are you going to come with me?" she asks. Cara is a childhood friend of Erin's who also left the ritzy enclave of their youth for the big city, although, unlike Erin, she chose a job that fell within the spectrum of respectable careers. She heads up pledge drives at the local public television station and can be seen on TV with amazing regularity, earnestly asking for donations while wearing a cashmere sweater and tasteful gold earrings. Her gentle voice, wavy blond hair, and curvy figure are prized by the station's management, as she never fails to bring in the pledges, even when the economy is bad and people don't normally feel guilty about watching *Antiques Roadshow* for free. She gets a lot of letters from prison as well, guys who watch TV all day and express their gratitude in tight, jittery handwriting for "*Nova, Frontline,* and your awesome titties."

"I can't," I say apologetically. "Proms, remember? I don't get home until two in the morning."

"Oh yeah, that's right," she says, softly rapping herself on the head. "I think the chemicals they use in this place are getting to my brain," she adds, gesturing behind her to George. "Are you looking forward to your next prom?"

I smile. "Yeah, I am. But partly for the wrong reason, I think," I admit.

"Oh? Do you have your eye on high school hotties? One of my clients brings her seventeen-year-old son in for trims sometimes, and it's all I can do to keep from licking his ear," she says dreamily. "But I think once they're eighteen, you're in the clear."

I smile and we both lean to the side and press our backs against the metal railings as a huge man with a silvery-gray ponytail barrels past us, taking the stairs two at a time. "No, it's that I'm attracted to William," I say. "I mean, it's not even as though I know him that well yet, but I just have that feeling, you know?" Erin nods, a familiar smile on her face. "And I *really* shouldn't be attracted to him. For everyone's sake."

Erin's eyebrow goes up from behind her sunglasses. "Gay?"

I shake my head slowly and the eyebrow goes higher. "Married?" she asks incredulously. I nod and she sighs. We sit silently for a long minute and she says, "Well, that guy with the ponytail is my one o'clock, so I should go." She walks up the steps and is about to open the door to George when she turns and faces me, shading her eyes with her hand. "This is what you didn't tell me about him when I cut your hair last week, Iley. Right?"

I nod while grinning and shrugging like a dope. "Yeah. But it wasn't like I was lying. I just didn't say it."

She crosses her arms over her chest and wags her finger at me in dramatic schoolmarm style. "Iley, nothing escapes me in front of that mirror. I see *every*thing. Besides, not telling is sort of the same as lying." She turns and walks into the salon and I think to myself, well, I guess that's true. And you, Miss Erin, ought to know.

Twenty minutes later I am crouched on the ground at the Boston Common, scratching my head as I watch the scene unfolding before me and trying to figure out whether this is worth the film. Sitting on a patch of dirt is a hedgehog that someone has discarded—not a real one, of course, and not even a plush one that might have fallen from a child's hand, but a resin one with stiff metal spikes, the kind that one might wipe his shoes with before entering the house. The eyes are painted with bright white corneas and angry, little black pupils, and the spikes look painful to the touch. Two jumpy birds and an inquisitive duck are regarding the faux hedgehog with interest, circling and chirping and quacking, and I decide, what the hell. I take a few quick shots, knowing full well that nothing will come of this, because in the Iley Gilbert aesthetic, animals fall somewhere just above Anne Geddes babies on the list of verboten subjects. But there is something sort of compelling about the evil little rodent-cum-Hammacher-Schlemmer mudroom accessory.

Put out by the clicking of the shutter and whirring of the film, the birds and duck wander away and I leave my camera at my face and move my head around, searching for something serendipitous as my mind wanders. What the hell does it matter if I'm attracted to William, I ask myself. He's married, but what's the harm in having an extra reason to look forward to these proms, besides the parade of sequined gowns and shellacked hairstyles? It's not like I'm some kind of animal, unable to control its instincts and urges, unwittingly going through life guided by an autonomic combination of food, sex, and sleep. I finish by looking through the viewfinder at the same place I started, the unmoving, plastic hedgehog sitting placidly in the dirt. Even though its spikes are forbidding, I can't resist the urge to touch one of them, and I reach out to finger a few. They inflict more pain than I thought they would, and I draw my hand back quickly, angry with myself.

Filing and doing some light errands was what the temp agency assured me when they called early this morning and asked me to show up at the Massachusetts Eye and Ear Hospital at ten o'clock. But I'd have to say that this temp assignment seems to be light on the filing and pretty heavy on the errands, as this is the fourth box I've been asked to walk across the street in just under two hours. I don't really mind; the weather is lovely and warm, with that bright May sunshine that brings smiles to normally crabby Bostonian faces, but I can't figure out why this isn't a chore for the mailroom. When I return to the office after bearing my fourth white, unmarked, Styrofoam cube to a wild-haired guy in a white lab coat, my curiosity gets the best of me. I turn to the office manager, an obese woman wearing a dark denim muumuu and those glasses with lenses that are supposed to get lighter and darker according to whether one is inside or outside, but never quite work correctly.

"Laura," I say, as she clicks her purple fingernails against the keyboard, "do you mind if I ask something about those packages that I've been carrying across the street?"

She doesn't even look up from her monitor. "Eyes," is all she says.

I stand very still for a minute. "Excuse me?"

"They're eyes," she repeats, turning to face me. Her lenses are too dark for this light, and with the space between her eyebrows and cheekbones totally unreadable, I can't make out her expression. "They're for the research departments, across the street. We order them from eye banks around the country. But they're too delicate to trust to the mailroom." As if to illustrate her point, a mail cart speeds by in the hallway, and three packages fall from the cart onto the floor. A second later, a shaggy-haired guy wearing a Patriots T-shirt and ropy, gold chains runs up behind the cart, places the packages back on, and sends the whole thing down the hall again with a firm push.

"I can see that," I say, and we trade a smile. "So, eyes. Hmmm."

"Yeah, about fifteen or so in each box. I hope that doesn't upset you," she says, reaching into a glass jar of Swedish fish and extracting a green one. "Some people, I tell them it's beakers or test tubes or something. But you seem like you can handle it."

"Oh yeah, yeah," I say, nodding as I remember how I

nearly tripped when stepping off the curb with the second package of the morning. I imagine the eyeballs springing from the box, rolling into the gutter, and looking around in every direction, then I chuckle quietly as I think about what a great photograph that would make.

"That's the spirit," Laura says, getting up and clamping my shoulder with her meaty hand. "Oh, and it's time for your lunch break," she adds, glancing up at the clock.

I'm not really all that hungry, but I walk to the White Hen Pantry, or as my flamboyant college friend Billy used to affectionately refer to it, the White Hen Panty. The White Hen Pantry is a sad sort of convenience store, the poor stepbrother of shinier New England purveyors of all things non-nutritious and overpriced. The sludgy coffee sits in a cracked pot on a stained burner, and the fabric roses by the register are caked with dust. I wander around the store and settle on a mini-box of Lorna Doones and a foil package of mixed nuts, rationalizing that at least the nuts might have some protein.

As I approach the counter, I see an unkempt, twenty-something woman with a threadbare windbreaker and sweat pants, and a small girl who looks about three years old. The child's hair is uncombed and she looks exceptionally tired and stressed for such a tiny person. She is wearing a pink sweatshirt with the word "Princess" spelled out in glittery, magenta letters across the chest, and there is a stain of something orange by the hem.

"Kiss it, honey, kiss it for good luck," the woman orders, pushing something in the girl's face. The girl obliges, puckering up and giving an obligatory peck to what looks like a little piece of cardboard. The woman takes it back, hunches over the counter, and begins furiously attacking it with the edge of a penny when I realize what it is: a scratch ticket. She stamps her foot when she realizes it's a loser and orders the girl to kiss another, then another, and another.

"I want Chiclets," the girl whines as she caresses the gum and candy display beneath the counter. "Mommy, I want Chiclets."

"No!" Mom replies sharply. "You shut up, or I'll make you sit over there and wait for me," she says, pointing to a sagging stroller by the door. The scratched plastic frame and wheels have long ago lost their luster, and the fabric has faded to a sickly pinky-peach hue. In the center of the seat is a naked, bald baby doll. "Now kiss this one, we're going to get lucky, OK?" The girl frowns and turns away from the counter, finally relents, and graces the card with the unhappiest kiss I've ever seen. She quickly whips back around, her little arms folded over her chest.

"That's $5.97," says the cashier, rousing me from my observation of this pathetic scene.

"Oh, I also need a pack of Marlboro Lights," I say, pointing to the endless rows of cigarettes behind the counter. As he reaches for the cigarettes, I slide my arm to the right and surreptitiously grab two boxes of Chiclets, in orange and peppermint. "And these," I say quietly, pushing them across the counter. He glances at the woman, still hunched and breathing through her mouth as she pushes the penny across yet another card, and smiles ruefully at me as he places the cookies, nuts, cigarettes, and a book of matches in a plastic White Hen Pantry bag.

I take my change and grab the bag in my left hand, the gum in my right. On my way out the door, I drop the Chiclets into the stroller, in the small of the baby doll's back.

Six

William is pushed up close to me, so close that I can feel his breath, warm and smoky, in my ear. If I turned just a little to the left, I could probably feel the brush of his long, curly lashes against my temple. He opens his lips slowly as I close my eyes, then he screams at the top of his lungs, "I'LL TAKE THE LEFT SIDE OF THE ROOM, YOU TAKE THE RIGHT, OK?"

It's Friday night again, and we are at the prom of the Pierce School for the Deaf here in Boston. Upon arriving, I was struck dumb by how quiet it was here in the gym, and then I took a good look around and realized that had these been hearing students, it would have been my noisiest prom yet. Everyone's fingers were fluttering a mile a minute, with no breaks in the action. Kids silently ran to and fro across the gym, greeting their friends with hugs, kisses, and complicated, gleeful hand gestures that made me wish I understood sign language. A kindly teacher with dentures and a tweed blazer acted as an interpreter for me, and helped me check the students in while demonstrating how to sign "camera," "photograph," and "prom" after I expressed interest in learning a few words. I got a giggle and a few snickers when I tried "dance" and evidently ended up signing "sex" instead. Another teacher, this one a spritely, wavy-haired woman who could have passed for a promgoer herself, helped William and signed instructions to the couples in front of the camera.

Then the music started, and the quiet was shattered. It was the loudest music I've ever heard in an enclosed space in my life, and that includes the time I took my teenage cousin to see Kid Rock. I could feel the thump of the bass deep in my chest, and the screaming guitars conspired to make my ears bleed. William took one look at me and hollered apologetically, "I SHOULD HAVE WARNED YOU. THEY MAKE IT REALLY LOUD, SO THEY CAN FEEL THE VIBRATIONS. ALSO, SOME KIDS CAN HEAR A LITTLE BIT, I GUESS, SO THIS HELPS THEM HEAR THE MUSIC."

"OK, NO PROBLEM," I screamed back, my head pounding.

Now the evening is drawing to a close and the couples are slow-dancing to a Jon Mayer song, which sounds much less romantic and sensual when played at a volume that could scare off a herd of cattle. I've taken the right side of the room as William told me to, but I'm enjoying watching the kids too much to take any photographs right away. They can either communicate or dance but not both at the same time, and it's fun to see who is lost in the moment and simply embracing, and who stops dancing for a few seconds at a time to sign something sweet and sentimental. I decide to go for the split-second after the signing stops and before they begin embracing again, where their faces are joyous and open, and take several shots of different couples. William ambles over as the next slow song starts and shouts, "HOW ABOUT THAT DRINK TONIGHT?" I'm afraid I'm going to lose my voice if I try to compete with Norah Jones, so I simply nod and smile.

We pack up, count the money, say our good-byes to the teachers of the Pierce School, and drive off in search of a bar. We find one, a small place with an excellent jukebox and a shrine to Elvis, tucked away on a little side street. As I slide onto the stool, I realize that my ears are ringing. "Are your ears ringing?" I ask William, and three people look over at me.

"You're shouting," he laughs as the bartender walks over. "No more Pierce School proms for you. What do you want?"

"Do you have Caffrey's?" I ask the bartender in a voice that I'm sure is inaudible, but to my surprise, he can hear me fine and nods in response. A moment later I'm wiping foam off my upper lip and grinning as William turns to face me.

"So how do you like it? The job, not the beer." His eyes twinkle in the glow of a nearby Elvis candle.

"I like it," I reply. "I'm dying to know how you got into it, actually. You started to tell me in the car before, then we got pulled over, remember?" A young, burly cop, all puffed-up swagger and testosterone, took issue with William's busted taillight, and was set to give us a ticket when I popped out of the car, walked around, and told him that we were on our way to pick up a friend who was being released from the hospital. He took a good, long time to look me up and down as I blathered about our poor friend's injury, then sent us on our way with a warning.

"Yes, what you did was very impressive," he recalls, pushing a lock of hair behind his ear and nodding. "So about eight years ago, I was working as a freelance photographer, you know, for magazines and things like that, and I had a friend who worked in the darkroom of this studio that shoots proms and weddings. They needed someone else in the darkroom, and so I took the position for a little extra cash. We'd get baked and then work on people's prom photos," he says, laughing and shaking his head at the memory.

"Mmm, just like a real artist," I muse.

"The guy—what was his name?" he asks, looking at the ceiling as "Common People" blares from the jukebox. "Irving, his name was Irving. He needed someone to come with him to the shoots and seemed to think I was the most responsible one," he says.

"Shows what he knew," I say flirtatiously as I sip my beer.

"Ha, ha. So I helped him for a few years, and then his mind started to go a bit. He had to have been at least seventy when I started there. I think he realized he needed to retire when he put his camera in the microwave one day," he says sadly.

"Ooh, yikes," I cringe as I turn to face William. I keep my legs neatly crossed, but the Caffrey's is starting to work its magic on my empty stomach, and what I'd really like to do is wrap them tightly around him.

"So I sort of took over his business, kept all the same clients, and here we are," he says, gesturing with both palms in the air. He drops them to the bar and starts fiddling with a blue cardboard coaster. "It ain't *Vogue*," he adds, sighing.

"Eh," I say, shrugging. "Who wants to take pictures of blond, bitchy anorexics all day?" Just as the words leave my mouth, a lanky blond in a suede miniskirt reaches across me to retrieve a drink from the bartender and shoots me an annoyed glance. "Oops," I say to William as I start my second beer.

He laughs. "The truth is that we do take pictures of people like that at the proms. Some of these girls, they're a bit scary, aren't they?"

"Oh, yeah," I agree, thinking back to the precocious girls at The Regency, licking their chops while looking at William, a man twice their age, and the girl getting felt up behind the school in Revere. "Except tonight. Tonight they seemed sort of sweet. Maybe that was only because I had no idea what they were saying," I admit.

He gives me a look of recognition and tilts his head. "That's funny, Iley! I sometimes wonder the same thing. Maybe some of those kids are drug addicts and jerks, but you can't tell because they're signing."

"So, but you must do your own photography on the side, right?" I ask, getting back to the career question. My query is met with a quick flash of William's eyes and a sense of resignation, and I immediately wish I hadn't asked it.

"I used to," he says quietly, so quietly I can hardly catch it with my hampered hearing. "I have a darkroom but I don't get into it as much as I should. It's like, I get busy with all of this stuff, and then I just lose my motivation to shoot my own work. I used to like found objects, stuff I would discover wandering around the city," he says into his beer glass.

"Me, too!" I say. "I just took a picture of two birds and a duck investigating a fake hedgehog. I mean, animals are a bit gross in photos, but there was something funny about it," I babble. "Well, I'm sure you'll get back into it sometime," I say encouragingly as I resist the temptation to grasp his hand.

"Yeah. Yeah," he says, in a not very believable voice. He searches the spot in front of us for a long minute, as though there's a message hidden in the wood grain of the bar. Just as I wisely decide that this is definitely not the night to ask any questions about Mrs. William Jasper, he pulls some bills out of his wallet and puts them on the bar. "Want to head out soon? I'm dying for a cigarette," he says, casting an evil look at the NO SMOKING BY ORDER OF THE COMMONWEALTH OF MASSACHUSETTS sign posted behind the bar.

"Yes, of course," I say. "Who are these people, telling us we can't smoke in a bar? Don't they know that smoking goes with drinking?" I ask defiantly as I try to hand him a fistful of cash.

"You get no argument from me," he grins, handing the money back to me. "The beer's on me; you deserve it. You're a natural at this prom stuff. I'm not sure if that's good or bad," he laughs, as we head out into the springtime air and light up.

"I think for now it's good," I decide aloud, as I look at him through the clouds of wispy smoke.

The darks are always what emerge first once the paper is in the developer tray, so the first thing I see is the hedgehog's beady black pupils staring up at me. Within a few seconds, I can tell that this photo is going to be a bust, because it's positively bursting with unadulterated cuteness. One of the little birds has been caught in the middle of a spirited jump, and Christ, the duck even looks like he's smiling, as though he's on loan from an AFLAC commercial. I yawn and fight to keep my eyes open; it's only ten in the morning and quite dark in here, after all. After William dropped me off at two o'clock this morning, I not only couldn't fall asleep for a long while, but was also kept up all night pissing the two pints of beer I drank after the prom.

When my bladder beckoned once again at eight-thirty and my eyes flew open, I was disconcerted to find myself eagerly counting the hours until this evening's prom and remembering how nice William's behind looked on the bar stool last night. I leaped out of bed and decided to get in some darkroom time, forgetting that the quiet and dark always conspire to make me drowsy if the circumstances are right. (Once I tried developing photos while drunk on Finnish vodka and nearly passed out face-first into the water bath, such is the cocoon-like atmosphere in here.) And unfortunately, Rithy isn't next door to keep me engaged in lively conversation about his still lifes and the giant rats in the alley behind the restaurant. It's graduation weekend at Boston University, right where the largest of

Rithy's family's restaurants is situated. This means double and even triple shifts for everyone, to make sure that all the graduates and their families can be kept in chicken satay and the award-winning pad thai.

I develop a few more photos—trite, boring ones of flowers that I took the same day as the hedgehog—and decide to pack it in for the day before I become too frustrated. I step outside into the bright light and see Don meandering around in front of the door, the way he always does at this hour. Poor Don looks not too much older than I am. He's a veteran of the Persian Gulf War who suffered post-traumatic stress disorder and subsequently developed a life-destroying drug habit. We met a few years back when he began taking part in a methadone program that was run out of a tiny space down a side street next to the New England School of Photography. Every morning Don would come for his methadone, and if I happened to be here, we would exchange hellos and he would ask about my photography.

Last year the methadone clinic lost its funding and abruptly closed its doors forever, probably bowing to pressure from local businesses who complained about the disheveled people staggering zombie-style on the sidewalks and streets nearby. The only problem was that some of the program's recipients couldn't remember (or perhaps didn't want to remember) that it was closed. The clinic provided a tiny bit of structure in their lives, and they were loathe to let it go, instead preferring to show up every morning at ten o'clock for their imagined daily methadone injection and group therapy. One by one, they eventually stopped coming, but Don continues to loiter for several hours each day, waiting in vain for help that will never come.

"Been developing something nice?" he asks, his eyes dead and glassy behind the droopy lids. He's wearing a too-small white sweatshirt with the phrase "Fort Lauderdale, FL: Spring Break Capital" splashed across the chest in vibrant neon colors; I'm sure it's something that a college student recently discarded without a care. This is the question that Don asks me most frequently. Sometimes he throws me a curve ball and puts a twist on the question, asking if *I've* been developing into something nice, telling me that it's crucial to keep growing as a person while he fiercely scratches all over his body.

"Not today, my man," I say, shaking my head. "Just a bunch of crap."

"Yeah," he says, peering around the corner at the boarded-up door to the clinic. He picks at his scalp, forcing his greasy black hair up into messy little spikes around the crown of his head. "I know what that's like."

"Hang in there, Don," I say, giving him a sad smile as he casts another longing glance at the door. I turn and walk down the street, thinking about what I am going to wear to tonight's prom.

" 'You Can Go Your Own Way,' " I say triumphantly into William's ear, bending over and leaning in close to him as he peers through the viewfinder at the empty backdrop. "What do you think of that?"

He straightens up and looks puzzled for a second, then

says, "Fleetwood Mac? That song from the seventies, I remember it. That's a good one, Iley." We have unofficially started a little game, in which we think of passive-aggressive lyrics from songs from our childhoods and try to best one another. In the car last night, we'd gotten to talking about the music at the prom again, where the deaf kids unwittingly danced to songs about a girl's fat ass. William suggested that we try to see who has the best song, and came out of the gate strong with The Monkees' brassy "I'm Not Your Stepping Stone."

"It's like they're saying 'fuck you' without actually saying it, which I think is the cornerstone for the kind of song we're talking about," he decreed as I let my head loll against the headrest and stubbed out my cigarette in the Volvo's overflowing ashtray.

"Yeah, I thought it was pretty inspired," I say, putting my hands proudly on my hips and hoping that William takes notice of my carefully chosen prom attire. Tonight I've decided to wear a close fitting, pink V-neck sweater, a necklace with a sparkly star that sits right above my cleavage, and low-slung, dark blue jeans. "You know, because in the verses he talks about how much he loves this person, then he repeatedly tells her to go to hell in the refrain, right? How confusing can you get?" I ask as the first of the promgoers from Wakefield High stream into the dingy catering hall.

"Yeah, sounds like love to me," he says in a tone of voice that's hovering somewhere between heartbroken and hopelessly bitter. "Well, looks like it's showtime," he adds, nodding in the direction of a growing crowd of kids, all hooting and hollering in that collective pre-prom roar that

I'm quickly coming to recognize. A fat, balding man in a gray, threadbare suit is telling the kids to shut up and listen to the photographer's assistant, then there's a hush and a long silence, and I realize with a start that he's talking about me.

"OK!" I yell as a girl in silvery stilettos with four-inch heels stumbles onto the dark green carpet, nearly twisting her ankle. "Please line up against this . . ." God, what color is this, I think to myself as I glance at the peachy-tangerine wall that's been sloppily painted with dark green, anemic-looking vines and huge, lumpy posies. ". . . orange wall," I decide, walking over and taking a spot beneath a posy that's easily bigger than my head. "I'll check you in and then he'll take your photos," I say, pointing at William.

"Yeah, yeah, we know the drill," a tall, handsome kid says to me in a jaded voice as he walks over to the wall with his date. "This is my third prom," he adds, immediately setting himself up for a solid *thwack* on the shoulder with the baby blue, rhinestone-studded satin clutch his date is holding. He doesn't even flinch. "Tammi, I told you, you didn't even *live* here when Dana took me to the prom when I was a sophomore. Can I help it if your family was still in New Hampshire then? *God.*" Tammi gives a little sniff, and I slink away, smiling as I try to remember when these kinds of things used to matter so much.

I get down to work, checking in a very pimply couple who create a look of consternation on William's face as soon as they step in front of the camera, a popular couple who wear what looks like couture clothing and positively reek of weed, and a shrunken, disabled girl who is with her dad. "Sarah, you look wonderful tonight," I say, even though one side of her face is disfigured and there is a sticky-looking stain on the toe of her right patent-leather shoe.

"Thank you," her father says, winking at me with tired eyes. He is wearing a hopelessly outdated jacket and tie, the kind of clothing that clearly says, *I gave up my vanity years ago when things you can only imagine in your worst nightmares began demanding my attention.* "We might need some help with makeup, if you don't mind."

"Of course; it's no problem," I say agreeably as he hands me a little, silvery tube of lipstick. I start to take the cap off, then think better of it as I watch Sarah gnaw her lower lip as though she's working her way through a tough cut of meat. "We'll do it when she gets up there; girls always want their makeup to look fresh in the photos," I assure him.

I walk over to William, who is shooing away the popular pot-smokers—they've decided that the camera loves them and have confused William's backdrop for the red carpet, waving to all their friends and posing. He gives up and simply turns his back to them, until they get bored and walk away in a huff. "Hey, there's a girl coming up who I think has some special needs, I just wanted to let you know," I say, slipping the lipstick in my jeans pocket.

"That's nice of you," he says, smiling at me.

"Well, I'm just trying to make your job easier. That's what I do!" I exclaim, giving him a shit-eating, mock-sycophant grin.

"No, I mean it was nice of you to describe her that way.

My assistant two years ago really liked the word 'retard.' Hey, did you see those poor kids with the acne?" he asks, his eyes wide. "Don't they have medicine for that now?"

"I think so. But I think I heard it was dangerous. Doesn't it make them crazy? Or horny? Or something; I can't remember," I shrug, and William laughs.

"You're funny, Iley," he decides, and our eyes meet for a long second. "Well, back to the photo line for you," he says. It almost looks as though he's blushing a bit, but I'm sure it's the peachy-pink cast of the vile walls of The Wakefield Manor. "Oh, and I think our next guest must have taken some of that acne medication," he adds quietly, holding back a smile. I turn to see a very pregnant girl outfitted in a prom gown that's been let out at the waist, a lemon-yellow confection with little daisies at the hem. She studies me with narrowed, kohl-rimmed eyes as I check in her and her date, a little, high-voiced guy who doesn't seem like he'd have any notion of how to get a girl knocked-up. I suppress the urge to gape, mainly because I think she may punch my lights out if I do.

It's all downhill after that; how can you top a promgoer in her seventh month? As I'm checking in one of the last couples, I get a strange sense of déja vu, and I can't put my finger on why, until they walk away and I watch them pose for William. The girl, a skinny thing with wispy, blond hair, too much goopy lip gloss, and a limp, pink dress, looks an awful lot like the one I saw getting ready to have sex behind the school in Revere. I stare at the couple for a long minute—it's not the same guy, not by a long shot. Well, I figure, these girls all sort of look the same to me, frankly.

* * *

We've been driving for nearly an hour now, in search of a bar that isn't too grimy or a restaurant that isn't home to waitstaff awash in novelty pins, and coming up empty. Even though neither of us has said so, it's clear we've given up on finding a place to get a beer, and are instead simply cruising around, talking and laughing, listening to the radio and smoking. Just like high school.

"Don't you think it was shitty, how they laughed at that girl and her dad when they danced?" William asks in a pained voice as I shift in my seat to get a better look at him. We've turned onto a small side street with few streetlights, and I momentarily entertain the fantasy of him asking me if I want to "park."

"Of course it was shitty," I reply blithely. "All kids are shitty at that age. But I think it upset her dad more than it upset her, if it makes you feel any better," I say as I light another cigarette, inhale deeply, and blow the smoke out the window into the brisk midnight air. "*I* saw a girl pissing and a guy puking when I went outside for a smoke, right after they served dinner. She had her dress bunched up around her waist like she was stuck in some fucking chiffon beanbag chair," I spit, and William howls with laughter.

"I told you that they always find a way outside, Iley," he says triumphantly as we turn back onto a major thoroughfare, with an eerily lit Shaw's supermarket on one side and a string of weird little retailers on the other. "Ham," he says, nodding his head in the direction of one store as we wait for the light to change. "Why do they need a whole store for ham?"

"I dunno," I giggle as I realize I'm having the most fun and relaxed time I've had in quite a while, just talking with someone with whom I feel incredibly simpatico. And when he looks over at me and gives me a smile that makes my heart and crotch flutter, the very same way they did when I was riding in a car with a boy in high school, it makes me inhale sharply and force myself to look out the window.

"I guess we should start heading back," he sighs after a long silence. We both watch as the stoplight turns from yellow to red, signaling the WALK sign to illuminate for people who would never walk across this pedestrian-unfriendly thoroughfare anyway. "It's getting late," he adds in a sleepy, unbelievably sexy voice, and I decide to kill the fluttering for good.

"Yes, I've been meaning to ask you. What does Mrs. Jasper have to say about you staying out so late after prom?" I tease.

After a few beats of silence, he says, "Well, Mrs. Jasper—her name's Kendra—is out of town a lot." Each word leaves his lips as though it's coated in something acidic. "She's into art restoration." He stares straight ahead and grips the steering wheel, and I'm about to say something about what a great career that must be, when he continues. "She works part-time at the Smithsonian and teaches two days a week at Georgetown."

I arch one eyebrow as we get on Storrow Drive and a gigantic Cadillac SUV, whale-like both in size and hue, cuts us off and gifts us with a series of annoying honks. "In D.C.?" I ask, puzzled.

"In D.C.," he replies, stubbing out his cigarette in the

ashtray and rolling up his window. "She's there to teach classes on Thursdays and Fridays, then spends Saturdays at the Smithsonian. She comes home on Sunday, and then leaves again on Wednesday night," he says in a steely voice. "Every week."

"OK," I say softly. I join him in staring straight ahead at the road, and we don't speak again until we reach my apartment and I quickly jump out of the car.

Seven

"So, like, how do you know when something would make a good picture?" the guy with the Starfleet Academy T-shirt asks me with genuine interest as he leans on the desk.

"I don't know," I shrug as I glance at the clock behind his shoulder and regret having begun talking about photography. It's five past five, five minutes longer than I'm required to stay at this software development company in Cambridge, and I want to get the hell out of here. "You just know, I guess."

"Wow, cool," he drawls, scratching his scraggly goatee and obviously in the midst of forming a new line of questioning. I pull out my keys and put them on the desk in an effort to stem it. "You drive here? Because I'm walking to the garage, too," he says hopefully as he looks at the keys.

"Nope, I rode my bike," I say, picking up my silver key ring and waggling my bike lock key at him. "It's just downstairs," I add, sounding a bit too grateful. I stand up and sling my bag over my shoulder, nearly knocking a cocoa-encrusted coffee mug off a low filing cabinet behind the desk. It was here when I arrived this morning, and if anyone harbored any hopes of the temp washing it, they will be sorely disappointed. "It was nice to meet you, Phil," I say as I make my way to the door.

"Don't you have a bike helmet?" he asks in a disbelieving voice. "You should really wear a bike helmet."

"I know I should," I retort. "Of course I should." *Jackass.*

When I walk in the door twenty minutes later, dripping with sweat and dying to drop onto the sofa, Erin is already there, thumbing through *Vanity Fair* and pushing Gary's head away from her. "Keep your fur on," she tells him irritably. "We'll go in a minute."

"You want me to take him?" I pant as I lean against the chair by the door. "I'm already up." She looks up and studies me for a second and must see my numb expression, the kind that can only result from sitting behind a desk all day.

"Naw," she says, rousing herself from the sofa and causing Gary to leap around with anticipation. "I need the exercise anyway," she yawns as she smacks herself on the stomach. Erin has one of the female body types frequently seen in her kind: in proportion, but somewhat round-cheeked and chubby, the result of a lifetime of a bit too much drinking and time spent lolling in ski lodges. Bitsy embodies the other body type, preternaturally thin and stringy from tennis and sailing, and never lets Erin forget that this is the preferred look for a woman of their standing.

"Thank you," I say, heaving a sigh of relief and taking her spot on the sofa as she and Gary shuffle out the door. I

turn on the TV and notice a little plate on the floor with a neatly arrayed pile of Triscuits. It's funny how some habits die hard. Erin is wearing a black T-shirt and a striped skirt with an uneven hem today, and she spent the entire day with her hands in strangers' hair, yet automatically and without fail, Erin removes foods from their packages and presents them in a manner more pleasing, even when she's all alone. Boxes and jars, with their bright, common colors and loud, brassy product names on the labels have no place at the Brooks table.

I flip around until I find a rerun of "King of the Hill," and after a few minutes, Gary bounds in the door. Erin follows a few steps behind and chases after him, nearly breaking her neck when she trips on his leash and stumbles across the kitchen floor. She unclips the leash, throws it on the table, and sits on the sofa with me. "Boomhauer, now there's the kind of man I would like," she decides, nodding at the TV. "He's good-looking and good-natured, and you can't understand a single thing he says." She sighs. "I'm sure my mother has plans for me to meet all sorts of jerks this weekend," she says angrily.

"Well, they're proud of their daughter; she's got such a high-profile position at Harvard and all," I tease as I bite into a Triscuit and immediately choke on a scratchy little shard of cracker.

"Someday," she promises. "Someday I'll tell them what's going on. In the meantime, I should probably dig out some clothes for my trip," she adds, but doesn't budge. A syrupy ad for an Internet dating service comes on, the founder as soft-spoken and earnest as Mr. Rogers as he explains their special matchmaking criteria.

"You think this is religious?" I ask as Erin lights a cigarette and picks up her magazine again.

"What, the guy?"

"No, the whole site, the whole thing," I say, gesturing to the TV. "There's just something so . . . so weirdly serene and gentle about it, it reminds me of the old ladies downtown who ask if you know that Jesus died for your sins." Gary lumbers onto the sofa and gives me his patented "shove over" look. When I don't, he starts nudging me, so I relent, and the three of us study the ad's rosy-cheeked, turtleneck-wearing couples blathering on about how they found true love.

"Well, there's only one way to find out," Erin decides, handing me her cigarette and putting the magazine next to the plate of Triscuits. She walks into her room and appears a moment later with her laptop. "Ohhh-kaaaaay," she says, typing in the Web site name and waiting. "All right, it's not saying anything about religion yet," she says warily, as I watch her pupils move back and forth. "Hey, look, a personality test! Should I take it?"

"Sure, why not?" I ask, tickling Gary under his chin. Normally he likes this and responds with low growls of pleasure, but today it seems to be annoying him.

"Let's see . . . this is a very weird list," she says slowly, her eyebrows knitting together as she spins the laptop around to face me. I study the screen for a moment; there is a list of words with check boxes to the left of every one. At the end of each word is a period, which lends to the personality test a strange sense of pretentiousness. It reads:

- ❑ Warm.
- ❑ Accepting.
- ❑ Guarded.
- ❑ Aloof.
- ❑ Funny.
- ❑ Risk-taker.

And so on for another fifteen words or so, adjectives that aim to capture a stranger's essence via DSL lines. The weirdest word on the list by far is *obstreperous* (complete with period). "Erin, what is 'obstreperous'?" I ask as Gary lets out a low moan. She turns the laptop back around and begins typing.

"This dictionary Web site says it means 'argumentative or difficult,'" she says after a minute. "That sounds like a lot of people I know," she laughs as the show ends and the up-tempo, twangy theme song begins. "This part of the test is free; I'm going to do it!" she decides, squinting at the monitor screen.

"OK," I say, but her personality test is immediately cut short, as Gary lets out an enormous burp and throws up on the arm of the sofa. "What the hell?" I ask, leaning over to survey the mess, a pulpy pile of something electric yellow. "What *is* that?"

"There was a Twinkie in the street," she says meekly. "He just seemed to be enjoying it so much. I'll clean it up," she sighs, getting off the sofa.

"You got that right," I call after her. "You poor guy," I say, turning to Gary and rubbing behind his ears. He looks at me sleepily, and I picture his online personality test (Upbeat. Purebred. Flea-prone. Gregarious. Easily nauseated.). I chuckle a little, and then decide to take pity on Erin and help her with the Twinkie cleanup.

William withdraws the fork from his mouth through gritted teeth. He grimaces and gives a big shiver, the same way Gary does when he realizes we've snuck a heartworm pill into a bit of cheese.

"Oh. Oh. Ew," he groans, putting the fork down on the card table they've set up for us.

"Why did you eat that?" I ask, pointing to a plate that is said to contain vegetarian lasagna, but actually bears a distinct appearance to plastic vomit. "You said never to eat at these things," I scold him playfully. Tonight we are in Millis, about forty-five minutes outside of Boston, and the kids are working their way through their prom meal.

"I know, I know," he says, sitting in a folding chair and running his fingers through his hair. "I didn't have time to eat; I got distracted taking pictures earlier."

"Yeah, the light was so nice today, wasn't it?" June sunshine, clear and crisp on my face as I rode my bike to the darkroom. "What did you shoot?"

"Oh, just some buttons I found in the alley outside a fabric store downtown. The colors of the buttons just looked cool against the charcoal-gray pavement," he says, pushing the fork around in the yellow, congealed mess on the plate. "Blue and rust and jungle green and lavender. The contrast was great. Hey, listen to me, talking just like an artist," he muses, smiling up at me as he sets the fork down.

"What, you don't get to do that often?" I ask. He doesn't

answer, just shuts his mouth and sits silently for a few seconds. *You can talk to me about art whenever you want,* I think. *I'm not in D.C. I'm here. Right here.* Instead I point to the manic deejay and whine, "I cannot listen to one more Hoobastank or Matchbox Twenty song tonight, OK?"

"It's not so bad," he assures me as he stands up. "Be glad you weren't doing this job when the Backstreet Boys were more popular." He spies a camera on the table; it's my own Nikon, with the yellow embroidered strap. "That yours?"

I nod. "I brought it from home—you never know what you'll see, right?" I ask, remembering the sight of the girl with the prom dress over her head. "Back to the dance floor?" I say as I peer at a red-faced kid who has mistaken a scissor-like, jumping jacks move for dancing.

"Yeah," he says distractedly, catching sight of the kid, whose date is now backing away as though from a rabid animal—moving slowly, never taking her eyes from the crazed thing. "You want to run out for a minute beforehand?" He doesn't say what for, doesn't need to. I smile eagerly and wait for him to walk out to the dance floor so I can admire his loose-limbed gait and glossy hair, then slip my camera around my neck and duck out an exit by the ladies' room.

"I am SO HIGH!" I hear a girl shriek as I step out the door and light up. She is sitting on the pavement, next to the far side of a row of bushes, her face as pale as her white satin gown, her black and white beaded purse a few feet away. Two girls are trying to rouse her, each grabbing an arm, and one, two, three-ing, but all they're succeeding in doing is dragging her butt through the bushes a few inches at a time.

"ASHLEY!" one screams, pushing her glossy lips up close to the tendrils that frame her friend's face. The tendrils, once assuredly bouncy and curled to soft perfection earlier today at the salon, now hang like limp fettucine noodles. "Ashley, get up! They're announcing king and queen soon, and we don't want to miss it!"

The other friend, a snub-nosed girl with glittery eye shadow and a dress with a too-tight, strapless bodice, nods dramatically. *"Yeah,* Ashley. We're not waiting anymore, OK? Come *on,"* she urges, folding her hands across her chest and nearly forcing her breasts out of their tentative restraints.

"OK, OK," Ashley drawls, giggling, playing with her hair, channeling Anna Nicole Smith. She crawls to retrieve her purse and lifts her arms in the air. When the two friends say their one, two, three, I focus my camera, and as they pull the wasted Ashley to her feet, I take the picture. They're right under a light, so I don't even need a flash. But even if I had, it wouldn't have mattered—they're so distracted they don't even notice.

On my way back in, I decide to hit the ladies' room and have to suppress a smile as I pee and listen to two shy girls who talk about their senior-year boyfriends and how "tonight is the night." I can only imagine that they are talking about one thing, and I dally at the sink long enough to confirm my suspicions.

"My sister said the first time it hurts," confides the one with a generous sweep of glitter across her hairline, like all the figure skaters have nowadays. I glance at their expressions in the mirror; they've got the faces of soldiers about to go into battle, and I decide it's time to step in.

"It doesn't necessarily hurt," I say, drying my hands on a paper towel as they both turn to stare at me. "It just . . . takes a little while to get to the point where it's really fun."

"What, you mean like a few minutes?" glitter girl asks as her friend's eyes grow wide.

"Mmmm, no, I mean like a few months," I say evenly. You know, just in time for your boyfriends to go off to college and dump you for some coed hotties. "Maybe I'm wrong, though," I add with transparent cheeriness after seeing their crestfallen faces. "Maybe you're fast learners."

"Mr. Frechette said that *I'm* a fast learner," I hear one of them say forcefully as I leave the ladies' room and get swallowed up in the strains of Hoobastank. "He told me that I understood how to conjugate all the French verbs faster than anyone in the class. So I'm not worried."

I'm drunk. I'm drunk with William in an Applebee's, pressed up against him at the bar and ignoring the voice in my head that's saying, *Wife in D.C., Iley. William belongs to somebody in D.C.* "This place is horrible," I decide aloud as I look around at the other bar patrons: two guys in khakis and polo shirts, talking to one of the blond bartenders; a lone, sullen woman hunched over a mixed drink; a couple in their fifties, obviously waiting for a table as they compulsively check their watches; a group of forty-something women with color-damaged hair, cheap pumps, and drinks like strawberry daiquiris and piña coladas.

"I know," William says, starting in on another beer. "But we can't be too choosy, right? I didn't see any other place to go, other than that freaky dive."

"Check out the piña colada," I say, nodding at one of the

women in the group of noisy revelers. "I didn't even know they made that drink anymore."

"Oh, yeah, that reminds me," William says as I rest my elbow on the bar, place my chin in my hand, and turn to face him. He is flushed from the booze, and his eyes are swimming. For a split second, I wonder if I should stop drinking, so I can drive us home later. I may not always bike sober, because I figure that the only person I could injure would be myself. Cars, with their hulking metal and machinery, are a different story. "I rented *American Splendor* the other day, and it had that song about the piña colada in it."

"I *love* that movie," I coo. It's true. I do.

"Me, too. So anyway, the lyrics to that song are definitely the worst. The guy in the song is reading the personals in bed next to his 'lady,' as he calls her. Then he takes out an ad himself, because he's bored with said lady," he explains, laughing.

"That's pretty bad," I say. "Then what?"

"You don't remember it?" he asks. "Well, it is thirty years old. So he gets a response, and he's all excited, and it turns out to be her, and they find love again."

"LAME!" I yell, and begin to laugh raucously. How did I end up here, post-prom and talking about "The Piña Colada Song"? I order a kamikaze and gulp it down.

"So you never finished telling me about your conversation with the girls in the bathroom," William says, peering at me through narrowed eyes. He studies me a split-second too long, and instead of glancing in another direction, I lock eyes with him and don't look away, even as one of the khaki-wearing men chortles with delight over something the bartender has said to him. "What was their story?"

"Sex," I say, feeling like a new recruit about to jump out of a plane after uttering that one simple word. Heart pounding. Throat constricted. Excited. Here we go. "That was their story. They were going to have their first time after the prom with their boyfriends, and I was giving them some pointers."

He looks intrigued. "What did you say?"

"Oh, not much. Just that it might take awhile before they really get into it," I shrug.

"Did you say anything about what it feels like?" he asks, leaning in close to me with his lips parted. He looks at me expectantly as I watch his pupils enlarge. Does he want me to talk dirty to him here at Applebee's, with the Sox game blaring from the TVs over our heads and the squealing daiquiri drinkers on our right? Hell, I decide, I'll try anything once—and if I've misread him, I'll just blame it on the booze.

I turn forty-five degrees on my bar stool, then lean over and press my chest against the upper half of his right arm. "I told them that if it's with the right person, it feels really, really incredible," I lie in a low purr. I let the tip of my tongue graze the spot behind his earlobe before I pull back and sit upright. After a few seconds, I look over and his eyes are locked on the bar and he's gripping the edge, his expression intense. The TV flashes to an image of the bright lights at Fenway, and the screen throws a white glare onto our section of the bar and anything metal in it. The beer taps. A set of keys belonging to the lone drinker. William's wedding band.

"I think I need to use the bathroom," I say suddenly. "We're not going to get any more drinks, right? So maybe I should just meet you outside?" He nods and I trot off to the bathroom, where I splash cool water on my face. I pace the floor for a minute and look out the tiny window. It's a typical overdeveloped suburban horizon: Linens 'n Things, Best Buy, another chain restaurant, Borders. And across the highway, between a break in the big box retailers, sits a small sign for a Comfort Inn. I study the sign and think about what my list would look like if I filled out an online personality test:

- ❑ Lonely.
- ❑ Horny.
- ❑ Bored.
- ❑ Obstreperous.
- ❑ Risk-taker.
- ❑ Impulsive.

I swing open the bathroom door and march through the restaurant and out to the parking lot, my breath coming out in short bursts. William looks up when he sees me, and gives me a rueful smile. "You ready to go home?"

"No," I say, looking him squarely in the eye. I point to the sign for the Comfort Inn. "I want to go there."

In homage to the recently deceased photographer, we've checked in as Mr. and Mrs. Cartier-Bresson. The dead-eyed girl with the lank ponytail working behind the counter didn't even bat an eyelash, just handed William the keys and directed us to the far staircase. We walked up in silence and let ourselves into the room, which was completely dark and smelled of cheap polyester bedspread and Pine-Sol. Never one to waste time, I quickly became sober enough to turn on a small metal desk lamp and start yanking off William's shirt. Now the room looks like a cliché, as though this is a movie, and a set dresser was hired to meticulously create the scene: Pants in a bunch on the floor. A bra draped over a chair. Shoes kicked to the far reaches of the room. My thong in a knot at the foot of the bed. And William and I, rolling around on top of this itchy, flowered bedspread, kissing as though each other's mouths contain some life-giving force, and touching one another in a way that feels much more familiar than it should. It's the feeling of pure attraction, of lust, really; and the experience to read the person and know instinctively which way to move. For an instant, my mind flashes to the girls from the ladies' room, and I am filled with gratitude that I am thirty-one and not sixteen.

It's hot in here now; much hotter than when we came in, and we're both so sweaty that we seem to slip effortlessly across the slick surface of the bedspread. I lie on my back, the sweat pooled between my shoulder blades adhering me to the flowery surface, and before too much longer, William is inside me. I grab his hair as he lowers his lips down next to my ear and lets out a long, relieved sigh; it's the sound of someone who hasn't visited this dark and delicious place on a woman's body in a long time and was worried that perhaps his passport had expired.

I breathe deeply, listen as he gets more and more excited, and think of Erin. No, no, not in that way. Instead, I think about how she and I always commiserate about how most men don't understand that a woman rarely comes the first time she's with a new guy, even if the sex is amazing. Sometimes *especially* if the sex is amazing, because that can mean that your heart is in it as well as your body, and sometimes you're just not relaxed enough. So few men comprehend this phenomenon, and instead see it as a blow to their sexual prowess, that she and I often wish they would teach it in Sex Ed as fact: Hair grows under your arms starting at about age twelve. It's normal to wake up and find something a little wet and sticky on the sheets. Your Adam's apple growing larger is what makes your voice deeper. Women rarely come the first time. I let this roll around in my head as I roll around with William on the bed, try to pace my breathing to his, and hope he understands.

Only something happens. Before I know what's going on, my skin feels hot and tight, my back is arching, and I grab William and press him to me as I become every woman you've ever heard on the other side of the motel room wall, moaning and shouting with unrestrained pleasure. A few minutes later, William provides the complementary piece to the motel scenario, making me smile from ear to ear as he knocks the cheap headboard against the wall with every frenzied thrust.

Eight

"These are good from a technical standpoint, Iley," my friend Craig says as he turns the pages of my portfolio and nearly knocks over a burnished chrome saltshaker. He moves the saltshaker to another table. "But kind of safe, don't you think?"

"Well, how dangerous are those?" I ask snippily, gesturing over to the bar. We're at 12 Newbury, a chic restaurant that regularly features up-and-coming photographers in mini-exhibits that line the long wall behind the bar. After going to undergrad with me, and then getting a graduate degree in photojournalism, Craig's desire to travel the world and take gritty photos was abruptly cut short when his longtime boyfriend was killed on a photojournalism assignment in Rwanda. He found his way to the restaurant business, quietly working here as the maître d' and serving as the curator for the bar's gallery. He gave me a little show a few years back, and

I'd recently decided that perhaps 12 Newbury was ready for another.

"Temper, temper," he admonishes, wagging his finger at me.

"Sorry," I say sheepishly. I'm definitely not my best today: my hair is dirty and itchy, my eyes have bags you could store last winter's sweaters in, and I'm completely exhausted. From fucking William until two-thirty in the morning, that is. "I'm sort of tired today, I didn't mean that, Craig."

"Well, I'm glad someone had a fun night," he says in a voice that is meant to sound kicky and fun, but instead comes out as inordinately sad. "In any case, I agree with you, OK? This show *isn't* very exciting," he says, pointing to the still lifes of wine bottles on the wall. "And these photos aren't selling. But I know that you can do things that are more interesting than what you have in here. Have you been shooting very much lately?" he asks, leaning back in the black leather banquette.

"Yeah, yeah," I assure him, although I can't actually visualize any photos I've taken that I've been excited about recently, and I make up my mind to start visiting some new neighborhoods for inspiration. "Oh, don't look at that," I say quickly as he leans forward and pulls something from the pocket in the very back of the portfolio. I try to grab it from him, but he's too quick, holding it above my head.

"Oh, God," he groans as he turns the photo around in the air. It's the hedgehog and my fowl friends from the Boston Common, in all their cute glory.

"I'm going to send it to the six-year-old daughter of a

friend of mine, don't have a conniption," I say, rolling my eyes. "It's not part of the book."

"It's so . . . sweet," he says, smiling against his will as he lays the photo on the table. "This can't be the same Iley who took a picture of all that blood on the sidewalk after those homeless guys got into a fight over a supermarket turkey, can it?" he asks, laughing. He peers at me, at my tired but happy eyes, my stubble-burned jaw line, my mysterious half-smile. "Wait a minute. You're not in love, are you?" he asks suspiciously, leaning forward and resting his arms on the table.

"No, no worries there," I say firmly as I shake my head, tuck the photo back into the pocket, and zip up the portfolio.

Tonight we're in Malden, just outside of the city, at a ramshackle little catering hall that suffers from delusions of grandeur and calls itself The Manor. Even though it's been less than twenty-four hours since William and I were naked together at the Comfort Inn, I can just tell from the way he is looking at me that tonight will command a repeat performance. The pre-prom photos have been shot, the meal consisting of a fatty piece of beef and gray green beans has been served, the kids are dancing, and I'm counting down the minutes until we can get out of here. Get out of here and get a drink. Get out of here and get out of our clothes. I practically lick my lips with excitement as I focus the camera on a bored-looking couple gripping each other and swaying on the dance floor. I'm looking at them but thinking of William, and it's only after I've taken a few pictures that I realize that they've moved out of frame, and now I'm taking shots of a vinyl upholstered chair on the far wall. I shake my head and move a few steps to the left, where I knock into a blond, mulleted kid with ripply front teeth and deep, pitted acne scars.

"Hey, watch where you're going," he sneers, the smell of hard liquor wafting out of his mouth and settling in the air between us.

"Sorry," I say tartly. "Take it easy, man."

"It's cool," he nods. He's obviously the type of person who only responds well to those who treat him as shabbily as he treats others, and it appears I've passed muster with my bitchy retort. I wonder briefly what life must be like for him at home, and I see him eyeing me, taking in my jeans, mint green baby tee, and black ponytail. "You party?" he asks.

"What?"

"I said, 'You party,'" he repeats, annoyed. "We got some good stuff out in the limo. All the way in the back, around the corner," he says, striding away from me.

I take several more pictures and talk to a gregarious teacher who shares a depressing anecdote about how one of her students thought that Alaska and Hawaii were off the coast of California, because that's where these states are included in little boxes on maps of the United States. Then I take off William's Canon, slide my own Nikon around my neck, and give the "Going out for a cigarette" signal to William. I step into the warm air, walk around the corner, and am immediately flagged down by my pockmarked friend. He's standing by a gigantic Hummer limo, which is gleaming and ridiculously outsized. Next to him is a pudgy, dark-haired girl whose eyes are rimmed with red and whose lipstick is smeared beyond repair.

"How do you guys get out here?" I ask, lighting a cigarette.

"Bathroom windows," they both answer at once.

"Impressive," I say, blowing smoke into the air and watching as the girl slumps against the Hummer's shiny black door.

"You want to see inside?" my new mullet friend asks, shoving the girl out of the way and opening the door. She slowly crumples into a pile of flesh and pink satin on the pavement, and he peers over at her for a few seconds before deciding, "She'll be fine." I peek into the Hummer limo, and through the clouds of smoke, I can make out about six kids in there, in various states of undress and all baked out of their minds.

"Who's that?" one asks, squinting at me and shielding her eyes with her hand. She's got blood-red fingernails and a drooping white carnation corsage pinned to her wrist.

"She's cool," my friend answers, and I step into the limo.

"You gonna take pictures?" a kid with a buzz-cut and tongue stud says as he points at my camera. He's got his jacket off, and his cummerbund's tied around another guy's head. "Take a picture of thith," he orders, pointing his tongue out at me. I oblige, and soon everyone is posing. I get a shot of a curvy, red-haired vamp with her high-heeled, strappy shoes off and her feet splayed in the air. Another kid insists I take a picture of him sparking up a giant bone, so I do. A morose, sad-eyed girl who is quietly studying her hands doesn't even notice when I take a photo of her. The crowd is getting pretty boisterous and

I'm starting to worry that perhaps I should head back inside, when a loud, "SHUT UP!" comes from the furthermost part of the limo, where I've been hearing rustling of fabric and suspicious slurping noises since I got here. A girl's head pops up, and I instinctively click the shutter. And as I do, I realize who this is. The blond promgoer. Her hair is a mess and drooping in knots around her ears, her spaghetti straps hang limply around her shoulders, and her dress is rumpled and unzipped. She narrows her eyes at me and slides back down behind the seat, and I decide that now would be a very good time to go back in.

The prom ends according to protocol: take a few final shots of the room during the last dance, make small talk with the principal, count the money. William and I gleefully scramble into the Volvo at midnight and go off in search of a drink. I am tingling with anticipation, and when he tentatively suggests that we should skip the drink, I agree immediately, knowing full well that he doesn't mean the evening would end here. We end up in a king-size bed at a Best Western, where I offer silent thanks to my trusty bike for giving me such robust thighs and supple hamstrings. Many a girl would be thrown to the other side of the bed, or perhaps even across the room, by a man bucking wildly beneath her for the better part of thirty minutes. But not me.

I'm dozing on the sofa with Gary at my feet when Erin comes in, wearing a canvas tote bag on her shoulder and an ill-fitting, pale blue polo shirt that barely covers her stomach. She looks as though she's in costume, getting ready to take her place in the front row of a preppy parade.

"Nice outfit," I croak from the sofa as I slowly hoist myself up. William and I stayed at the Best Western until well after three in the morning, and my voice is thick and scratchy from cigarettes, my body tired and achy from everything else.

"The bag will be good for storing Gary's toys," she says, ignoring my comment and placing the bag on the chair by the door. It has lime green webbed handles and is embroidered with a tasteful BEB monogram. These are Bitsy's initials, and she would undoubtedly scream if she knew that this bag would soon be home to Gary's drooly tennis balls and rubber chew toys. "God, you look awful," she says, studying me as I stretch. "Are you sick?"

"No, I was out really late . . . with William," I answer, trying to look sheepish. But I can't pull it off; I'm sure I only look euphoric.

Erin opens her eyes wide. "Oh no. Did you sleep with him last night?" she asks, her voice filled with dread.

"Well, um, yeah. Both nights, really," I say, lying back down and rubbing my eyes. "Friday and Saturday. We were out after Friday's prom and . . ." I trail off, holding both palms in the air as though I don't know how it ever happened. At the sound of the word "out," Gary runs to the door, and Erin swats him on the butt before moving the canvas bag off the chair and sitting down heavily.

"Iley," she says, her voice sounding strained. "You're having an affair?"

"No!" I say, sitting up on the sofa and muting *The Breakfast Club* on TBS. I'd been watching it and wondering how many of the kids at the proms might have ever seen this movie, and whether they found it patently ridiculous or accurately reflective their own lives. "I'm not having an *affair*, Erin," I snap.

"Well, William's married, isn't he?" she snaps back. "I mean, isn't that what an affair is?"

"He's married, but only just, all right?" I reply, annoyed. "His wife is never around, she's in D.C. half the time, and it sounds to me as though they've got this only marginally alive relationship," I say.

She doesn't say anything for a minute, just tugs at the hem of her polo shirt and stares at the floor. "Well, just so long as you know what you're doing." She gives me a glance that makes me squirm, because the look is very critical yet I know it's not on purpose; it's an autonomic response, one friend's involuntary urge to protect another.

"I saved a police blotter for you," I offer a little too helpfully, holding out the *Herald*. "There's a really good one in here about a fish thief at Haymarket who made off with over two hundred dollars' worth of mackerel. They use the phrases 'fish tale,' 'something fishy,' and 'holy mackerel.' Reporting at its finest."

"I'll have to check it out later," she says quickly. "I have to change out of this stupid shirt and go help Furious George at the salon. We got in some new styling carts, and he wants help setting them up for tomorrow. They're white and going to look horrible in a matter of weeks, but of course he doesn't care," she spits, looking at me again with dismay. She cocks her head and gives a dramatic pause. "Did you know you were going to do this? Is this why you didn't tell me William was married right off?"

"I dunno," I reply honestly. "I don't think so." Erin smiles and looks at the floor, then wordlessly heads into her room, leaving me with Gary, the jock, the hood, the rich girl, the geek, and the basket case.

"Fucking hell," I hiss as I yank the paper out from under the enlarger, slam down the metal frame, and inelegantly plop the photo into the developer bath. It's a hot Tuesday morning in the darkroom, and everything is coming out all wrong. I should have known that this would be a bad day when Don didn't even recognize me on the street, just dumbly stared as he tipped a movie theater-size box of Mike & Ike into his mouth when I said hello. Now this has simply become an exercise in wasting costly photographic paper, as I expose negative after negative and disappoint myself with the results. I shot a roll and a half of film yesterday and covered so much ground on my bike that my calves are sore. Cambridge. Watertown. North Allston. And back to Brighton. There are a few strong pictures: a diner sign juxtaposed at a funny angle to the entryway of a nearby church, a phone pole so covered with staples from long-gone band posters and roommate-wanted flyers that the staples themselves formed a cross-hatched design, the moss-covered dashboard of an old Mustang. But there are lots of dogs, too, not to mention the half roll that I wasted in the back of the Hummer.

I hear Rithy on the other side of the wall, his timer clicking off and then buzzing. He takes way too long to turn off the buzzer, and I punch the wall. "Sorry, Iley," says a muffled voice after the buzzer stops.

"No, I'm sorry," I apologize to the wall as I sit on a small stool next to the photo chemicals. I forego the tongs and pluck out the uninspired picture of ivy growing from in between bricks with my fingers, and drop it in the fixer. I know this one's not a keeper, so why treat it gently? "I'm not having a very good day over here."

"Any day that I'm here is a good day," he replies. "I will be here more this summer. Business is not so good since the new Thai place opened down the street."

"Oh yeah," I say as I start to work with a new negative, this one of the guy with the tongue stud. It's indescribably stupid and I won't do a thing with this photo, but the composition seems good, and I'll take anything right now to bolster my confidence. "Thai Garden?"

"Thai Kitchen," he answers irritably. "*Our* restaurant is Thai Garden."

"Sorry," I say again. "Maybe I'll come and eat there again sometime," I add, remembering the time I took a first date there and Rithy's cousin accidentally spilled a pitcher of Thai iced tea on his pants.

"Yeah, maybe you come," he says over the sound of his buzzer. "This time Nan doesn't wreck your friend's pants," he laughs mirthlessly, the shameful memory of the bad service seared into his brain. "I don't know if I'll be there, though, so you tell me ahead of time if you're coming. I don't work as many hours now."

"All right," I say, watching as the glint of the silver tongue stud appears in the developer tray. I consider whom I would bring to Thai Garden and then smile when I think about him.

Lisa and I have just finished the last of the paperbacks and are moving onto the seasonal items, which means row after row of bottles of sunscreen, followed by plastic beach toys, water wings, nose plugs, and goggles. She and I were assigned to work together this evening at what must be my most peculiar temp job yet: doing inventory at a gigantic, downtown CVS. When the agency called yesterday and informed me of this opportunity, I rolled my eyes and nearly laughed into the receiver. But then I remembered that I'm running low on photo paper, I need a new flash, and I'm hoping to foot the motel room bill for a future adventure with William, and I said OK. The store closed early at nine o'clock to allow all of us to file in and receive our directions from a friendly, bearded guy who is now walking around in his socks, padding between the Hair Color/Hair Styling and Feminine Hygiene/Incontinence/Baby Needs aisles and shouting out helpful hints as we scan the items.

Lisa and I were put on Seasonal/Magazines/Books/Candy, which comes with its own set of challenges. First of all, cellophane bags of Hershey's Kisses and Kit Kat minis are floppy, which means it can be hard to get the UPC code flat enough to scan. Also the books and magazines sit in tiered racks, so you'd have to pull out each and every one, which is time-consuming. But Lisa is bright, freshly graduated from Boston University and planning to move to New York to work in radio production as soon as she can, and we hatched a plan. While everyone else immediately started scanning their shampoo bottles and nail scissors and panty shields, we sat on the floor and began to strategize. We decided that if every item were facing the right way with its UPC code flat and readily accessible, it would go much more quickly. So we spent the first hour turning everything around and upending the books and magazines, and now we're scanning with rapid-fire efficiency.

I'm scanning a pair of SpongeBob water wings as my mind drifts back to my conversation with Erin, who I haven't really seen much of since Sunday. Is she right, did I really know that things were going to go this way with William? I remember the feeling in my chest the first time I went to his studio, the care I took putting on mascara when readying for our first prom, the way it took my breath away when The Pixies were pouring from the windows of the Volvo. But did I honestly have designs on a married man so early on? I don't think so, I decide uneasily as I reach to scan a six-pack of squat, green mini-canisters of propane. I remain lost in thought and take a deep breath, then abruptly knock into Lisa.

"Are we done?" she asks, surprised as she holds up a small squeeze bottle of lighter fluid.

"Meet in the middle, that was the plan, right?" I say. I look up and down the aisle. "I finished my half of that side, and my half of this side."

"Me too," she says, smiling and tightening her blond ponytail. "Excuse me," she calls to the bearded guy, who is wearing a concerned expression as he walks briskly toward the Cold and Cough/Allergy aisle.

"Yes?" he asks, holding his clipboard against his chest. He's got a scanner hanging from his belt loops, bigger and more formidable than ours, molded in red plastic with several multicolored buttons on the keypad.

"I think we're finished," Lisa announces, and two jokers working across the aisle on vitamins and dietary supplements snap their heads up and stare at us.

"Really?" he asks. We hand him our scanners and he nods, evidently impressed. "Good job." He smiles.

"So can we go?" I ask, shifting from one foot to the other. It's nearly midnight, I need a smoke, and my back aches from leaning over all those bags of Twizzlers.

"Oh no, no," he says cheerily. "I can't let anyone leave until we're all done. It's the store's policy, not mine—we need to have everyone go at the same time." Lisa and I look at one another with our mouths agape, and he runs off to manage a DayQuil caplet catastrophe.

"Well, at least we've got something to read," Lisa shrugs as she walks over to the magazine section. She selects a few women's magazines and tosses them to the carpet. They land in a messy but slightly artful array, as though they were fanned out and then picked over in a doctor's waiting room. We each take a magazine and sit in silence, reading about the new color palette for summer, Brad Pitt's upcoming film, and how to know if your guy is The One. I rarely read magazines like these, and I'm struck by just how many articles focus on the importance of hair removal, the bikini zone in particular. I had no idea that so many men place so much value on a neat and tidy hoohah, as Erin likes to call it. I think about my own, covered in dark, wiry hair that itches when I ride my bike for too long on summer afternoons, and flip the pages back to a soft-focus Sally Hansen ad for a home waxing kit.

"See her?" Lisa interrupts my hair musings and holds out her magazine. Featured on the page is a model/actress of the moment, her shiny blond hair lustrous and her smile large and vapid. "My friend is interning this summer with this woman's stylist in New York City," she says. "She doesn't know how to match clothes or anything," she announces a bit triumphantly, pointing to the picture.

"Whenever she dresses herself, she ends up on those worst-dressed lists. So Melissa—that's my friend—she literally has to help her boss pick out this girl's T-shirts and skirts and jeans and stuff."

"Pathetic," I say, scanning the body copy of the Sally Hansen ad in my own magazine. Hmm, maybe this waxing thing wouldn't be too difficult.

"Also, she has three French bulldogs that go everywhere with her," Lisa continues. "They shit all over everything and everyone acts like there's nothing weird about dogs crapping indoors at a photo shoot."

"Does your friend have to clean it up?"

She nods pitifully. "Sometimes."

"That's too bad," I say, thinking about how unpleasant it is to pick up Gary's brown bombs. Except that he's my pet and there's only one of him, so I feel quite sad for this Melissa person. "Well, I'm going to take a little stroll," I announce to Lisa as I stand up and stretch. I peer around the store until I find what I think is the appropriate aisle, then go off to do some hair-removal research.

Nine

It's the next morning, and I am alone in the hot apartment, sweating and crying as I sit on the bathroom floor. This waxing thing didn't go the way I planned at all, and I've got burns on my inner thighs, stringy bits of wax everywhere, and some very raw, red skin on my hoo-hah. It's too mortifying an injury to warrant a visit to the ER, but in all honesty, I feel as though I could use some robust painkillers, stat. Nurse Gary is on call, however, trying to push his way into the bathroom and growing more anxious with every yelp I give from behind the door. His furry ears are always attuned to any sounds of anguish in the apartment, and he will faithfully appear at my or Erin's side at the first strains of weeping. He is so skilled at providing comfort that he can even discern between hysterical laughter and explosive tears; Erin's can sound so similar that even I've been fooled, at times pausing outside her bedroom door and hoping she's OK. But Gary always knows which is which, an awe-inspiring feat for someone who cleans his butt with his tongue.

"I'm OK, honey," I sniff as I choke back tears. I can hear Gary panting, readying to give me comfort, but I don't open the door. The last thing I need in here is dog hair and clumps of wax adhered to his thick coat. I peel as much wax off as I can, repress the urge to vomit from the pain, and walk out of the bathroom naked from the waist down, wiping my eyes and searching for a cigarette.

The next day things look worse, not better. The torn skin on what must be the most sensitive area on my body is starting to ooze, and I can't sit down for more than a few moments at a time. Riding my bike is out, as is taking Gary on any walk longer than five minutes. Naturally, we're also in the middle of a June heat wave wherein the thermometer is hitting an unusually warm eighty-five degrees, and the sweat that normally trickles down my inner thighs without my noticing is burning me like napalm.

It's Wednesday, and all I can think about is this Friday's prom. There are only two weekends of proms left, which means four evenings with William, and I am loathe to give any of them up. As I search the Internet for the phone number of my HMO, it's not lost on me that I am more concerned about how this waxing mishap will affect my nights of sex with William than it will the health of my skin. I sigh as the pre-recorded message efficiently outlines the different departments and their extensions: internal medicine, press one; pediatrics, press two; ob/gyn, press three; medical specialties, press four; mental health, press five. My index finger hovers over the "3" on the keypad for a second—does this injury fall into the realm of gynecology?

Dermatology? Insanity? I impulsively press the button, and after explaining my predicament in a vague yet urgent way, I'm given an appointment with my doctor, who had a cancellation today. I grab the key to my bike lock out of habit, and then hurl it to the floor in anger when I remember that I need to take the T like every other chump.

"Hello Iley," Dr. Barrett says warmly, which immediately puts me at ease, or as much at ease as one can be when her vagina is in searing pain. She crosses the room and takes a seat on the small stool before setting my intake slip and a small pile of pamphlets on the counter. Dr. Barrett is direct and open, a stately African-American woman with a no-nonsense hairdo and little makeup. "I understand you've had some burning and a possible infection?" As soon as the words are out of her mouth, I know what the pamphlets are for: STDs. I'm sure of it. I can tell by their bright-colored covers and crummy illustrations, and my mind immediately flashes to a pamphlet we were forced to read in high school entitled "Chlamydia Is Not a Flower."

"I had an accident," I blurt out. "A waxing accident. I'm very embarrassed." Best to get it out in the open now that I'm not in the secondary stage of syphilis.

Dr. Barrett inhales through her nose and nods sagely. "I see it more often than you think. Let's have a look," she says as she puts on gloves, opens my gown, and gently pokes around for a few seconds. "You really made a mess here," she decides, shaking her head. "I'm glad you came, though, because this is getting infected." She gestures for me to sit up. "If you want to do more, um, grooming, I would recommend going to a professional. But even then, they can do damage unless they have a lot of practice," she warns.

"No, I think I'm done with this sort of thing," I say, forcing out a laugh. She rolls the chair over to a small computer workstation and calls up a screen that looks like it's on loan from an early IBM computer museum.

"I'm just looking over your chart, as long as you're here and we have a minute," she says. "You still smoke?" she asks, looking up at me reproachfully.

"Yeah," I admit. "I'll try to quit soon."

She doesn't reply to this, and continues to press the keys as I watch the all-caps words scroll across the bright blue screen. "Still on the Pill?"

"Uh-huh," I nod. I stayed on it after Matt and I broke up, because I loved the way it helped to control my menstrual cramps, and Dr. Barrett saw no reason for me to stop taking it even after he was out of the picture. Now I'm grateful that I chose to stay on it, since my and William's frenzied motel-room visits don't exactly allow for the deliberate unrolling of a condom or the patient insertion of a diaphragm. Last Saturday, we barely made it inside the room before we had all of our clothes off, my back pressing uncomfortably against the hard, plastic fire evacuation map bolted to the inside of the door. I hug my arms to my chest happily and smile as I remember it.

"Well, remember, anytime you're with someone new, you've got to use condoms until you're sure that this person is safe to have sex with, and is monogamous as well," she continues. She looks up to see my mouth hanging open—how did she know I was with someone new? "I sometimes see these waxing accidents with new relationships," she explains evenly, barely suppressing a smile. I laugh and tell her that, yes, I have been sexually active with someone new. I also assure her that everything is cool, perhaps a bit too flippantly.

"It's important, Iley," she says sternly. "A lot of people claim they are monogamous, but aren't. You can only rely on the Pill for certain things—I tell that to all my patients." She stands up, shakes my hand, leaves the antibiotic cream prescription on the counter, and walks out of the room. And as I gingerly pull on my underwear and take off my stylish paper gown, my smile fades when I admit to myself that Dr. Barrett is right. My relationship isn't monogamous. He isn't only mine. He isn't even single.

There isn't a lot to say about Kendra, except that William and I rarely mention her, and I generally choose not to think about her. Sometimes if William describes something mundane he did during the week, such as a new recipe he tried, or a visit to the Target in Watertown, then I know he's talking about things that were done with Kendra. He never says that these activities were carried out in her company, but we both know that they were, and this tends to kill conversation. If he talks about things that get him excited, get his eyes sparkling as he explains them, like a the purchase of a pair of plaid pants at The Garment District or a new gallery exhibit, then I know she wasn't there. This is confirmed by his declaration that "you should have been there/you would have loved it/it's too bad you couldn't have seen it." I know I should have been there, I think to myself as I study his hands while he advances the film on the camera. Of course I would have loved it, and it's too bad I couldn't have seen it.

But it's all right, I tell myself, as I put on my most blasé look in the face of these descriptions. I don't long for the new recipes and the trips to Target—these are the activities of the married, the labor-intensive chores of day-to-day living. I'd love the plaid pants purchases and the gallery visits, but I don't need them. Some days, it might be better if I didn't know what I was missing, but it's not worth getting upset over. I don't want any more than what I've got.

Erin and I are sitting at the bar in Charlie's Kitchen in the middle of the afternoon on Thursday, she sucking down a margarita, and I, a screwdriver. Because it's the height of wedding season, she is expected to work both Saturdays and Sundays for several weeks in a row, and as a result, gets two days off mid-week. She doesn't like doing "wedding hair"—updos, elaborate braids, and loopy, shellacked hairstyles—but it's part of the job, and the salon needs her. The pressure is intense, she once explained to me after a particularly bad morning at the Four Seasons bridal suite, where the mother of the bride threw a show-stopping tantrum. But she's getting better each year; at one of the first weddings she ever did, Erin and the bride both ended up weeping in frustration over the failed hairstyle. Furious George quickly shipped her off to a four-day updo clinic at the Vidal Sassoon School in Montreal, and she's been much more confident ever since. She still doesn't like it, but at least she doesn't make anyone cry.

For my part, I should be taking photos or in the darkroom, but my hoo-hah is still so tender and painful that it seemed that an afternoon spent on a bar stool was more in order. After watching me walk around the house like a gunslinger from the Wild West last night, with my thighs parted and my toes outward, Erin pointedly asked what the hell was wrong with me. I told her and we had a laugh, and she suggested that some booze might do the trick.

It's dark in here, dim as always, with Faces playing on the excellent jukebox and the black-clad, tattooed bartenders leaning against the beer taps and watching a re-run of "The Powerpuff Girls" on a wall-mounted TV over the bar. Erin picks at her plate of beer-battered French fries and listens with interest as I tell her about the mystery girl I've seen at a few of the proms. "She's real cheap," I say as I gesture to one of the bartenders for another screwdriver. Vodka, it goes down so easy and mixes effortlessly with my Finnish blood. "Too much makeup and really skanky-looking gowns."

"How many gowns can she have?" she asks, wiping ketchup from her fingers onto a paper napkin. "I mean, if she's with all these different guys, is she wearing a new dress at each prom?"

"I don't think so," I say slowly. "I'll have to look," I add, thinking about all of my ridiculous prom outtake photos from behind the schools, in the parking lots of catering halls, and in the Hummer. "She just . . . she's just gross, getting felt up one week in a parking lot, and then giving a blow job to some other guy a few weeks later," I say. "I mean, it's her decision to do that, but . . ." I trail off. There's something about my harsh judgment of the unfaithful promgoer that is starting to make me feel queasy, and I chalk it up to the rapid intake of screwdrivers. But not Erin. She gives me a little smirk and wordlessly turns back to her fries.

A few long seconds pass, and a bartender with black pigtails makes a dramatic gagging sound when a Bowflex infomercial comes onscreen, the models' abs oiled and bulging. She flips the channel to an ancient episode of "All in the Family," and busies herself at the bar. I don't recognize this episode and am glad. For some reason, whenever I watch a re-run of this show, it's always the one where Gloria has a miscarriage. I've seen it no fewer than five times in the last two years. Either it's a very popular episode, or I have bad luck and am destined to see Sally Struthers' tear-stained face on a regular schedule for the duration.

"Want to go outside?" I ask.

"Of course," Erin says, feeling in her black canvas bag for her cigarettes and lighter. "We'll be back in a minute," she says to the pigtailed girl, who doesn't even acknowledge us, such is the frequency with which she hears this line since the smoking ban went into effect. Then Erin turns to me and says, "Iley, I just hope you know what you're getting into."

"What? I'm never going to see this girl again! Prom season's almost over. I won't even remember her in a few months," I reply, but I'm pretty sure this isn't what she means.

She confirms my suspicions. "That's not what I mean. I mean what we were talking about on Sunday. You and"—she snaps her head from side to side, scanning the virtually empty bar—"William. Just be careful."

I give an annoyed sigh. "I am, Erin. Do I look worried?"

I ask, catching a glimpse of myself in the mirrored panels above the jukebox on our way out the door. To be truthful, I do look ever so slightly worried.

* * *

Back in Boston for tonight's prom, very close to home, at the Boston Performing Arts Academy on a litter-strewn street, just a stone's throw from Fenway Park. I asked William on the way over if the kids were going leap on cars in front of the school à la *Fame*, flexing their toned limbs and singing about how they're gonna live forever, and he chuckled and reached over to ruffle my hair. I leaned into his hand as he did this, and his fingers remained on the back of my neck for another few blocks, caressing the base of my hairline and turning me on so completely that thought I might jump out of my seat.

The kids are just as I'd hoped: mostly sporting dyed hair and eccentric-looking ensembles, or the occasional traditional tux-and-gown getup spiced up with unexpected twists like fluffy orange slippers or a tiara assembled from neoprene and felt. Here, finally, is where I'm seeing my Duckies, with their outrageous shoes and stylish glasses, and I'm elated. For my part, I've worn my most attention-getting Fluevogs, the neon green sling-back sandals with the yellow whipstitching on the heels, and the crowd approves. At last, the music is beyond reproach: The Strokes, Interpol, The Hives, vintage Joy Division, and even a few Pixies songs. I'm finding it hard not to jump into the fray and start dancing, and I notice that William seems to be feeling the same way, tilting his head to the beat and lip-synching some of the words as he snaps photos on the dance floor.

I'm having a great time until I realize that I need to scratch at my slowly healing hoo-hah *right now*, so I hobble with my legs clamped together to our equipment area, grab my camera and cigarettes, and head to the bathroom. As soon as I open the door, I realize I won't even need to go outside to get my fix for either nicotine or photographs: this is where the action is, with kids of both sexes packing the place and filling the air with a thick cloud of smoke. I race into an empty stall, yank down my jeans, and scratch with relief. Then I come out and light up, leaning against a sink and watching with interest as a guy with huge aviator sunglasses and a purple faux fur wrap around his neck caresses the foot of a tiny Chinese girl with at least ten tiny pigtails sticking out from all over her head. She is sitting on a nearby sink, and when I ask if I can take their picture, he puts her big toe in his mouth and gives me an evil grin.

This is, naturally, the most expressive crowd yet, posing dramatically and working it for the camera lens as though they've been waiting for me all night. I get a shot of a tall, blond guy with a touch of lipgloss and blush looking wistfully out the window, a spindly, hollow-chested, dark-eyed girl doing a ballet move for me against the mirror, stretching her leg above her head as though it might snap at any moment, and another of a fat kid with dreadlocks and a cerulean blue suit. I also take a photo of four feet clad in Doc Martens, visible through the open space at the bottom of a bathroom stall door. The walls of the stall are shaking violently by the time I leave, and no one seems to notice or care.

When I get back to the prom, I am surprised to see that

things are winding down a bit, and I take a look at my watch: eleven-fifteen. I give William a quizzical look as he walks over to me. "It's some city ordinance," he explains. "Everyone needs to be gone and the school needs to be all locked up by midnight."

"What?" I ask, disappointed. "But this is the first place where I've really liked the kids and the music," I say, waving to my ballerina friend as she glides by with a handsome guy wearing an enormous Afro.

"I know," he agrees sadly. "That's the prom paradox. But," he says with a bit of mischief in his voice, "the up side is that you and I will have some more time together." He gives me a sweet, eager grin, and I respond with a sickly smile before we begin packing up. Once we are at the car, he says, "Where should we go?" He waits patiently for my answer, looking at me with those gorgeous eyes for a few seconds before shoving everything into the car.

I wait for him to slam the trunk, and I lean against the back of the dusty Volvo and sigh. "I can't tonight, William. I'm having a problem," I say, looking down at my crotch.

He immediately mistakes this for a menstrual issue and says with evident earnestness, "Oh, that sort of thing doesn't bother me. But that's OK."

"No, it's not that," I admit, massaging my forehead with my fingers and looking at the ground. "I . . . I had an accident with some wax down there. It's not really worth getting into," I say, feeling sheepish.

"Oh my God," he says sympathetically. "You poor thing, are you all right?"

"Oh yeah, I'll be fine," I assure him as I watch two

nitwits in Red Sox jerseys get into a yelling match outside of the sports bar across the street. One already has a black eye, and looks as though he'll get the other one to match in a few minutes. "It's just that things are kind of sensitive, and not in a good way."

At this, I expect that William will drive me home, but he quickly looks at his watch and says, "Well, you want to go to the movies instead? If we book it over there, we can make a midnight showing. Can you walk all right?" he asks with concern.

"I can," I say, smiling broadly. We walk to the nearby multiplex, built on the site of Boston's enormous, decaying Sears store that was razed to build this monstrosity, and choose a movie together. There isn't a wide selection at this hour, so we're stuck with something that borders on action-adventure, but I don't care. When the lights go down, I pull in close to William. We share a bucket of popcorn you could bathe a newborn in, and our slippery, butter-coated fingers touch every few seconds, bringing a little grin to my face each time. As a chase scene unfolds on the screen, I realize that I feel completely like I'm on a date, a good date, an early date with someone I have high hopes for. I'm totally relaxed and happy, the way I always feel with the first stirrings of love.

Oh, shit.

Ten

The next night's prom passes nearly imperceptibly. By this time, I'm on auto pilot and can check in each set of kids in a matter of seconds, snap the pictures of the king and queen without even caring about their names, am able to robotically make small talk with the chaperones. I take my smoke breaks but no photos; I didn't feel like bringing my camera tonight, and am instead focusing all my excess energy on William. Studying him from across the gym, trading jokes with him, touching him. And in the ultimate prom paradox, this prom goes extra-late, so by the time we're all done, it's well past one o'clock, too late for movies or food or drink. So William has driven me back to my apartment, and finally we "park," making out in the Volvo on this steamy night and sweating as Hooverphonic quietly plays on the car stereo. I'm just itching to take off my clothes, but thanks to my waxing mishap, I shouldn't. So I pull away from William's lips, take my hands from his chest, and flop down face-up in his lap. He's incredibly hard, pressing against the back of my neck, and I feel like the ultimate cock tease on prom night.

"I'm sorry," I say. "I'm being a tease."

William reaches down and starts playing with my hair, running his fingers through the dark strands. "It's all right, Iley. We can talk instead. There's something I wanted to ask you anyway. Do you like what you're doing?"

I gulp. Does he mean artistically? Morally? I hope he can't see my puzzled expression in the dim glow of the streetlamp a few feet away.

He waits a few seconds, and then clarifies. "I mean, do you like taking these kind of photos, working with me, that sort of thing. Because our last proms are next weekend, as you know," he says, looking down at me. "And I wanted to know if you wanted to continue on through the summer and fall, helping me with weddings."

I picture it and my mind immediately flashes to images clicking through a View-Master, my favorite childhood toy prior to being given my first camera at age eight. The little, square pictures appear, one right after the other: a glowing bride, a kindly priest, a father-daughter dance. A bouquet toss, a plate of sticky wedding cake, a "Just Married" sign on a limo. William and I laughing, talking about photography, having mind-blowing sex in motel rooms. With each silent click, my summer and fall unfold in neat succession. I turn to him, my face impassive. "OK," I say.

"That's great," he says enthusiastically. He pulls his knees toward his chest, lifting my head toward his. We start kissing and before long we're both panting and sweaty again, William straining against the seams of his jeans. I drop back down into his lap facedown this time, unzip his fly, and take him in my mouth. It's been a while since I've done this, but it must be like getting back on a bike, because William's eyes are rolling back with pleasure and he's groaning as he grips my hair in his hands. When he comes with a loud shout and a blind, accidental swipe of the steering wheel with his arm, I pray that the horn doesn't wake Gary and send him to the window. I smile up at him as he catches his breath and looks at the vinyl roof.

"That was incredible," he whispers, looking down at me. "I owe you one," he adds, grinning.

"All right," I agree, wishing I could take advantage of his offer right now and wondering if the dampness in the cotton panel of my sensible underwear is going to hinder the recovery process down there.

"Hey, I have to ask you something else," he says as I start to sit up. "Why did you try to, you know, get waxed?"

"Oh, it was stupider than that, William," I correct him in a wry voice. "I tried to do it to myself. I guess I did it because it seems like something guys might like. So, the answer is 'self-improvement,' I suppose."

"You silly thing," he chides as he touches my face. "You don't need any improving."

"You're in darkroom three, right?" Therese asks gruffly as she shoves a brown plastic jug of developer across the metal desk. Therese is the middle-aged woman who oversees the darkroom spaces, an obese, sullen specimen of a person who serves as both a cautionary tale and grim reminder of the reality of the photography world. A graduate of the school where she currently works, she lost her passion to be the next new thing early on, and instead settled for a career wherein she watches others trying vainly to go where she wasn't able. So on three weekday afternoons and Saturday mornings, she sits at this table, dispensing chemicals and collecting darkroom fees, hating and hiding from behind a transparent wall of regret.

"That's right," I say, trying to neither match her bitterness nor cheer her in any way. The first year that I rented darkroom space here, I decided to give Therese a little gift at Christmastime, a token really, to thank her for doing such a thankless job. I think it was a tin of fancy hot chocolate, something that came in a Christmas tree-shaped container and looked appropriately festive for the season. When I handed it across the desk and placed it in her thick fingers, her face registered such an expression of surprise, panic, and sadness that I realized my mistake immediately. Unused to this sort of generosity from the enemy, Therese mumbled a low thank-you and threw it unceremoniously in a drawer. I'm sure it's still there to this day, clumped and caked and a total waste of gourmet cocoa beans, and I've never tried to be anything more than efficiently breezy since.

"Well, you gotta tell that little Chinese kid that he's overdue on his fees," she says, writing my name in block letters in the ancient logbook. One of its green vinyl covers hangs by a thread from the spiral binding, and the other is completely detached, sitting on the corner of the desk.

"What?"

"That Chinese kid," she repeats impatiently, picking up the logbook in both hands and tapping the short side on the desktop, trying to get the curling pages to align. "Joey, right?"

"Ah," I say, nodding, as I think, Rithy hasn't paid his fee? The idea is shocking. "He's Thai, not Chinese," I inform her as I pick up the developer.

"Whatever," she replies with a dismissive wave, a hand gesture that clearly means *they all look the same to me.* "Whatever he is, if he doesn't pay up soon, we can't let him keep coming here." I swear that a little smile plays on her lips as she announces this.

"OK," I say as I walk away from her, not giving her the satisfaction of seeing the worried look on my face. I wonder what's happening with Rithy, I think, as the developer pours from the jug and into the tray with a hearty *glug-glug-glug*. Probably nothing, I decide as I start in on a new photo I took recently, a collection of flattened and tightly bound cardboard boxes standing upright in a supermarket parking lot. There were so many labels and stickers on the short side of the boxes that, once flat, they all stuck out to make a frilly mane of food company names and logos. An unknowing observer might even need a few seconds to figure out what this image is, which means it is by far my favorite kind of photograph.

I trill a little song as I create a few prints of the boxes, and then print a few from the Boston Performing Arts Academy just for fun. I'm in such a stellar mood by the time I leave that I take the long route home, pedaling leisurely along the Charles River and wondering if Erin has read today's *Herald* yet. I stop off at the corner deli and buy a paper, just in case she was too busy at the salon, then leave it open to the police blotter on the kitchen table. I even pause to read one entry entitled, "Hot Buns," about a mystery ass grabber who lurks in crowded lines in a North

End bakery on Sunday mornings. Apparently he waits until after mass lets out, when the din in the bakery has reached a fever pitch and the place is so packed with hungry churchgoers that customers can barely move, and then helps himself to a few handfuls of flesh before fleeing. "I know we got good buns here, but this is ridiculous!" crows Salvatore Comperchio, the bakery owner. Brilliant.

I've got it in my head that I want a picture of William and me having sex. It shouldn't be too difficult, really; just get plenty of booze in him after the prom and ensure that he's properly enthused about getting a room afterward. I feel pretty certain that we'll end up naked together tonight, but I'm hedging my bets just in case and have dressed to excite: short black miniskirt, low-cut, sleeveless tangerine-colored top that ties on the side, and a little white cotton cardigan. I've left my underwear at home in their drawer, am all healed from my waxing nightmare, and am ready for some sweet action. I slip into the front seat of the Volvo at five-forty five, and William casts a glance at my bare thighs. It's more a look of concern or disdain than one of arousal, and I chain-smoke all the way to St. Albans, wondering what the hell is going on. When we arrive at the school, I wait until William has joined me in yanking things from the Volvo's trunk to gently shrug off my sweater. He does a quick once-over of my top and skirt and gapes, his eyes wide.

"What are you wearing?" he asks, biting his lip.

"You don't like it?" I say, doing a little pirouette.

"Iley, this is a *Catholic* school," he says a bit hysterically. "See?" He points to the spire on the church in the lot adjacent to the low brick building.

"Ohhhh. You did tell me that we were going to St. Albans," I admit. "I guess I just didn't think about what that meant. I'm sorry, William," I say, and I mean it. "I'll put the sweater back on. That should make it a little better, at least."

He sighs and his expression softens. "It's all right. I'm sure it will be fine, don't worry about it." He looks me over again, this time more slowly and with evident enjoyment. "You do look wonderful, you know."

"Thanks," I say sweetly, as I give him a tender squeeze on the arm. I slip into my sweater and we walk inside, past two nuns who look disapprovingly at both of us. I smile as I think to myself, if you disapprove of us now, sisters, just wait until later.

St. Albans gym looks just like every other gym, save the framed image of Jesus over a door near the entrance and the nuns gliding across the polished wood floor. Brother Edward, a round-faced man with shiny skin and a scar on his forehead, pumps William's hand up and down and virtually ignores me as I pull out our tripod and backdrop, readying for the crowd. When the kids start to arrive, it's almost refreshing to note the absence of piercings and pregnancies, but other than that, they look and seem remarkably like all the others. There are rude ones and sweet ones, ones who preen like peacocks and ones who pose shyly for William, ones who dance self-assuredly and with rhythm, and ones whose moves are on loan from MIT's robotics lab. All in all, it's a fairly standard prom, and when I lean against the wall with a bored sigh, I'm joined by a cute, sandy-haired guy who looks to be about my age. He's got a medium build and is wearing an ill-fitting suit with a too-long rep tie and an overly starched shirt. I turn slowly to look at him.

"Thomas," he says in a soft voice, and holds out his hand. "Full-time history teacher, part-time unwilling chaperone." He smiles a nervous but earnest smile, and I notice that his teeth are aligned in a peculiar way, wherein one of his two front teeth is nearly in the middle of his mouth. It reminds me of paper bag puppets from childhood, with one felt tooth glued squarely in the center of the bag's bottom panel.

"Iley," I say, shaking his hand. "Full-time aspiring photographer, part-time prom photographer's assistant." I give him a small, perfunctory smile. "What kind of history do you teach?"

"World history," he replies, pushing his hair from his forehead with one deft swipe. He has pretty, light brown eyes and long lashes.

"Huh. They let you teach that here?" I ask dryly.

He laughs. "They do. Although I think you might be confusing World History with Earth Science, where they *do* learn the history of evolution, by the way. In this school, anyway." He looks closely at me. "So I take it you're not a Catholic school graduate."

I shake my head violently, and this makes him chuckle. "Well, I'm not either, but teaching positions in history seem to be a little hard to come by 'round here, so I took the first thing that sounded good," he explains. When he says the words "'round here," I notice the slightest touch of a Southern accent, and I lean in closer to listen, in an effort to decipher where he's from. He follows suit and leans in closer as well, and I can smell the faint scent of cinnamon wafting from his lips. "I don't even know most of the saints' names," he admits, sounding sheepish. "Sometimes I sneak comic books into the school's daily mass. Hell, this ugly suit isn't even mine!" he laughs, holding out the tie as though it's an unwanted appendage that was grafted onto his body without his consent.

"Yeah, you don't really seem like the St. Albans type," I agree, as I scan the gym and catch William studying us. My stomach does a little twist and I'm trying to ignore this sick feeling, when Thomas clears his throat and shoves his hands deep in the pockets of his borrowed trousers.

"Um . . . maybe I could call you sometime?" he asks, suddenly looking as panicky as a high-school kid asking for a slow dance. I blink at him for a few seconds as the lights dim in preparation for the coronation of the king and queen. I glance at William, who is talking jovially with a nun, and then look at my sandals.

"OK," I say finally. "Yeah. I'm listed in the book, under E. Brooks. That's my roommate Erin."

"Yeah?" he says with thinly veiled disbelief. He peers at me as though I've just told him a real whopper, like my phone number is 1-800-54-GIANT (the Boston-based company that replaces your busted windshield during your lunch hour) or 867-5309 (Jenny, of course).

"Yeah," I assure him, nodding slowly. "In Brighton." We stand in silence for a few seconds, and I point to my camera when the class president takes the mike to announce the king and queen. "News is breaking, I have to go," I say in a mock-important tone, and hear him laughing as I walk away.

* * *

"Wha . . . what's going on?" William slurs after I've quickly wriggled out of my skirt and top and am setting my camera on the low dresser across from the king-sized bed at the Courtyard Marriot. We've checked in as Robert Frank and Cindy Sherman, I've gotten William bombed out of his mind in the hotel bar, and now I am going to get this photo with my little Nikon. I leap onto the bed and wrestle him out of his pants, and he draws me close to him, breathing hard as I pull down his boxers. I nearly kick the cable release off the bed in my excitement, but grab it at just the right time, tucking it under the ball of my foot as I climb on top of him. Since my waxing accident took us out of commission for so long, we're both horny as hell, thrashing around and quickly wrapping the slippery comforter into a lumpy ball of polyfil. William sits up so we're face-to-face with one another, and I wrap my legs around him, bobbing up and down and using my free hand to grab the cable release. When he starts to breathe even faster, grabbing my back and pushing himself into me with crazed intensity, I know it's almost time. I can barely concentrate enough to do it, but I manage to grasp the end of the cable release in my fingers, and *click*, the flash goes off just as I throw my head back and scream with pleasure.

"What was that?" William asks seconds later, suddenly sober. "Iley?"

"I took a picture," I sigh as we fall down onto the bed and I rest my head on his shoulder. I run my fingers up and down his damp chest and smile up at him as he plays with my hair. "You know, we are photographers, after all. You and I should take some cool pictures, right?" I get up and fish around in my bag for some cigarettes and light one for him and then myself. Thank God for smoking rooms.

"I guess," he drawls, sounding sleepy. "OK, whatever, just be cool about it." He takes a few puffs on his cigarette and reaches for the glass ashtray on the nightstand. "You know what I mean," he adds as I lie back down on the bed.

"Yeah," I say with quiet resignation in my voice, leaning against him once more and trying to ignore the empty feeling that rises in my chest. "I know."

"So how did you like St. Albans?" he asks, changing the subject and tipping my face toward his. "I think you really made a splash there with your outfit. I told Brother Edward you were Brazilian, by the way."

"You what?" I screech, laughing as I flip over onto my stomach. I swat him on the chest. "Why?"

"Because he kept looking at you in a way that seemed disapproving, and I got nervous. So I told him that you were interning with me on some foreign exchange photography program," he replies, shrugging and smiling. "I figured that since you tried to do a Brazilian wax recently, it wasn't that much of a stretch." He shivers a bit as the air conditioner cycles on, revving with a noise that sounds as though it's readying for liftoff.

"It's cold in here. Let's get under the covers," I suggest, and we unfurl the comforter and slide between the soft sheets. "Brazilian, well that is something," I say, shaking my head and grinning at him. He pulls me close to him and we lie in silence, listening to the air conditioner and the occasional *ding* of the elevator down the hall.

"So who was that guy you were talking to?" he asks just as I drift off to sleep.

"Oh, just some history teacher," I say drowsily. "Seemed nice, doesn't buy into the Catholic school thing at all, which was sort of funny." I stretch my legs, my toes getting caught in the tight folds of the sheet.

"It seemed like you two were hitting it off," he muses in a voice that is straining to sound offhand, but isn't. He sounds jealous; just the tiniest bit. I like it.

Another hung-over Saturday morning in the darkroom, where I'm equal parts exhausted and energized, head pounding from lack of sleep and buzzing from a night of sex. It's a perfect day outside, sunny and warm and clear, and I toyed with taking Gary for a long walk along the river, but ultimately decided not to. I was just too excited to develop the picture of William and me to endure Gary's loping gait and incessant sniffing for hours, and instead gave him an abbreviated jaunt around the block before racing here on my bike. I breezed past Don, who gave me a friendly wave and asked me if I was developing into something good, and swallowed hard when I decided I didn't want to consider the answer to that question. No junkie is going to make me feel bad about myself, I decided, as I pulled the film from my camera and got to work.

Now I've got a perfect little negative of the photo of us, and it's just as I'd hoped. While not erotica (the light and composition aren't good enough for that) and not quite porn (you can see that my boobs are real, and neither of us has the dead-eyed look of the very high), it strikes something in between. My legs are wrapped tightly around William and both of our heads are tipped back, with his hands grasped firmly around my lower back. It looks like two people teetering right on the precipice of a very intimate and intense moment, all mounting tension and excitement, just waiting for that explosive few seconds. Which is exactly what it is.

I make a very small photo, maybe the size of a business card, and give it a quick run through the photo dryer. I crop it from the larger piece of paper and return to my darkroom space, where I stand silently for a few seconds as I think about where to keep it. My messenger bag? My jeans pocket? I want it to be accessible but protected, and I falter for a second before putting it into the pocket of my bag. Then I take the negative and put it in the same spot.

I finish up in the darkroom, step outside into the bright light, and decide that Gary really would love a long walk after all. I've got enough time to go home, get him, and bring him down to the river before readying for tonight's prom. My last prom. I want to do something to celebrate tonight and wonder briefly if I should bring a tiny flask, like I've seen so many students carry in the breast pocket of their tuxes. When I stop my bike at a light near our place, I gingerly open my messenger bag to check for the photo and negative, which of course are still there. I chide myself for being so paranoid, then run up the steps to our apartment, shouting Gary's name. He's on his leash and ready to go in no time, and as he pauses to sniff a discarded piece of fruit leather in the street, I think about what to do with the photo. I don't want to leave it in the apartment, yet I don't want to carry it in my bag all the time. It should be close to me, but not obvious to others.

Gary turns his nose up at the fruit leather and gives a little gagging sound. "Yeah, you got that right, Gary," I laugh. "That stuff tastes like you're chewing on a strawberry shoe." I've never understood fruit leather myself, and you know that if Gary doesn't show interest, it must really be an unappetizing item.

I'm yanking him across the street and away from a crumbly bit of bagel, when I suddenly think of Heidi and Clayton, old college friends of mine who both played guitar in local bands and were madly in love with one another. Clayton's band enjoyed more success than Heidi's; I always thought it should have been the other way around, but perhaps his band's name, Need More Cowbell, had something do with it. The upshot of this success was that Need More Cowbell got gigs all up and down the East coast (and eventually even a spot on "The Conan O'Brien Show"), which meant that Heidi and Clayton were going to be separated for a time. The two of them had a real zest for everything life had to offer, and apparently, rip-roaring libidos to match. So before Clayton went on the road, they decided to make an audio recording of themselves having a marathon sex session to help them through the long nights.

Because Clayton was frequently bunking with bandmates, I'm not sure how much quality time he was able to spend alone with the recording, but Heidi told me that she listened to it all the time. Their private, erotic soundtrack got her through many a lonely night. But then something happened. Eventually, it lost its ability to arouse her. She explained that it was like when you get an amazing new CD, and you thrill to every note, every chord change, and every hook, because each feels so fresh and seems so perfectly placed in every arrangement. But then you get used to the CD, and with each listen, you know what to expect: where the key changes from major to minor, the drum solo, the three staccato notes at the end of the song. So it was with their erotic recording. She would anticipate every gasp, every moan, every squeak of the bedspring, and it did nothing for her anymore.

She thought for a long time about how to re-purpose the recording and came up with an idea so brilliant I thought it should be trademarked. She began listening to the CD during her commute to work, a forty-five-minute trip to downtown Boston that brought her to a job that she hated, working as a paralegal in a stodgy law firm. While surrounded on all sides by unsmiling, navy-blue-suited businessmen reading their *Wall Street Journal*s and sneering at her sticker-covered messenger bag, she would quietly plug in and thrill to the sounds of her own panting and moaning. An entitled-looking woman shoving past Heidi on the escalator lost all power to wreck Heidi's day if her ears were slowly filling with the sound of her boyfriend noisily climaxing. It gave her such a thrill, she said, to know that the only things separating the crowd from this X-rated scenario were a couple of thin rounds of foam that covered her tiny headphones. She claimed it made her feel naughty and deviant in front of all these losers and squares, as though she and Clayton were stripped naked and doing it right there on the T.

When we reach the Charles, I walk with Gary to the

river's edge and let him lap at the dirty water, then laugh aloud when he lifts his head and attempts to shake off several pieces of grass that have stuck to the damp fur beneath his chin. I quickly hold my camera to my face and take a few quick shots of him flailing, then grab his head and pull the wet grass off. As I let the camera fall against my chest, I think, *wait a minute.* I pull the camera strap over my head and study the minuscule zippered compartment in the back for a few seconds. It's so small and narrow, and such a tight little space that I have never been able to fathom what might possibly be able to fit in there, other than some loose change, all in dimes. I take a quick little breath and pull the photo from my bag, then fold it in half and tuck it into the compartment with a little zip. I slide the strap back onto my neck, light a cigarette, and smile as Gary and I continue walking, narrowly avoiding two aggressive joggers who sneer at my smoke. I feel like Heidi on the T; there is literally no more than one quarter inch of black webbed nylon separating the world from my exquisitely dirty and amazing photo. I feel naughty and deviant already.

Eleven

"Don't you feel like dancing?" I ask William dreamily as I sashay in front of him. We're at our last prom, at a new, gold-toned and pink catering hall in Framingham, and the kids are all slow dancing in the low light of the gaudy, dusty rose ballroom. The song blaring from the deejay's speakers is Top 40 bubblegum pop, pure treacle really, but it's having an effect on me nonetheless. It makes me want to put on a shiny gown and throw my arms around William's neck.

He gives me a wide, closed-mouth grin. "Not here, unfortunately. But we'll dance later. I promise." He holds his camera to his face and takes two quick shots of a tall, gawky couple that wouldn't look entirely out of place wearing their orthodontia headgear to prom. The girl, all spindly elbows and knees and ankles, blinks spastically as the flash goes off.

"Well, I'm going to hold you to that," I say flirtatiously

as I step out of the way of a tall, curly-haired kid wearing a tuxedo and camouflage high-tops. "Nice sneakers," I tell him warmly, and he nods and smiles at me. I watch him walk to the men's room and consider aloud the idea of getting a pair for myself tomorrow.

"I don't like it when regular people wear camouflage during wartime," William says forcefully. "I think it's disrespectful. You know, to be mixing fashion with something that people wear when they get killed in battle." He gives me a challenging look.

"Huh," I reply, mystified. I've never heard this philosophy before, nor have I ever heard William disagree with me, and neither is sitting too well. I suddenly wish I had decided to pack that little flask for my last prom after all, but I decide that a cigarette will do for now, so I gesture to the doors and dash outside into the balmy air. I walk around to the back parking lot, where I immediately spot my element: kids smoking, kids kissing, and, in an assault on my nose when I round the corner, kids smoking some very strong weed. The odor is unmistakable, and I'm surprised that they're gutsy enough to be smoking it here.

"Hey," I say to a girl wearing a lavender slip dress and pointy-toed sandals. I light a cigarette, and without warning, the sheer exhaustion of the season's proms and my post-prom parties comes crashing down on me. I sit, heavy-lidded and fatigued, right on the asphalt, with my back against the painted brick building. I take off my camera and place it on the ground next to me, and draw my knees tightly to my chest.

"You OK?" she asks, looking down at me. She is wearing gigantic, silver hoop earrings and an elaborate matching necklace, and the jewelry actually looks quite pretty against the pale simplicity of the dress.

"I'm fine," I say, nodding. A few kids tumble to the ground next to me, peppering me with questions about my camera and whether or not I'd like to get high. My replies go something like: this is the kind of camera everyone used to use before digital cameras; yeah, developing pictures by hand takes a long time; no, I don't like to use those super-long lenses that the photographers on the sidelines of the Pats games use; yes, please, I would love it. And so a fat joint is quickly passed to me and I inhale deeply, closing my eyes and listening to two guys mercilessly taunt one another about which of the two looks more gay.

When I open my eyes and the joint comes back to me again, I take it eagerly and notice that a few more kids have joined us outside, laughing and leaping around in the parking lot. I nearly gasp aloud when I realize that one of them is my little friend, the slutty girl, the one I hate to see for reasons that I don't like to think about. And suddenly, thanks to some kid's mighty powerful stash and the fact that I haven't smoked in well over a year, I am now quite baked and laughing raucously at her. I point and snicker and loudly announce to the girl in the lavender slip dress, "See that girl? She's been at, like, four proms with four different guys."

The two debating boys snap their heads around to look at her, and they give a loud, Ricki Lake-inspired *woooooooooo*. "You sure?" asks the kid with the iridescent blue cummerbund and bow tie (the one who looks more gay in my opinion, although no one asked me). "I think she's here with Rory, man," he laughs to his friend, a dead-eyed, skinny guy in a too-big tuxedo and scuffed shoes.

"Well, you better tell Rory she's been screwing guys all over eastern Massachusetts, OK?" I cackle, feeling deliciously vicious.

"What's that?" bellows Rory from several feet away, pausing from feeling up his date to stride over to us.

"Can I see this?" the girl in lavender asks me abruptly, pointing to my camera. She is joined by a girl wearing ruby red lipstick and black braids, and before I can answer, they've picked up the camera off the ground and are playing with it.

"Yo, she says that your date's a slut, man!" brays the kid with the blue cummerbund, opening his mouth so wide I can see portions of the masticated prom meal in his molars. The two girls are joined by a third, and they are all posing for one another, clicking the shutter and advancing the film with indelicate motions. I struggle to get to my feet quickly, getting no help from either of the guys, who are now face-to-face with Rory. His date has wisely decided to hang around with the three girls who mistakenly think they are now on a magazine shoot, posing and preening in front of the lens. "Make love to the camera!" one shrieks, and as I glance over, I see that Rory's date has her narrowed eyes firmly fixed on me, with a look that suggests she would like to tear me limb from limb.

"Look, it's no big thing," I sneer dismissively at Rory. "So she's been at some proms with different guys, whatever." I say this loudly and give her a look right back, complete with a self-satisfied grin. *I know what you're doing*, the look says to her, *and now so do they.* Rory bellows to his date, and I see that now she's in the center of the cluster of girls, as they all throw my camera back and forth. I take two long strides toward the noisy group, when a tiny door on the side of the building swings open, and a red-faced man with enormous eyebrows and a cheap suit barrels toward us. Before I know what's happening, it's all screaming and yelling, kids stamping out cigarettes and throwing contraband in the bushes, and everyone scatters. I see my camera fall in slow motion to the ground, and watch as my mystery prom girl races away with Rory, her head turned and her eyes trained on me until she's out of sight. I pick up the camera with a sigh and walk back inside, ignoring the principal's pleas for me to describe who was out here smoking.

William has kept his promise, and it's simply divine here in Room 112 of the Best Western, where we've left all the lights off save the one near the bed, and are dancing around in slow circles. The cheap bedside clock-radio has been tuned to an easy listening station, and Spandau Ballet's "True" crackles from the small speaker. I rest my head on William's shoulder and he holds me tightly to him, his hand pressing into the small of my back. I've taken off my shirt, and I am trying mightily to ignore the feel of his wedding band pushed against my vertebra, inhaling deeply and concentrating on the song lyrics. He buries his face in my hair for a minute and then kisses my neck, breathing slowly and smelling of the cheap scotch we drank in the catering hall's bar after the prom was over.

"Hey," he murmurs as we turn the corner by the bed and my skirt grazes the *TV Guide* hanging off the low dresser.

"Hmm?" I ask, resting my chin heavily on his shoulder, closing my eyes, and nearly drifting off to sleep. I re-open them and immediately search for the thin stripe of light under the doorway. This swath of yellow-white illuminated carpet has become my reference point in the last several weeks, a sort of GPS system on the highway of my relationship with William. When I wake in a strange, new motel room with him sweaty and sleeping next to me, for a nanosecond I am supremely disoriented, until I spot the light beneath the door and remember where I am. The light is both comforting and unsettling, as its location is never the same two weekend nights in a row, reminding me that I'm not at home and certainly not visiting anyplace for an extended stay.

"I'm so glad you're going to stay on to help me with the weddings. *So* glad," he says earnestly, pulling my head off his shoulder and pushing the hair from my face. He traces my top lip with his index finger as a seventies love ballad begins. "Really. I would have hated to see you go after prom season." He pulls me over to the bed, where he sits down on the edge of the thin comforter and begins kissing my breasts. I lean forward and gasp as he buries his face in my chest, and then I fall onto the bed, where he slowly takes off my skirt and slips my thong down with deliberate care. I follow suit and slide him out of his clothes, unzipping his jeans very carefully and lifting his green, vintage Le Tigre polo shirt over his head inches at a time. When I lean back, with my head resting on the Best Western's sorry collection of pillows, William rolls on top of me, and our bodies move slowly and perfectly in synch. It's the most tender of our motel room visits yet, with William's rhythmic, soft breathing filling my left ear and my arms wrapped around him as though I could pull him even closer to my heart if I tried a little harder. A person more romantic than I would likely call it making love.

The tiny photo of William and me is gone. I will never get it back. Someone at that prom in Framingham removed it from the zippered compartment in my camera strap while I was high, and with any luck, the photo is in the bushes or the garbage. I will never know what became of that print, and I have to be OK with that. I can't stop time and change what happened. On the plus side, my camera didn't sustain any damage. This will come in handy, since I have a portfolio review coming up with a gallery owner in tony downtown Newton, and my current collection of recent pictures feels rather uninspired.

"Pfffft!" spits Erin disgustedly, as Gary tosses his head to and fro and a bit of dog shampoo lands on her upper lip. "Sit still," she orders, and his rear immediately hits the bottom of the tub, his soapy tail wagging cheerily. It's hot as hell in here, even with the window open, but thanks to some very rainy afternoons and Gary's playful leaping through mud piles on the local ball field last night, his bath can't be delayed any longer, so we've bitten the bullet and put on our swimsuits to give the old boy a bath. Well, Erin is wearing a swimsuit: a hot pink and lime green skirted number, better suited for a dip at the club. I am wearing a black T-shirt from my old job at the camera shop that reads FIND YOUR F-STOP in large white type marching across my chest, and a pair of cutoffs.

"You're a good boy," I coo, scrubbing under his chest and pulling out a small clump of dirt. I pick up one of his paws to wash it, and he immediately mistakes this for the "shake hands" cue he so excelled at while at obedience school as a puppy. He moves his paw up and down as I try to soap it up, and Erin laughs.

"Such good manners," she boasts. "Bitsy would be so proud." Gary comes from a long line of Airedales bred by a famous, top-notch breeder in Connecticut. These are the type of dogs you see trotting around the ring and getting their genitals grabbed at the Westminster Dog Show each February. We let Gary watch the yearly competition but generally change the channel when the Airedale takes the floor, because we don't want him to feel inferior, trapped in our messy apartment as his distantly related cousin prances before an adoring crowd.

"You got that right," I say, hosing down his legs with the special spray attachment that Erin stole from the salon, and giggling at the sight of his legs. With his fur soaked and lying flat against his damp skin, they are spindly; weak looking, even. Erin laughs loudly and Gary looks embarrassed, so she and I trade a quick glance and get back to the bath in silence. When he is rinsed for the final time, squeaky-clean and smelling vaguely of chamomile, we towel him down, and I awkwardly lead him through the living room. As part of our well-practiced repertoire, Erin already has the door to the apartment open, and I pull all ninety pounds of wet dog onto the porch and down the steps. I am barely able to take off the towel before he's shaking himself dry, spinning his head and torso in opposite directions as the water droplets fly.

"Whew!" I say, leaning against the porch railing and watching as Erin comes out with a pack of cigarettes. We smoke for a few seconds in silence, watching Gary's quick-drying show.

"So who's Thomas?" Erin asks, her lips wrapped around the cigarette.

"What?"

"I forgot, when you went out earlier to get coffee, someone named Thomas called," she says evenly.

I put my hand on my hip and tilt it out at a dramatic angle, and with the mock insouciance of a teenager, I roll my eyes and bray, "Just a boy I met at the dance."

"Really?" she asks, smiling as Gary lopes back into the house and jumps onto the dry, plush towel Erin has placed on the sofa for him. "Good boy!" she shouts into the front window.

"Yeah, really," I answer, smiling as I remember his soft blond hair and his too-long tie. "Some history teacher from a Catholic school we went to. Wow, I didn't think he would call." It's been at least a week, and truthfully, between worrying about the lost photo and daydreaming about William, I'd almost forgotten all about him.

"Nice?" she asks, re-tying the lime green Spandex string on her flouncy skirt.

"Very nice," I say. "Cute too. And single, I'm assuming." I pause with my mouth open. "I'm not sure what to do." I scratch behind my ear for a minute, stalling for time. "You know."

She looks at me and nods. "I know. But William isn't your boyfriend. Don't forget it." This last sentence is delivered in a loaded tone, one that's full of challenge and barely masked worry.

"I know he's not," I scoff, flicking my cigarette butt on the ground, stamping it out, and picking it up. "Of course he's not," I repeat forcefully, trying to convince both of us. "I just wonder if it's a good idea to . . . bring someone else into the picture." I pause for a second. "No pun intended, of course."

"Ah, I'll never tire of hearing you make that joke, Iley," Erin says sarcastically while giving me a wry grin. Gary bounds out the front door and Erin scratches him on his back. He responds with a low, contented growl and sits down on the porch. "But seriously," she continues, locking her gray eyes with mine, "don't let the thing with William keep you from going after more . . ." She drifts off. "Possibly something that could work out better for you," she finishes carefully. "At least call him."

I smile and wonder if she remembers that this is the same advice she gave me about William. Just call him. And we're all seeing how well that's working out.

Twelve

I rub my eyes fiercely with the heels of my hands until I see a drifting rainbow of blobby shapes behind the lids; the fluorescent light in this little basement office is starting to make me nutty. I'm at the Westin Hotel, buried in the bowels of the accounting office, on a temp job that actually involves porn. Porn movies, that is, and people who rented them after their hotel-room bill had already been closed out. Also: room service, dry cleaning, bar tabs, and hotel salon haircuts. The guests' credit cards are duly charged for their goodies after checkout, of course. But apparently the hotel also follows up with a little itemized list of charges, a mailed printout that quashes any doubt that someone might have gotten away with something, and prevents flustered phone calls from guests who forgot about that late-night tumbler of scotch or impulsive viewing of *American Vixens 2: Jugtastic*. Or so implies Javier, the short, dark-eyed, twenty-something from the accounting department who has been put in charge of overseeing me. He hands me a pile of printouts and sits down next to me, explaining how I'm to cross-reference the name and room number with the extra charges and then input them into a database. After entering the information into the right fields, I hit "PRINT," and an itemized list for each guest should spit from the printer.

"It's not that hard, really," he says, a bit disappointedly. I sense he was hoping for someone younger than himself and a bit more malleable, not an over-thirty woman with a long ponytail and purple mary jane sandals. He's wearing a burnished silver Westin pin on his lapel, and I can tell he's entrenched in the service industry culture, speaking respectfully to his superiors on the phone and striding around the small room with a self-imagined sense of importance. But he seems like a nice guy, so I decide to try and make this a little bit fun.

"Javier," I ask, as I key in the first of my hedonistic guests, "what was the craziest bill you've ever seen? You know, things that people bought or did after they supposedly checked out." I look over and arch one eyebrow at him.

He looks furtively around the room, and after realizing that we're the only two in here right now, smiles and replies, "People get a lot of movies. You know . . . porn movies." He lowers his voice for the last two words.

"Yeah, I figured," I say, grinning. "What else?"

"Booze," he says without pausing. "Always lots of booze. Also we have this really delicious steak in the restaurant, it's huge," he boasts. He runs his hand through his wavy, black hair. "It's expensive too. One time, one room ordered eight of them, I think. Oh, and when the Mary Kay convention came to town last year, we sold a lot of chocolate brownie sundaes after accounts had been closed out." He abruptly turns back to his monitor when someone enters the room, a middle-aged woman with a blond shag and a seersucker pantsuit.

I spend the next two hours keying in names and room numbers, forcing myself not to think about what the suites look like here and envisioning myself in one with William. I'm about to mentally explore the bathroom, with the two of us lounging in a warm, bubble-filled tub, when I decide I need to stop. I sit straight up in my chair and close my eyes, inhaling deeply.

"Are you all right?" Javier asks, a matte black Westin pencil stuck jauntily behind his ear now.

"Yeah. Yeah, I'm OK," I assure him.

"You can take a ten-minute break in another fifteen minutes or so," he says. "I know it's tedious work. The last temp went to the ladies' room and never came back." He shakes his head sadly.

This cheers me a bit, thinking of some poor girl sitting on the toilet in the potpourri-scented bathroom and deciding that she could not possibly key in another room number. I turn back to my work and make up my mind to think about someone or something else while I perform this mindless task. But what? A few room numbers later, I settle on Thomas. A small part of me wants to call him; it's flattering to know he's interested, and he was so endearing. But a bigger part of me feels guilty. Why should I feel guilty? I ask myself angrily as I grab a printout that lists a dry cleaning bill for $242. I refuse to feel guilty, I decide. I mean, *I'm* the one who is single! I shout silently. *I'm* the one who should be dating. Not William. I realize I'm stabbing the keyboard in anger when I see Javier looking over at me.

"OK, break time," he says nervously. He walks over to check my progress. "Wow, you're quite efficient."

"Thanks," I say, receiving no pleasure from this compliment. Emboldened, I point to the black phone on the edge of the desk and ask, "Can I make a local call?"

He hesitates, and I can see the cogs in his head turning, as he envisions himself cast out from the Westin family of hotels for agreeing to let a temp call Kuala Lumpur. "All right, as long as it's local," he says firmly before walking back to his desk. "Dial nine for an outside line."

I dig Thomas's phone number out of my messenger bag and dial the number. It rings twice and he picks up.

"Hello?"

I am shocked. I was expecting to leave a message—it's eleven o'clock on a Tuesday; why the hell is he home? "Hi, this is Iley," I croak. I clear my throat. "We met at the prom." I realize how ridiculous this sounds, and we both laugh a little bit. "I'm sorry—I wasn't expecting you at home."

"I'm a teacher, remember? And it's summer, so school's out," he says in an amused voice. "Sorry you didn't get my machine."

Busted! "Oh yeah, that's right," I say sheepishly. "Anyway, Erin said you called, so I just wanted to, um, get back in touch." I start tapping a Westin pen on the desktop.

"Well, I'm glad you did," he says warmly. A long pause follows, and I suddenly wish I hadn't decided to do this here. "By the way, your accent is excellent."

"Huh?"

"Your accent. Brother Edward told me you're Brazilian," he explains.

I laugh. "No, no, no. I'm not Brazilian. William—that's the guy I work with—told him that I was, because he was concerned about the skimpiness, I guess, of my outfit. In retrospect, it *was* a little revealing."

"It was?" he asks innocently. "I didn't notice." A beat of silence passes. "I'm just kidding, of course."

I snort with laughter. Coming from nearly any other guy, this mock sarcasm would sound lecherous beyond belief, but between his slight accent and earnest voice, it's positively sweet. "So," I say.

"So, should we go out sometime?" he asks, taking a sharp breath in. "Maybe a movie and dinner? I like to do 'em in that order, because then you have lots to talk about during dinner."

"That's clever," I say, impressed. I push William from my mind and swallow hard. "OK."

"Well, I suspect that with you, we won't have to worry about things to talk about anyway," he says, and I can tell from the sound of his voice that he's grinning. "Maybe I'll check into what's playing and we can talk later about plans?"

"Yeah," I agree, smiling. "That sounds pretty nice." We say quick good-byes, and I hang up the phone. Javier is watching me with wide eyes, his chin pressed into his hand.

"You went to the *prom*?" he asks, incredulous.

As I mount my bike with my mini-portfolio strapped tightly to my back, I'm fighting back tears and swallowing hard, reminding myself that I'm never, ever to cry after a meeting. But this morning it's nearly impossible not to, since the owner of the Valeria Gallery in Newton looked me square in the eye and told me that my photos were technically perfect but very uninspired. Perfect silvers and dozens of black-and-white gradations do not a winning photograph make, he said tersely, and I knew that he was right. That was the worst part, the painful recognition that he was not telling me anything that I didn't already know in my heart. Rejection is one thing when you believe in your own work, when you feel strongly about your talent. You can brush off the criticism, no matter how harsh, because you have bedrock faith in yourself and can breezily claim that the person judging your work is blind/crazy/jealous.

But this is the first time that I was in agreement with a gallery owner; the photos *are* dull, the zest and energy drained from my normally engaging images. My portfolio provides a window into my distraction of late, and I've signed on for a whole summer's worth of this distraction. I can barely see through the tears as I pedal through traffic.

In many respects, weddings are easier than proms—well, this wedding, anyway, which is at a large, sun-splashed restaurant in Salem. The bride is remarkably easygoing, although that may be due partly to the fact that she's thirty-six and partly to the fact that she downed a few glasses of wine as she readied for her walk down the aisle. When William instructed me to take the obligatory picture of the bride applying her makeup in the mirror, she stuck eye shadow applicators in her ears for me, which I found hilarious and her mother found inappropriately frivolous. "Ma, Chris loves me whether or not I have eye shadow on my eardrums today," she said as she removed them, and I cackled.

Now William and I are standing near a window and photographing the cupcake tower, a wedding cake-shaped confection made entirely of several tiers of cupcakes. The frosting looks absolutely delicious, soft and buttery and in pastel shades of green and yellow and lavender, and I'm finding it hard not to reach out and grab one. "Damn, those look good," I say as I lick my lips.

"No sampling," he warns, giving me an affectionate wink.

"I know," I say, rolling my eyes. "I have to say," I add, looking around the room at all the guests as they enjoy their fancy brunch, "so far, weddings seem pretty easy."

William laughs. "*This* wedding is easy," he corrects me. "The bride isn't nuts, there are only about eighty guests, it's a daytime event, and this place has great light. Also it's Sunday and we didn't have a wedding yesterday, so you're not all tuckered out from staying up too late the night before." I know he intended for this comment to refer to the actual work of shooting the wedding, but we both immediately think of other reasons we might be up late together, and we lock eyes and smile.

"Well," I shrug, "for my first one, I'm having a pretty good time." The event manager, a prim-looking woman with white-blond hair and a neatly tailored pink suit, clicks over to us on sensible heels and tells William that it's time for the bride and groom to cut the cake.

"Cupcakes," I correct her, as she begins to wheel the

table over to the center of the dance floor. William gives her a hand, trying to spot the cupcakes in case one should unceremoniously plunk to the floor, and the cupcake tower makes it there without incident. The bride and groom each push a cupcake in one another's mouths, and the crowd roars with laughter. William takes shots of them and I take shots of the crowd watching them; we're a good team, in the middle of the action but not intrusive. A tired-looking waitress wearing a frizzy ponytail and a dirty black apron wheels the cupcake tower into the kitchen, and a few moments later, dozens of tiny plates emerge, each with its own adorable cupcake in the center.

Based on the weddings that I've attended as a guest, I know that once dessert is served, things start winding down fast. There will be a bit more dancing—sloppy, drunken moves on the hardwood floor, with single male guests coming on to bridesmaids way too strong. Lots of insincere good-byes between extended family members who rarely see one another and prefer it that way; an overtired kid slumped in a chair, the satin bow on her dress untied and dragging on the floor; the bride and groom whirling maniacally through the room as they try to thank everyone for coming.

I watch William as these events unfold around us, and he takes a small envelope from the bride's father and smiles. I wonder what kind of motels there are in Salem, and then feel a bit queasy when I realize it's only four-thirty. Our after-prom trysts were always under cover of darkness, but with daytime weddings, there will obviously be trips to motel rooms in broad daylight. This fills me with a sudden surge of seediness that takes me by surprise, and I rest my hand on the small, now-empty placecard table to steady myself. Dark, light, it shouldn't really matter, should it? I treat them the same in photography, working with light and shadow carefully and respecting what each can add or take away from an image. But it is true that light obviously does have more power. If you're not careful, it can illuminate way too much.

I'm poking around in Rithy's darkroom space, which is against the rules, but I don't care. It's clear that he hasn't been here for some time. The plastic trays that normally contain the photo chemicals are bone dry and tipped up on their sides, leaning against the back wall of the deep sink. The giant basin that usually contains rapidly circulating water is on the floor, the gaskets and plastic tubing disconnected. The garbage can is empty, with only a crisp, black garbage bag lining it. No discarded contact prints, aborted attempts at dodging and burning, or film canisters. The whole thing makes me very nervous, and I scuttle into my darkroom to think about it and develop some pictures.

Once there, I find I can't concentrate. Cowed after my visit to the Valeria Gallery, for the first time in a while I lack self-confidence, and I chew my thumbnail as I consider whether or not to develop my most recent roll of film. Sure, the discarded Adirondack chair with the flowers growing up through the splintered slats looked interesting this morning, but who knows what might appear on that photo paper now? I hurriedly shove everything back in my bag, and walk out of the darkroom, my head down. On my way out, I stop to see Therese, who is sitting in a puddle of sweat behind her metal desk.

"Hot enough for you?" I ask brightly. She grunts in response. "Any news on Rithy—I mean, Joey?"

"Yeah," she says dully as she scratches at one of her underarms. She's wearing an unflattering, yellow sleeveless top, and there are crescent moons of perspiration encircling each pit. "He's not coming here anymore. Told me he can't afford it. So we're looking to rent that space to someone else, if you know anyone." This is the highest number of words that Therese has ever deigned to speak to me in one conversation, and I'm sure it's only because she enjoys bearing bad news about an aspiring photographer.

"Did he say why?" I ask, trying to sound nonchalant. Best not to fuel the schadenfreude.

"Naw, just that he don't have the money," she says, shrugging as she clicks and retracts her pen with a stubby thumb.

"Wow," I say, my dejection starting to show through, which makes Therese smile slightly. I walk outside and light a cigarette immediately, now worried not only about the future of my photography, but Rithy's as well.

"Well, that wasn't quite what I expected," Thomas says grimly as we take a seat in one my favorite Spanish restaurants in Cambridge. I would have to agree; the foreign film was billed as a captivating glimpse into the life of a gay bullfighter in a very conservative culture, but ended up being a preachy, paint-by-numbers exercise in teaching tolerance.

"I feel the same way," I admit as a big basket of bread materializes in front of us. A young, multiply pierced waitress stands over our table, and I order a glass of sangria.

Thomas asks for beer. "It was disappointing," I add, shaking my head. He looks vexed when I say this, and there is an awkward silence. It's broken by a very overweight man sitting two tables away who asks the waitress in a loud voice whether or not there are low-carb items on the menu.

"I'm on the Atkins diet," he announces.

Thomas raises his eyebrows at me, and I smile. "It looks like he's on the *Chet* Atkins diet, maybe," I say cruelly. "You know, eating things like you'd find in the deep South. Fried stuff." Thomas laughs out loud, albeit a bit politely. "I, um, I don't mean to sound bitchy," I say, backpedaling as I realize that it's entirely possible that he has an obese brother or father or old buddy. "It's just that, well, I'm pretty sick of this low-carb business," I say, lifting my sangria glass to my lips.

"Oh, I understand," he says as he shakes his head. "That was funny," he adds, a slow smile spreading across his lips. "Plus, I always like any reason to talk about Chet Atkins. Since I am from Tennessee, after all."

"Really?" I ask. "Your accent isn't so strong." The waitress plops two laminated menus on the table, but neither of us makes a move to read them.

"Well, I've been in New England for awhile, so I guess it's gotten diluted," he shrugs. In this light, beneath a string of tiny yellow lanterns, his hair has a burnished sheen, and it repeatedly falls across his forehead in a way that makes me want to brush it out of his eyes. We finally decide on what to get (several tiny plates of delicious tapas) and settle into predictable first date questions and answers. He's talking about what drew him to teaching history and I'm midway through my second glass of sangria when I realize there's a question he could answer for me.

"Do you ever cover current events, that sort of thing, in your class?" I ask as a troop of waiters and waitresses carrying a dish of flan with a candle in it wind their way toward a large party. They sing "Happy Birthday" in Spanish, and the birthday girl looks as though she would prefer to fall through the tiled floor than make a wish on her birthday flan.

"Sure, that's how you make history relevant," he says excitedly. "Why?"

"Well," I say, spearing a piece of spicy chorizo with my fork, "do you think that it's disrespectful for regular people to wear camouflage clothing during wartime?"

"What do you mean, people who aren't in battle?" he asks, confused. He sets down his forkful of garlicky potatoes and leans back in his chair, the pose of a person preparing to give something serious thought. I notice that he's got a brown belt through the loops of his jeans, and it's been dressed up with an oversized, slightly tacky gold buckle.

"Yeah, exactly. Do you think that people who wear camouflage as a fashion statement are disrespecting people who are currently fighting in Iraq? For instance."

He folds his arms over his chest and thinks for a few seconds. "I . . . don't . . . know," he admits. "It's an interesting question, I'll have to think about it." He sounds so contemplative that I can't help but laugh at him.

"It's not a homework assignment, Thomas," I say, pushing my hair behind my ear and leaning forward with my elbows on the table. "Don't worry too hard about it," I tease.

"Well, I'm going to think about it anyway, and then maybe I can tell you the next time I see you," he says as the waitress clears our plates. "You know, like extra credit." I give a half-smile as the muscles in my chest and stomach clench.

"OK," I say, trying to stay in the moment. We split the check and head outside, where I light a cigarette the moment my feet hit the sidewalk.

"You smoke?" he says, looking at me out of the corners of his eyes.

"Yeah, is that a deal-buster?" I ask, with a bit too much challenge in my voice. Mainly because I'm not sure what I want the answer to be.

He takes some time to think, and we walk in silence for what feels like minutes. When we reach the corner, he takes a long look at me. "No," he decides. "I think it's all right."

"Really? It tends to be a black-or-white thing for most people."

"I know. But I don't look at stuff that way. Sometimes you have to make sacrifices, I think," he says as we round the corner.

"Well, this is me," I say, pointing to my bike.

He does a double take. "You rode that here?" he asks. I nod proudly. "But you look so . . . put together," he finishes bashfully. "How do you ride in a skirt?" he asks, pointing to my black denim miniskirt with the unfinished hem.

"Carefully," I reply, and we both laugh.

"Well, I should get on the T. My dog is waiting for me," he says.

"Oh, I have a dog, too!" I say joyfully. "Gary. He's an Airedale." I bend over to unlock my bike and nearly lose my balance as the sangria burbles through my veins.

"Mine is named Guy. He's a Finnish Spitz; they're pretty unusual," he says, grabbing my elbow so I don't fall over. "Are you going to be OK riding home?"

"Oh yeah, I'll be fine," I assure him. "Finnish Spitz, I'll need to look that breed up," I decide aloud. "I'm one quarter Finnish, by the way."

"Well, you and Guy will have a lot in common, I'm sure," he says. "Want to meet him sometime? A dog date?" He gives me a look of pure eagerness, the same expression Gary often fixes me with when there are Snausages just out his reach.

"All right," I sigh, won over by his total lack of self-consciousness. What could a dog play date hurt? Some Frisbee fun in the park by day, some sweaty sex with William at night. I may need to get a date book soon to keep this straight.

Thirteen

Erin has just walked in the door, the very picture of heat-wave weariness, with her hair glued to her neck and her face covered in a slick layer of sweat. Despite her obvious discomfort, she is smiling broadly.

"What's happening?" I ask from my damp spot on the sofa. I've got the fan pointed on myself in a futile attempt to cool down, and a bowl of ice cubes beneath my bare feet. My toes are so cold that they are turning a raw pink, the color of undercooked ham, but I don't care. "Good police blotter today?"

"Better. Where's Gary?" she asks, peering around the corner into the kitchen. Because of his English heritage, Gary doesn't do well in the sultry weather and tends to react poorly, usually in the form of extreme stomach distress.

"He's sitting in the tub with a bowl of ice water, don't worry," I assure her. The claw-footed monstrosity in the bathroom is the coolest place in the apartment, and as long as he stays there with his belly pressed to the smooth porcelain and his mouth near a bowl of frigid water, he should be fine.

"Well," she says, clapping her hands together, "do you remember that client of mine with the lung thing?" She is referring to an unfortunate woman who took an extravagant vacation to Belize last winter, only to return with a peculiar malady, a lung problem that stymied even the most experienced disease specialists in Boston. She was confined to the hospital for weeks and then returned home, where her breathing was so labored that she couldn't leave her bed for more than a few minutes at a time. Trapped and depressed, she complained to her husband about her illness, her bad fortune, her hair. Since he couldn't fix the first two, he decided to focus on the third and phoned Erin with a very strange request. After Erin was satisfied that the woman wasn't contagious, she packed a bag and gave her a lovely, easy-care cut, right there in the bedroom of the enormous Beacon Hill brownstone. The woman eventually recovered fully, but not before getting two more stylish haircuts from Erin in the comfort of her home.

"Yeah, of course. Wasn't she the one with the enormous, black dildo under her bed?" Erin had gotten an eyeful when she accidentally kicked a brush under the bed and had to root around under its fluffy dust ruffle for it. The brush wasn't the first thing she grabbed, unfortunately for everyone in the room.

"Uh-huh," she remembers, smiling. "Anyway, to thank me, she has given me an *all-expense-paid trip* for two to . . . Las Vegas! In the beginning of August. Want to go?" She flops down next to me on the couch and lights a cigarette.

"Vegas in August? What kind of gift is that?" I laugh. "It's going to be hot as hell, Erin," I point out.

"It won't matter. We'll be in pools and air-conditioned casinos and restaurants," she explains pragmatically. "It'll be fun."

"Oh, I'm going with you, don't you worry about that," I assure her. "I just like to complain." I pull my foot from the bowl of icy water and clamp my fingers around my frozen toes, trying to bring them back to life. "When do we go?" I ask, as I try to remember where my bathing suit is. I think the last time I wore it was when I went on a trip to a lake in New Hampshire that turned out to be much too cold to swim in.

"Whenever we want during the first two weeks in August. We've got three days, two nights, during the week. I figure that works out best for us anyway, since now you and I both work on the weekends. You know, at your weddings."

"Right," I say, looking around the room and trying to avoid her gaze. Working on the weekends at weddings, that's what I do now. Working at places where marriages begin, then doing the kinds of things that cause marriages to end.

Spurred on by the memory of Erin's infirm client, I have come to Beacon Hill this morning in an effort to shoot some memorable photographs. It's not that hard to do here; the neighborhood is photo-ready, with its ornate gardens and curlicued latticework on metal gates and imposing, richly hued doors. I try to tell myself that this isn't a cop-out as I pump my legs to make it to the top of the steep hill. Sure, the Beacon Hill trip is right out of Photography 101, the place where you always see young photography majors marching around with their new Minoltas, hunting for just the right composition. But you've got to start again somewhere, I tell myself firmly as I lock up my bike. I mean, the cherub that I love so very much was a Beacon Hill discovery, so perhaps this trip will be just what I need to bolster my confidence.

The next hour is a mixed bag at best. A beat-up, tartan plaid mini-backpack sitting alone on the pristine sidewalk looked sort of sad and compelling, until it was reunited with its owner, a pigtailed girl who sprang from a nearby brownstone and snatched it up in front of me. Her mother, a tall woman wearing a lime green knit polo dress and white Keds, looked none too pleased and gave me a withering gaze as she shuffled her daughter away. Two streets over, the window of a dry cleaner's featured a little handwritten sign that announced, SAL IS IN THE HOSPITAL UNTIL WEDNESDAY. FOR ALTERATIONS, SEE IRENE. Seated a few feet from the sign was a dour-looking old woman (Irene perhaps, exhausted from taking on all of Sal's alterations while he's convalescing?), and I was all set to take a picture of the sign and the nearby plastic bags full of laundry, when she moved from her spot and wrecked the shot.

I walk around some more and take some halfhearted shots of boring Beacon Hill standards, and unlock my bike. I ride down Charles Street, stop for a red light, and find myself face-to-face with a shuttle bus filled with panting dogs. The side of the bright red bus reads DOGGIE DAY CARE, and I think of Thomas for a few seconds and our upcoming doggie date.

When I ride up Beacon Street, I flip the bird at Cheers the way I always do, loathing the tourist trap that dupes Midwesterners into thinking they will belly up to a bar that remotely resembles the Hollywood set and get chummy with Cliff Claven. As I bring my arm down, I notice something that stops me. I quickly cut across traffic, grinning broadly at all the angry drivers who honk and shout, and lean my bike up against the railing outside the bar. A sweaty family dressed in "Cheers" T-shirts frowns as I stride past them and wreck their vacation photograph, and I give an insincere apology.

Sitting beneath the giant Cheers banner hanging off the railing is the distinctive decor of the homeless: a filth-encrusted sleeping bag, two plastic bags full of cans, a tattered gray blanket, and sloppy piles of books, papers, and clothing that's patently inappropriate for the weather, such as woolen gloves and a pair of ski pants. All of this beneath the jaunty Cheers logo, its yellow script promising fun and frolic within. Excellent. I take a few shots, and the decorator himself stumbles over to me from a nearby garbage can.

"Whuzza?" he says in a loud voice, causing the family in the "Cheers" T-shirts to scurry. "Whatcha' doin'?"

"Just taking a few pictures," I tell him. "I like what you've done with the place." He studies me for a long moment, uncomprehending.

"Izza government up at the State House, keeping me here," he informs me dully, pointing a dirty index finger up the street at the giant, gold-domed building. "They know I have the answers, and they wanna keep the secret. From the people."

"That's probably true," I assure him. "You probably do

have the answers." The door to the bar opens, and a muscle-bound guy wearing a blond, glistening crew cut and a black "Cheers" polo shirt strides toward us.

"OK, buddy, what'd I tell you yesterday?" he barks. "You can't put your stuff here." He sneers with evident disgust, and I pray mightily that someone this jackass knows and loves succumbs one day to mental illness or substance abuse so he can reflect on this moment.

"Yeah, yeah," the homeless guy mutters, scratching at his beard. He turns to me as the Cheers bouncer folds his thick arms over his chest and waits. "You got any money?"

"Yeah," I say, digging around in my bag and handing him five dollars. "You smoke?" He nods vigorously, and I give him my nearly full pack of cigarettes and a blue plastic lighter. I get on my bike and ride away, creating a perfect coda to Cheers, as I flip the bird to the bouncer.

I ride down to Downtown Crossing, bouncing all the way on the cobblestones, and decide that I should look for a bathing suit, in the likely event that I can't find my old one. As I'm locking my bike up in front of Macy's, I hear someone call my name. It has to be me; no one ever calls for an Iley otherwise. I look up to see Rithy, sweating and looking grim.

"Hi!" I say, delighted. I start to reach for my cigarettes then remember that I left them with my friend up at Cheers. "Where on earth have you been?"

His face falls. "Pad Thai Palace," he spits as a harried-looking businessman accidentally whacks him in the knee with his brown briefcase.

"What?"

"Pad . . . Thai . . . Palace," he repeats, too loudly and too slowly, and I immediately make a pact with myself never to speak in this manner to a foreigner again. "They opened down the street from our restaurant. Only pad thai, that's all they make. It's really cheap. Everyone go there now for pad thai instead."

"Oh, Rithy, that sucks," I say sympathetically as a group of teenage girls pour from the doors of the Bath and Body Works, giggling and sniffing one another's wrists. "So . . . wait," I continue, confused. I need nicotine. "So you can't develop photos because of Pad Thai Palace?"

He rolls his eyes. "Right!" he shouts impatiently. I reel back; never before have I seen Rithy so upset. "We're not making enough money, so I can't pay my fees. No customers, no photography," he says. "So today I go to Filene's Basement to find some cheap dishes for the restaurant. We broke some last week by mistake. I see you around, Iley." He walks across the street and marches down the stairs toward the Basement, his head down.

"I've really missed you this week," William sighs as he slides into the tub. Tonight's wedding was a nightmare, from frenzied start to drunken finish. The bride was a scrawny, overly tanned bitch, a girl who had obviously spent her entire life in breathless anticipation of this one day and wasn't about to make concessions for anyone. Her mother provided a telling glimpse of what the bride will someday evolve into, making sure that the flower girls' nail polish shades matched perfectly and *tsk*ing loudly when she learned that one of the bridesmaids would be wearing her glasses. No contacts, she asked? Well, *why not*? The father of the bride was a stuttering, sweating shell of a man, and the groom had an eye twitch that seemed to worsen dramatically over the course of the day. At the reception, the band announced the new couple in a way that didn't suit the bride, and she threw a fit. The hotel ran out of gnocchi for the pasta bar, and a preteen cousin vomited on the dance floor.

The moment William and I were off the clock, we headed for the hotel bar, where I began downing the first of a few martinis. William decided that to reward ourselves for this horrible wedding we'd just finished shooting, he would book us a room in this lovely, plush hotel. We quickly made a mess of our suite, energetically testing out every horizontal surface and nearly breaking a lamp. I'd wondered at the start of the wedding whether I'd be able to go to bed with William tonight, now that Thomas—uncomplicated, unmarried Thomas—is on my mind a bit, but surprise, surprise! I can always count on liquor and my own libido to get me into a compromising position.

"Yeah," I say dreamily as I shift over to make room for his legs. I am wasted and starting to get a bad headache, but it's so cozy and bubbly in the tub that I want to stay attentive and take it all in. Screwing in a strange hotel room is one thing, but something as intimate as a bath is quite another. "Did you really?"

"I did," he says, running his hands through his hair, the water pushing it black and glossy against his scalp. "I mean, you do know that I think about you when we're not together, right?" He smiles, and I lean my head against the beige tiled wall.

"I know, William," I sigh, and there's a long silence. We listen to the water lap at the edges of the tub, then to the slow, heavy sound of the elevator doors closing down the hall. "I do too." I look at him and decide that now is the time. "I have a date next week, William."

His face falls. He runs his fingertips across the water for a few seconds. "You do?" he asks, in a voice so pained it hurts deep in my chest. I lean forward in the tub and take his hands. "Is it a first date?"

I shake my head, then wish I hadn't, as it makes me dizzy. "No, it's not. I've—I've been out on one date before with this person. I don't really know where it's going, but I wanted to tell you." I pause for a second and realize I'm not even sure what possessed me to bring this up here, tonight. Perhaps I am a crueler person than I thought. Or perhaps I'm trying to protect myself by striking first, the way Gary does when he spots a more formidable dog.

"You've been out with this person before?" he asks, sounding as dismayed as a child. He frowns. "That really hurts my feelings."

"Well, it really hurts *my* feelings that you're married, so now we're even," I snap, my voice cracking as tears well in my eyes. I swipe them quickly with the back of my hand.

"Don't cry, Iley," he murmurs, as he scoots closer to me in the tub. He plays with a wet strand of his hair for a minute as I compose myself. This is ridiculous, I tell myself firmly, and try to take some deep breaths.

"I'm all right," I cough, grabbing a soft, cream-colored washcloth from a burnished silver towel rack and wiping my face. "It's just—well, you know. What we've got here has become a bit complicated."

He looks me in the eyes and then puts his head in his hands. He breathes heavily, and I wonder for a moment if he's crying. He lifts his head, and he's not. "I got . . . I got a bad thing going on at home. Kendra's only there half the time, and then when she is there, all we do is fight. It sucks, Iley! I don't know what's going to happen. But I like being with you," he says, touching my arm and then frowning again. "It *is* complicated, isn't it?"

"Yeah," I say, quickly sliding down beneath the water line and letting my ears fill with the sound of sloshing bathwater. I don't want to hear anything more.

Seven a.m. on a rainy Thursday, and I'm wearing a white lab coat and standing near a small table at the Shave Testing Lab at Gillette. The white coat isn't meant to make me appear more scientific or protect me from flying lather; it just gives the impression of cleanliness and professionalism, Wendy told me when I arrived here thirty minutes ago. The Shave Testing Lab is where Gillette tests prototypical razors, shaving creams and foams, lotions, and other personal care items, she explained to me energetically as I read and signed the two-page confidentiality statement. Men who work near the gigantic Gillette factory can sign up to stop by the lab on their way to work, whereupon each one is ushered into his own mini-bathroom consisting of sink, lighted mirror, vanity, and clothes hooks. Each is filmed lathering. Shaving. Rinsing. Slapping on after-shave. Before rushing off to work, they are asked to fill in a short survey that contains questions about their experience and how they would rate the effectiveness of the new items in question. After ten such visits, a volunteer shaver is eligible for a gift certificate to Legal Sea Foods, Bertucci's, or Hard Rock Café. My job is to bring the participants to their pre-assigned bathroom cubicles and make sure they return their surveys. When the temp agency called yesterday, I balked at the six-thirty arrival time, but perked up at the hourly rate, which—as one might expect from a multinational, vivisecting conglomerate—is incredible.

My first participant arrives at seven-fifteen, clutching a large cup of Dunkin' Donuts coffee and scowling. He's got bristly, black stubble that extends well past the collar of his shirt and must be a Gillette product developer's wet dream. After getting no reply to my greeting, I wordlessly lead him to his bathroom cubicle and walk back to my table. Two more men are waiting: a skinny, older man who drops his wet umbrella at my feet, and a fair-haired, smiley guy who looks as though it would take him several days to develop a five o'clock shadow. More men arrive quickly and I spend the next ten minutes making small talk as I check everyone in and walk them one by one to their bathrooms. Smiley guy's eyes light up when he sees he's in Cubicle Four—"I love this one, I don't know why," he admits to me as he loosens his tie. As I walk back to my table at the front, I furtively look at some of the shirtless guys as they shave. Some of them are humming, a bit loudly and off-key, and I wonder if they've ever thought about piping some music in here.

"This is a great place to meet guys," gushes Wendy, as I reach the end of the row of cubicles. So much for trying to surreptitiously see some skin. "Of course, now that I've got Joe and the boys," she says, beaming, "I'm not in the market. But if you're single and looking, I can certainly tell the temp agency to try to get you back in here!"

My mind loops on "Joe and the boys," said to me casually, as though I know or care who they are. I'm sure she's referring to her husband and sons, but this is one of my pet peeves, and I look up at her, distracted.

"What?"

"I said, if you're single, this is a good way to meet men," she repeats, unruffled.

"Oh," I say. I scratch my head. I shove my left hand in the pocket of my lab coat. I run the toe of my shoe through the puddle of water left by the wet umbrella, thinking of William and Thomas. "No, I don't think that would be a good idea for me right now," I decide.

Fourteen

Gary and Guy are in ass-sniffing heaven, getting to know one another as only two canines can, with their snouts deep in each other's backsides. Guy is a medium-sized, caramel-colored cutie with a curly tail and one of those funny dog mouths that looks to be smiling if you catch it at the right moment. He approached Gary with caution when he and Thomas arrived at the apartment to pick us up an hour ago, warmed to him slightly in the back seat of Thomas's blue Saturn, and is now behaving as though they could be long-lost littermates. We are at the Arnold Arboretum in Jamaica Plain, which is a beautiful and lush place to relax and play with one's dog, except it's full of strident, aging hippies. I've packed plenty of cigarettes to make them angry.

Thomas tosses a tennis ball in Gary and Guy's direction and processes what I've just finished telling him, the rich tale of Erin's double life. "So you mean to tell me that they've never once wondered why she doesn't talk more about work, or wanted to check out her office, or something like that?" he asks, incredulous.

"No, I don't think you get it," I say, sounding more impatient than I'd intended to. "I mean, I don't think they really care what she's up to. I think they're satisfied just to have this . . ." I trail off as I search for the word and then find it, ". . . veneer of everything being all right and glamorous and just as it seems it should be." I toy with sharing the story of Erin's brother Scott's crippling cocaine addiction but decide against it. Gary zooms past me, trots back, and pauses briefly before he runs to pee on a nearby tree.

"It just seems like a lot for Erin to keep straight, doesn't it?" Thomas asks while rubbing Guy's muzzle. "I'm not sure I could lie for such a long time. I'm not above little white lies, but the big, ongoing ones, I think I'd have a much harder time with," he says evenly. His statement is disarming, partly because it's made without any judgment at all, and partly because it sums up perfectly something in my own life that I'm none too proud of lately. I gulp, light a cigarette, and smile brightly at a woman who scowls at me and my smoke. She's got black, kinky hair and is wearing a dress that looks as though it had been stitched together in a hurry from ratty old bedspreads. Even her dog, an old, withered black Lab, is wearing a tie-dyed bandanna around his neck. Gary looks at them with mild interest and turns up his nose. There is a long silence that follows the impromptu discourse on lying, and Thomas clears his throat and tosses another tennis ball Guy's way.

"So where did you get this guy?" I ask, laughing at my inadvertent joke. "This guy, Guy."

He smiles. "He was my roommate's dog, but my roommate never took care of him too well. You know, he wasn't around a lot, or whatever." He pushes his hair off his forehead and exhales forcefully; it's hot as hell at the Arboretum today, under the cover of all the dewy leaves and trees. The seams of my bra are damp, and my sweaty feet squish uncomfortably in my mary jane sandals. I reach into my bag for a bottle of water and pour a generous amount into the collapsible canvas doggie dish that Thomas brought with us. "One time the dog was really sick, and Mike just went away and left me to take care of him. Oh, and the poor thing didn't even have a name—I just kept saying to Mike, 'I'm not always going to be around to take care of this guy,' and that's how Guy got his name."

I grin at this, and Thomas returns the smile, his eyes scrunching up in the corners. "Mike ended up getting involved with some girl from Utah, and he converted to Mormonism and moved to Salt Lake City. He didn't seem to want to bring Guy along, so that's how I ended up with him." He looks lovingly at Guy, who is sitting beneath a nearby shrub and energetically gnawing on a stick. "I used to complain about him, but I'm actually really glad he's mine now. Right, Guy?" he asks, and Guy comes over and laps some water out of the bowl.

"That's a good story," I decide. "Starts sad, ends happy." We stand for a moment and watch as a cocker spaniel and Dalmatian play with Gary and Guy. The hyper Dalmatian is too aggressive for everyone's tastes, and Guy lets out some thunderous barks before the Dalmatian's owner swoops in and leads her dog away.

"Hey, I forgot to tell you something," says Thomas suddenly. "I asked my summer school class about the camouflage question. And—

"I thought you didn't teach school in summer," I interrupt.

"Well, I teach one class, not at St. Albans, but at Waltham High School. It's just four weeks long, and the money comes in handy. Anyway, we spent a few minutes talking about whether or not it's inappropriate to wear camouflage during wartime."

"Really?" I ask, surprised. "So?"

"So, most of them seemed to think it was OK. I mean, you should keep in mind that the kids in summer school aren't necessarily, um, the cream of the crop," he explains diplomatically. "But they still made a good case. They basically said that at this point, most fashion is so divorced from the meaning—well, they didn't say divorced, but that's what they meant—that you can't really connect the two."

"Ha! I knew I was right!" I say triumphantly.

"Who was wrong?" he asks, bending down to pour more water in the dish. Gary's a water hog and has just lapped up the last of it, the droplets hanging from his damp beard.

"Oh, just a friend of mine," I say, pausing awkwardly before the word "friend." Thomas looks at me strangely, or perhaps not. Maybe I'm just paranoid and still reeling from our discussion about the distastefulness of long-term lies.

Darkroom time. I really can't justify putting it off any longer, and as an added incentive, I don't want Therese to derive any pleasure from thinking I'm not showing up anymore due to Rithy's absence. So I'm here bright and early on Friday, locking my bike and watching Don as he wistfully gazes down the alley.

"How's it going?" I ask him as I take my camera from my messenger bag.

He shrugs. "All right," he answers distractedly, still watching the door of the long-gone methadone clinic. He looks at the camera and something clicks behind his dishwater-gray eyes, the way it often does after I spend a few seconds with him. "You developing something nice today?"

"God, I sure as hell hope so," I laugh, thinking about my visit to Beacon Hill. "We'll see."

"Make sure you develop into something nice, too," he shouts philosophically as I swing open the door to the New England School of Photography. Once in the darkroom, I work efficiently and without emotion, having decided to approach this with the cool gaze of an architect or engineer. I'm just concerned with one photo at a time, I tell myself, as I use the tongs to move the backpack-on-the-sidewalk photo into the fixer tray. I try developing a few more, including the photos taken in front of Cheers and one I took of a discarded rose in the street, the kind that is actually made from a pair of cheap satin panties wrapped tightly and glued to a green, plastic stem. The photos are not stunning, but not terrible either.

While the pictures flip and sway in the water bath, I pull open one of the low drawers beneath the enlarger and grin when I come upon a few prints from the proms. Like a college freshman who ponderously speaks of the simpler times of high school, I find myself wishing for those days again, when William was just a hot photographer who would make me pant and scream post-prom, and not someone I'm more confused about with each passing day. I study two photos from the Boston Performing Arts Academy prom, the ones taken in the bathroom, and bite my lip as I close the drawer.

Saturday afternoon brings William and me to southern New Hampshire, in the backyard of a quaint Victorian done up in shades of slate blue and cream. This is the home of the bride's parents, old friends of William's former boss, who promised Irv that when it became time for Becky to marry, they would use his services. Since Irv is now in an assisted living complex and sounds as though he wouldn't know shutter speed from Shineola, William has taken on the job. Becky's parents are genteel, bringing us cool, frosty glasses of lemonade from the house as we set up under the tent, and Becky herself is an exemplary bride, standing barefoot in jean shorts and a Guided By Voices T-shirt as she politely asks if there is anything we need from her before she goes inside to get ready.

I can tell I will hate this wedding already because it's going to be the way a wedding really should be: a proclamation of true love between two sensible people about to embark on a lifelong journey. It's easier to laugh and snicker with William about the insanity of marriage when the groom is clearly miserable when saying his vows, or when you witness the mother of the bride screaming about the centerpieces, or when the bridal party is openly placing bets on how long the marriage will last. But when it feels so genuine and real, those are the days when I feel the most hollow inside.

William interrupts my ruminations with a little jab to my left arm. "Did I tell you that I took some amazing pictures the other day? Best ones I've taken in awhile, I think," he says playfully.

It's a challenge to match his level of enthusiasm. "I've been having the opposite problem," I say, my voice flat. "I recently got reamed on a portfolio review at the Valeria Gallery in Newton, in fact."

"Oh, I'm sorry," he says, frowning. He rubs my back for a few seconds and I catch the eye of Becky's father, who understands instantly that our relationship may not be of the traditional photographer/photographer's assistant variety. "That's hard. But, I mean, Newton? They're so stuck-up there, what could they possibly know about art?" he asks gently. He pops open a canister of film and holds the little gray lid between his front teeth.

"Yeah," I say, choosing not to tell him that I actually agreed with the gallery owner, stuck-up or not. "I think I'm just distracted these days," I add carefully. He looks at me as he puts the lid back on with a *snap*, and I wonder if he assumes that I'm talking about Thomas. *Good!* I silently yell at him before walking over to take a look at the bridal party. Then I think, *Good God, Iley, what's happening to you?*

The wedding and reception unfold precisely as I'd pictured them: glowing bride, deliriously happy groom, in-laws who smile at one another with genuine pleasure, cheery guests who don't drink to excess, a lovely band that fills the neatly groomed backyard with the sounds of swing and big band melodies. It's even a little cooler than normal for an early August day, and every so often, a light breeze carries the scent of flowers from the garden through the tent. The whole scene is heavenly, and it makes me feel like garbage. The reception ends not a moment too soon, and William and I pack up wordlessly as several small children race around the temporary dance floor that's been set up on the lawn. I know I should take a few shots of the little ponytailed girl spinning in circles or the toddler chewing on his dress shoe, because brides and grooms evidently love these outtakes of their pint-sized relatives, but I don't feel like it.

We get into the car and head for the highway. The windows of the Volvo are down and we're both smoking, and I don't feel like talking about where to get a drink, where to find a room, where to bed down for a few hours before slinking back to Boston. My sullenness is starting to overtake the entire car when I spot a sign for Canobie Lake Park, the eponymous, old-time amusement park. I smile for the first time in hours and point to the sign, which features the exit number next to a slightly demented-looking clown clutching a handful of lumpy balloons.

"Let's go there," I order, turning to William.

He turns to look at me. "Canobie Lake Park?" he asks, incredulous. "Is that what you mean?" He doesn't slow down.

I nod vigorously. "Yes. They've got great rides, William. A log flume and an old coaster and something called a Starblaster, which I've never been on," I say. "I think these places are even half-price after five o'clock, or something." He's wavering, his brow furrowing as he tries to decide which lane to get in. "Please?" I plead. "It would be really fun."

"Well, I'm not so sure about that," he says as he quickly pulls into the exit lane. I give a little trilling sound and wiggle around in my seat, crushing my cigarette in the ashtray and counting the moments until I'm screaming bloody murder on The Yankee Cannonball. When we arrive, the park is a mob scene, with pimply, harried high-school students outfitted in orange safety vests and attempting to direct traffic.

"Thatellite parking," a short kid with a terrible haircut and a prominent lisp dully informs William after we pay the thirty-four-dollar admission fee.

"What?"

"I thaid, 'Thatellite parking,' " he repeats more forcefully. "All the other lotth are full. You have to park in the thatellite lot," he says, pointing somewhere in the general direction of Vermont.

"Ugh," William says as we drive away in search of our far-flung lot. We circle the satellite parking lot for a good fifteen minutes, narrowly missing an exhausted father and his three yippy boys, and a pair of polyester-clad seniors contentedly gumming lavender cotton candy. "Here we are," he says flatly as the Volvo noses into a narrow parking space at the edge of the lot. I can tell he's crabby and agitated, and I take his hands in mine.

"Thankth for taking me here," I deadpan. "I really appreciate it."

He smiles against his will, and then we join hands and take the long walk to the park. Once there, however, his good cheer fades and he balks at going on the rides. No Wipeout. No Boston Tea Party. No Timber Splash, Giant Skywheel, or Crazy Cups. And shockingly, no Yankee Cannonball. "It's a wooden coaster, one of the very few of its kind left," I say encouragingly. "Why not?"

"I just don't feel like it," he replies, shrugging. "But you can go, and I'll watch."

"OK," I sulk. He waits in line with me for the twenty minutes it takes me to wind my way to the entry gate, and I am seated next to a pre-teen boy with glow-in-the-dark rubber bands around his braces. Because it's dusk and not quite dark out, they aren't glowing at full capacity, and it appears that he's got little bits of green bean stuck to each tooth instead. We lurch forward as we begin, and the ride on The Yankee Cannonball that normally gives me a rush and makes me holler like a fool doesn't. Every time we swoop down and I get a glimpse of William, my stomach tightens uncomfortably, and I know in my heart that it's not due to the dips and turns of the rickety coaster.

We meander around the park and I try to needle him into getting on some rides, with no success. I eat some fried dough with gusto and William gets a beer, and we take in a fairly anemic fireworks display for a few minutes. The park is quieting down considerably now, with parents dragging weepy, hiccupping children toward the exit, and teenage boys trying to reach second base behind the bumper car area. We find ourselves in front of the Starblaster, the ride that shoots you eighty-five feet into the air and then simulates free fall for a few gut-wrenching seconds.

"Last chance," I say to William, tipping my head all the way back and looking to the top of the Starblaster. "You want to go on this one with me?"

"You just ate fried dough," he warns.

"I'll take that as a no," I answer as I walk away from him and get in line for the ride. "Pussy," I mutter under my breath.

William ducks under the yellow webbed rope and stands next to me. "I'm sorry, Iley," he says. Two young mothers with tie-dyed tank tops and too-short cutoffs snicker loudly behind us, and William leans over and says curtly, "I'm not cutting the line, I'm just talking to her for a second." He turns back to me. "I just don't like this kind of thing. But I'll take pictures of you, all right?" he asks hopefully as he goes back under the rope. I reach the front of the line and am seated next to a teenage girl wearing a denim miniskirt and a tight, hot pink baby tee. She's got more baby fat than womanly curves at this point, and her little breasts sit atop a big roll of stomach flesh. We are securely locked into our harnesses by a sullen guy in his mid-twenties with beer breath, and I look over to see William focusing his camera on me.

"I'm Carly," the girl says to me, and just as the "ly" leaves her mouth, the Starblaster takes off, lifting us skyward with a speed that nearly brings my fried dough back up. The wind rushes past me, and it's exhilarating and frightening and intensely physical, not unlike other kinds of nights spent with William.

We bounce back to earth, and I answer breathlessly, "Nice to meet you. I'm Iley." And as soon as my name passes my lips, we're up again and Carly is hollering in my ear on the way back down. We are allotted one more blast into the stratosphere on this ride, and they give us a few seconds to prepare for this final launch.

Carly spots William shooting pictures of me and asks, "Is that your boyfriend?"

We take off again and I scream as loudly as I can, pushing this question into the heavens, way above the Starblaster. We lower back down and Carly instantly begins smoothing her hair. "I don't know what the hell he is," I tell her, shrugging. The surly guy unclips my harness and I wobble my way over to William. He is laughing and grinning, shaking his head.

"You ready to go?" he asks, lighting a cigarette for me.

"Yeah," I say. I feel euphoric from the ride, giddy and punchy from all that speed and rushing air. We start the long walk to the car, and William decides to come clean.

"I'm sorry I was so lame tonight, Iley," he say quietly, feeling in his pockets for his keys. "I don't like any of those rides because I've always been really afraid of them. I know it's stupid."

"Nothing can happen to you," I assure him. I look around our satellite lot and realize we are one of very few cars left.

He grasps my hand. "That's one of the reasons I like you so much, Iley. You're not afraid of anything."

Just afraid of having feelings for a person I can't have, afraid of the day I can't handle this anymore, afraid of what to do about Thomas. "Nope," I agree. "Not a thing."

We get into the car and I sit quietly for a moment, thinking about my ride on the Yankee Cannonball and the unusual perspective it afforded me way up there in the sky. Zipping down near the ground and feeling decidedly unhappy, even with the green bean boy laughing into my right ear. William interrupts my thoughts with a soft touch to my cheek.

"Motel?" he asks. He kisses me and pulls me close to him, and before long we're way past the point of no return, my Yankee Cannonball worries pushed uneasily to the back of my mind. We end up doing it right then and there, rocking the car and fogging the windows like so many teenagers after a date to the amusement park on a cool summer's night.

Another vivid, sweat-soaked dream, this one while I'm on the sofa well after midnight, having fallen asleep while watching *Clerks*. In the dream, I'm lifting lids of film canisters and looking for a fresh roll of film, but each time, I uncover something unexpected. One canister contains a silver-plated camera charm from a charm bracelet that was given to me as a teenager by my grandma. Another contains a handful of Erin's high-end bobby pins, except that they're all lumpy, as though they melted in the sun. Still other canisters are like clown cars, in that the items stored in them are actually much too large to fit into the tiny plastic cylinders. One has Thomas's gold belt buckle, and another has Gary's glow-in-the-dark leash. I pry open one that has a motel room key jangling on a blue plastic key ring, and another that has a white paper coaster with scalloped edges. But I know there must be film in here somewhere, and I need it. So I keep looking. Searching.

Fifteen

"You really are so pretty," purrs Thomas as he pulls down my bra strap and kisses me on the shoulder. My shirt is on the floor, the sleeveless one that Erin has to help me put on, with the twelve little buttons up the back. We are hot and heavy on his dark green Ikea sofa, and I'm not quite sure how I got here. I take that back, of course: I got here via Pinot Grigio Street, with a sharp left turn at Sex Drive and a little right turn at Little Bit of Sympathy Way. In other words, I am drunk, horny, and felt sorry for Thomas when he asked me up after our date and I initially demurred. It's not as though I'd have a real problem with sleeping with Thomas tonight and William next week. It's just that Thomas seems to really like me, and I don't think I can do this to him. My moral compass may be in disrepair these days, the needle spinning wildly, but it's not completely busted.

"OK, OK, hold on," I say as he unhooks my bra and starts to hungrily pull it off me. "Thomas. *Thomas*. Come on.” I slide my bra straps back onto my shoulders and pull away from him. He is rosy-faced and slightly wild-eyed, and I feel terrible.

“What’s the matter?” he asks, pushing his hair out of his eyes.

“I just don’t think I can . . . do this,” I say sadly as I clip my bra.

There is a long pause, and I pray that he reads between the lines. He doesn’t. “Iley, we don’t have to do this right now,” he replies, all compassion and understanding in spite of a prominent hard-on. “There’s no hurry.” I hear Guy give a little sniffle from the other room.

“No,” I say carefully as I reach for my shirt. “I mean that I don’t think we should do this anymore.”

He looks at me uncomprehendingly for a few seconds. “Wait a minute. Are you . . . are you saying you don’t want to see me?” He’s holding one of Guy’s chew toys now, turning it over in his hands. He looks at his fingers wrapped around The Daily Bark for a long minute; I imagine he figured that by now these fingers would be eagerly exploring inside my underwear, not gripping a squeaky newspaper. He looks up with one of the saddest expressions I’ve seen on an adult in a long time.

I put on my shirt and leap off the couch, because I don’t know what else to do. I impulsively open my mouth and the words pour out. “Look, have you ever been in a situation where you can’t see your way out of it, and you know it’s not right, but you can’t do anything about it?” I try to reach around and button some of the buttons, but it’s futile, and I’m sure I just look like a crazy, drunk gorilla instead.

He studies me for a few seconds. "Iley, do you have a problem with money or drugs or something? Because—"

"No!" I exclaim. "It's not that," I say, looking down and shaking my head.

"Well, sometimes if one of my students has a big problem, I'll tell them to step outside of themselves and look at the problem as though they were watching a stranger. That sometimes helps them find a solution."

He's so helpful and understanding that I want to scream, but I take a deep breath instead. "Thomas, I have to go," I say firmly. "I'm really sorry." I take a few more swipes at my buttons, give up, and pick up my messenger bag. So what if the back of my shirt is wide open, I think as I walk toward the front door of the little apartment. This night is beyond fucked-up already, how could my exposed back make things any worse?

"Iley, you can't leave like that," he says, his voice strained. He walks over to me, faces me, and then turns me around. He buttons in silence as I look hard at the floor and try not to cry. When the last button is through the hole and he gives the placket a little pat, I turn around to face him, say a gruff good-bye, and run down the building's four flights of stairs.

I push my sunglasses hard up the bridge of my nose, even though we're sitting in the airport bar and there is no natural light in sight. But my eyes are bleary from last night's drinks with Erin and puffy from weeping silently in my room about William. Or perhaps it was about Thomas. I don't even know anymore; all I know is that Erin and I decided to start our trip early with a well-aged, exquisite bottle of scotch, pilfered from the Brooks' liquor cabinet in Connecticut during Erin's last visit home.

"I think Gary is going to be sad to see us come back," Erin muses as she studies a woman with a stylish, asymmetrical haircut. Half an hour earlier, we dropped Gary off at the Bed and Biscuit, a posh, downtown doggie hotel that boasts private suites, room service, large-screen TVs tuned to Animal Planet, and tailored, individual playtime for each dog. He spends a few days' vacation time at the Bed and Biscuit roughly once a year, and Erin and I justify the expense by telling one another that he so rarely experiences anything other than the four walls of our cramped apartment, he should be able to loll around someplace luxurious. But really, I think it's because she and I love the paw print walkway, the bone-shaped bathtubs, the little jars of treats on every horizontal surface, and the framed, faux antique daguerreotypes of dogs that march up the wall next to the staircase. It's abundantly clear to anyone that these things were designed and placed here for the dog owners' aesthetic pleasure, not the dogs'. Yet we adore it anyway. It was the daguerreotypes that got me the first time we toured the place.

"I know, it's always embarrassing, the way he runs away with hardly a look back," I agree. "You at least want to think he's going to miss us a tiny bit," I add, thinking of a poor little cocker spaniel with the same check-in time as Gary, cowering and shivering and pissing on the floor in terror as its owner backed slowly out the door. Gary often holds weak-willed dogs such as this one in contempt, and I hope there will be no altercations later on at the snack bar.

"You ready to go?" Erin asks, putting twenty dollars in

singles on the bar and hoisting her black canvas bag over her shoulder. She sees me smile at the pile of cash. "The life of someone who works for tips—what can I say?" she says with a grin and a shrug.

We ready to board the plane, during which time no fewer than three airline personnel bark at me to remove my sunglasses, and once we get on and take our seats, I exhale and make a pact with myself. No thinking about William on this trip. No feelings of remorse about Thomas. And most importantly, no worrying about my entirely questionable photography career. Erin tightens her seat belt and lays several recent copies of the newspaper on her lap, rubbing her hands together with the look of a woman who is about to enjoy a splendid meal. She opens the first with a snap. "I haven't had time to read these lately, so I've been taking them home from the salon. 'Mission Hill: Elmira Jones, age seventy-three, called the police, claiming that her super changed the station on her radio without her consent. "I used to listen to the talk radio, but now it's that ugly kind of yelling music all the time," she said. The super claimed that he was only there to unclog her toilet, not to listen to the radio, and doesn't even like rap. After further questioning, it was determined that Mrs. Jones's grandson had changed the radio station.' Awesome," Erin decides aloud.

The trip goes without incident, with me spending much of my time staring out the window at the clouds and Erin occasionally chortling and reading me passages from the police blotter pages. I sleep for a little while and am plagued by dreams about Gary determining that he'd prefer to stay in residence at the Bed and Biscuit, rather than return home to our Brighton apartment. When I wake, I urgently need to pee, and I make my way down the long aisle toward the bathroom. There is an elementary school-aged girl padding around the plane in her socks, and she stops to talk to her brother a few feet in front of me. She looks at me with clear blue eyes, and although it's obvious I need to pass, she makes no attempt at scooting back to her seat or even turning sideways. Her parents are oblivious, noses buried deep in some in-flight magazines, and the girl gives me a practiced look of entitlement, turning to face me more fully and block the aisle. I gracelessly slide past her and relieve myself in the tiny bathroom, and emerge to find that she's planted in the same spot. I walk down the aisle slowly to give her some time to move. When she doesn't, I make sure my arm is where I want it, and I furtively elbow her in the side of the head as I pass.

The next two days pass in a blur, just the way they are meant to in Vegas. It's booze and swimming and slots and roulette (lucky number: 20), then more booze and some poker (Erin's game). A dark-haired, dicey guy named Carl insinuated himself into a conversation Erin and I were having at the pool yesterday afternoon and has been periodically meeting up with us since, and now he is sitting with me and Erin in the lobby of the Bellagio as we decide what to do next. He is remarking on the hotel's beauty and splendor, but I am unmoved by such ostentatious displays and instead prefer to focus my attention on a woman having a fight with her husband about which blackjack table they should try first.

"Now what?" Erin asks, suppressing the slightest of yawns. It's midnight, and she and I are both hurting from sunburn and too much alcohol.

"What do you mean, 'Now what?'" asks Carl in an amazed tone of voice. He gestures around the hotel. "We drink and we gamble." Erin and I look at one another and shrug, then walk into the casino. I quickly lose twenty dollars at a roulette wheel, then win forty. The dealer looks exhausted, her eyelids thickly painted with a shimmery lavender shadow that has migrated into her crow's feet, and I tip her a few chips and set off to find Erin. She is standing close to Carl at a craps table, by far one of the liveliest spots here. When it's his turn, Carl seems to really enjoy being the center of attention, and as he bends over to throw the dice, I notice what a nice ass he has.

"That's not bad," I say to Erin as I tip my chin in the direction of his backside.

"Yeah," she agrees, giving me the wide-mouthed grin of the wasted. "Don't wait up for me later, all right?" A big cheer spontaneously goes up around the craps table, as though to endorse Erin's upcoming rendezvous.

"OK," I say. "What's his story?" I ask as I start in on my fourth screwdriver of the evening. Or maybe it's my fifth.

"Who cares?" she laughs raucously. "I need to get laid and he's hot, that's his story."

"Fair enough," I nod. We stay for a few more games of craps, and I am relegated to third wheel status as the three of us stumble through the rest of the casino, with Erin and Carl knocking into one another and laughing as I amble behind them. After sitting alone at a slot machine and systematically losing eight dollars in quarters, I decide I've had enough of watching fruit and Liberty Bells spin before my bloodshot eyes. I find Erin and Carl at a poker table, and I whisper in her ear. "I'm going back to the room. You going to be all right?"

"I'll be fine," she says enthusiastically.

"Be careful," I whisper.

"Yeah, you too," she replies with utter sincerity, and I drunkenly giggle at this as I walk down the Strip toward our hotel. What on earth could happen to me here, where I'm surrounded by happy tourists and eager gamblers?

I stumble up to our room and drop onto my bed, when I am suddenly overtaken by a fit of loneliness. I'm alone in Vegas, drunk, in my hotel room. I pace the floor for a few minutes, feeling like a cat in a cage. I turn on the TV and flip the channels mindlessly as I bite at a hangnail on my left thumb. I smoke a cigarette. I start to run a bath, then realize that taking a hot bath in Las Vegas in August is just too perverse an activity to consider, then turn off the water and flop down on the bed again. I reach for my bag and pull out a phone number, then take Erin's cell phone and dial. Finally, what I really want to do.

The phone rings twice, and he picks up. "Hello?"

"Hi, William. It's me. Iley. How's it going?"

"It's all right," he says, his voice tight. He lowers his voice. "It's *Tuesday*."

"Wha—what?" I ask. Then I remember. It's Tuesday, all right. Which means that Kendra may be nearby. "Anyway, I'm in Las Vegas, all alone in the room. And—"

"I can't really talk now," he says in a suddenly officious tone. "We'll have to get in touch about that when you get back." She must be very near now. And before I can reply, he hangs up.

I throw the phone down in a rage, then pick it up and redial. No answer, so I leave an angry voice mail. "Don't hang up on me!" I scream into the phone and toss it onto the floral carpet. I turn the TV back on and scroll through the movie choices; they are all unbelievably lame, the kinds of films I might see if they were matinee price and I had nothing better to do on a cold winter day.

I strip down to my underwear and slide under the covers, thinking about William and Kendra and growing angrier by the minute. I flip off the blanket and root around in my bag for another piece of paper—this one with William's home phone, given to me to keep "in case of emergencies," he'd said awhile back. I pull Erin's phone out from under the fake mahogany nightstand and dial. He answers on the very first ring.

"I'm in my bed here at the hotel," I say, sliding back under the covers. "What are you wearing?"

"I said, I'm afraid that will have to wait until next week," he says slowly. Then, calling to someone obviously in another room, "Oh, it's just something about work; I'll be right there, honey."

Fuck him. Fuck him and his stupid art restoration wife. I'm going to make this as difficult as possible. "They've got porn movies here," I purr, breathing deeply. "I'm taking off my panties right now," I add, sliding them down past my knees. "Why don't you get comfortable?"

There is a long silence, followed by a sharp intake of breath. "Don't . . . call . . . me . . . anymore," he whispers angrily and slams the phone down again. I drop the cell phone on the bed and stare at the ceiling. Then I throw it as hard as I can against the far wall, yank my underwear back up, and fold my arms hard across my chest. I try to change the channel on the TV, but the remote won't work. That's because in my anger, I flung the TV remote against the wall, not the cell phone. And I don't feel like getting up. I fall asleep frowning, the light from the bright blue Movie Choices screen illuminating me in the hotel bed.

"Ahhhh," Erin says the next day as we prepare to take our leave of Las Vegas. We are at the airport, and she is wearing the pleased expression of a person who had a wholly satisfying one-night stand. She folds her hands across her belly and leans back in the plastic seat. "I think this trip was a success."

"Yeah," I say dully.

"Sorry I got in so late last night. Or early this morning, whichever." She actually arrived back at our hotel room at five-thirty this morning. I know because I'd woken up a half-hour earlier, gnashing my teeth and thinking about what my phone calls would mean for my relationship with William, and hadn't been able to fall back to sleep.

"It's no problem," I say honestly. "I'm glad you met Carl."

"Oh, and he had *such* good blow," she gushes, shielding her mouth with her hand on the word "blow." I smile; I always forget about how Erin's upbringing has left her with a real weakness for the white stuff.

She gets up to buy a bottle of water, and I focus my attention on a group of older teenagers, all boys, looking bored and sullen as they lounge around near a row of noisy slot machines. A few throw coins at one another in a way that is friendly but could at any moment turn antagonistic, depending on perhaps a too-hard throw of a penny or a sudden uptick in testosterone. It's clear that they're not tourists, and I wonder why it is that they are hanging out here, and what will become of them someday. Most of them are Hispanic, and there are a few white guys, and a couple of Asian guys. One of them reminds me a bit of Rithy, if Rithy didn't have the industrious family and the classes at Wentworth and the structured darkroom schedule. And then I remember that he no longer has the darkroom schedule, and I decide what I need to do. Well, at least someone will benefit from this trip, I think, as I watch Erin study the scratches on the side of her cell phone.

Much like my dream on the Las Vegas-bound flight, Gary seems a bit perturbed to be back in his old surroundings, looking sourly at the fifteen-inch TV screen and eyeing his Iams with disdain. "What can I do, buddy?" I ask as I give him a Snausage and watch him resignedly gnash it into tiny bits. "I'd like to live in a B&B too, but it ain't gonna happen." I pet him hard on his side, enjoying that solid, *thunk*ing sound that reverberates through the flanks of a large dog. The phone rings and I reach for it.

"Oh, hello, Iley," says Bitsy crisply. "So nice you're home today."

"Yes, well, Erin and I just got back from a trip late last night," I lie, immediately wishing I hadn't disclosed anything at all.

"Really?" she asks with mild interest. "Where did you go?"

My mind reels. Bermuda. St. Croix. Nantucket. Chesapeake Bay. Isn't that where her people go? Ultimately I tell the truth, because at least I can picture the place in my mind's eye. "Las Vegas. She was given the trip by a client." Oops.

"Las Vegas?" she muses. "With the dancing girls and Tom Jones? That Las Vegas? What sort of client at Harvard Business School would think my Erin would enjoy it there?" I hear the clink of ice cubes in a glass and the faraway sound of a lawnmower, and I think about how much Erin apparently enjoyed taking it from behind from Carl in the shower.

"I'm not sure, Mrs. Brooks," I say politely, praying for this conversation to end. "I can tell Erin that you called, all right?" Gary stands by the door and looks at me impatiently; he may have had twenty-four access to all-night, outdoor pooping at the Bed and Biscuit, for all I know.

"Well, if you got back so late, why isn't she there?" she asks. The call waiting beeps, and I heave a sigh of relief.

"She went out," I say hurriedly. "Look, there's a call on my other line, and Gary needs to go out. I'll tell Erin you called. It was nice talking to you," I lie, and pick up the other call.

"Hi, Iley, it's Thomas," a male voice says quietly.

"I'm really sorry, Thomas, I need to take my dog out," I sigh, exhausted from this morning's telephone challenges. "I can't talk now."

"Gary. I know your dog's name, Iley," he says evenly.

"Yeah, I know you know," I reply, kicking the toe plate on the refrigerator as I grab Gary's leash off the kitchen table. A long, uncomfortable silence follows. "Look, I'll call you back, all right?" But I know I never will. I hope that Thomas knows, as well.

I am sitting on the front stoop waiting for William to pick me up, a by-now familiar scene that should make me tingle with anticipation but today simply fills me with dread. His Volvo rounds the corner and my stomach tightens. The car stops and I slide into the front seat.

"Hi," I say, giving him a tight smile.

"Hey," he says, not looking happy, but not looking as though he is going to drive the car headlong into traffic either. He is wearing a short-sleeved Oxford shirt, and I study the curve of his elbow, the long flat plane of his wrist. I really missed these arms, I realize with a start.

"William, about the phone calls," I begin quietly, looking out the window.

We stop at a light. "Iley, that really was not cool," he says bluntly, looking right at me. I study his eyes for a second; he looks tired, not in the way where someone has slept badly for a few nights, but in the way where the tiredness is something pervasive, mind numbing, deeply fatiguing. "Things are so fucked up with Kendra—one minute she says she wants us to move to D.C., then the next minute she isn't sure she wants to be married. And your calling doesn't help."

"It was a one-time thing," I say through gritted teeth. "It won't happen again." We drive in silence for several miles, down Route 1, past the car dealerships and the steak houses and the furniture outlets. It's all ugliness in every direction, and the August heat and smog don't do anything to enhance the already revolting landscape.

We pull into the parking lot at the catering hall, a low-slung building with a stucco exterior and a frayed red carpet leading to the entryway. William turns to me and says a bit wildly, "Look, I *miss* you when I'm not with you! Do you understand?"

"I do," I say, my voice catching in my throat. I watch the florists unload a series of unattractive centerpieces, each packed with more than its fair share of carnations and baby's breath. We are even earlier than usual today, and I'd much rather set up inside the air-conditioned catering hall than sit here and argue with William in the hot car.

"I gotta . . ." he begins, then closes his eyes and puts his hand on the dashboard. "I don't even know what I gotta do anymore," he admits.

"Yeah," I say, staring straight ahead, knowing that a solution to this is not going to be found in The Friar Tuck's parking lot. "Just don't fire me, please. I really need money right now."

"You do?" he asks with concern, grateful to talk about something else. "What's the matter?"

"Oh, I need to help someone out who's in a bit of a jam these days," I reply, watching a bus boy step into the bright sunlight, light a cigarette, and shield his eyes with his hand as he surveys the pavement. I pull out a cigarette and light it, inhaling deeply.

"Well, I can give you some money, no problem," William says, much too quickly. It takes me by surprise and I look at him with a furrowed brow. Suddenly the bride's limousine arrives, and the belle of the ball emerges from the backseat, hauling her gown in a giant white bag and holding a makeup case with screenprinted images of Minnie Mouse.

"Time to go," I sigh, and we begin bringing everything inside. The wedding is by the book, and in light of our peculiar discussion in the car, I am relieved. It's always best when there's not too much to think about: just point and shoot. The justice of the peace performs a quick, emotionless ceremony in one small room of the hall, then the reception begins next door. Appetizers of soup or salad, entrees of chicken or beef, stale, little bread rolls and pats of frozen butter on small white plates, weak coffee poured from tarnished carafes. The bride and groom dance to "At Last," Etta James crooning the omnipresent "first dance" song as they lurch gracelessly around the floor. The obedient maid of honor even catches the bouquet. By the time the cake is ready to be wheeled out, I already know what it's going to be: a white, three-tiered, sticky affair that looks pretty and tastes terrible. I derive a strange sense of satisfaction when I see that most of the dessert plates going back to the kitchen are strewn with half-eaten pieces of cake and forkfuls of inedible icing. Through it all, William and I are barely talking, but we're not too tense, either. He catches my eye a few times and we trade a smile, which is encouraging.

At the end of the reception, we are alone in the back room, disassembling tripods and packing away lenses, and I say, "You know what? I think we probably shouldn't fool around anymore." I say it in a very normal, measured tone of voice, as though I might be saying, "You know what? I think my shorts are still at the dry cleaner's," or, "You know what? I think loose-leaf notebooks are better than spiral-bound."

William zips up a black canvas bag and leans against a small table. "You're probably right," he agrees, after a long pause. But of course, what people say and what they do can be quite different, and not too much later, I find myself searching frantically for that strip of light under the motel room door, so I can reorient myself. To where I have ended up, once again.

Sixteen

The next day finds me in the office of the infelicitously named Mr. Meany, at the New England School of Photography. Mr. Meany is an administrator at the school, and the one who determines darkroom assignments for nonstudents. I have brought a thick stack of greenbacks here this morning, in hopes of reclaiming some much-needed darkroom space.

"How can I help you today?" Mr. Meany asks, coming to meet me from behind a gray carpeted cubicle wall. He has white, greasy hair that's been cut into a loose, unappealing style, and he is wearing a rumpled green shirt and too-thin black tie.

"Yeah, I wanted to pay some darkroom fees for Joey Suchinda. Can I do that?"

Mr. Meany looks confused. "Is he a student here?"

"No," I say, stepping out of the way to let what is probably a work-study student pass by me with a sheaf of papers.

She has a large piercing across the bridge of her nose, and torn, striped tights, and Mr. Meany studies her with a pinched expression as she walks out the door. "He used to rent darkroom space, but then he stopped because he didn't have the money. But I'd like to rent some space for him."

"Well, I think that, um—what is her name?" he asks himself, furrowing his brow. "Oh, yes, Therese. I think that Therese can help you take care of that." He gives me a little nod and turns to go.

"The thing is," I implore him, "the thing is that I don't want him to know that I'm sort of his benefactor," I explain. Suddenly I'm itching for a cigarette. "So I'd like to set it up here in the office, if that's all right." Without my uttering one word about the sublimely unpleasant Therese and how I'm sure she'd blow it for me, he immediately understands. Mr. Meany and I are simpatico. He nods and I fill in some paperwork, then Mr. Meany decides that he'll call Rithy and tell him that he's the recipient of some mysterious government funding for non-students, and send a memo to Therese stating the same. Done and done. And it isn't until I'm back outside in the bright sunshine that I think about how spectacularly strange it was for William to offer me this money so readily, before he even knew what it was for. Was there some small, murky part of his mind that thought this was some sort of extortion—Rithy hush money to ensure that I wouldn't be making any more poorly timed phone calls to his place? Was there some small, murky part of my own mind that thought the same?

The next three days are spectacularly rainy, so much so that by the morning of the second day, I have to literally push Gary down the front steps when we go outside for his morning bathroom break. Thomas calls in the afternoon and I don't pick up; he drawls a short message for me and there is a long pause before he finally hangs up, as though he wants to add something else but then thinks better of it. I pass the time inside, smoking, snacking, thinking gloomily about William, looking at my portfolio. These are the perfect kind of days for spending in the darkroom, where it's dark and snug and the smell of the chemicals and the sights of your own work envelop you, and you forget entirely about the outside world. I should go, of course, but I don't want to. I tell myself that it's because I don't want to ride my bike in the rain, but I know in my heart that it's not a question of transportation.

Today may very well turn out to be the longest and most uncomfortable day of my life, I determine sourly as I look at my watch. It's Saturday morning, and I am temping for a Cambridge-based catering company—well, *the* Cambridge-based catering company, really, the one that provides Harvard University with all of the delectable food for its more upscale events. I am outfitted in a white Oxford shirt and black skirt, looking for all the world like a hopeless twit, and have been here since eight o'clock this morning, preparing for some giant outdoor alumni breakfast. Or maybe it's a breakfast for incoming students; I don't know. I don't care. All I do know is that when I finish here at noon, I need to race home, change, and be ready for William to pick me up at one o'clock. We've got a wedding that starts at two, and I've already plotted the best bike route home and mentally combed my closet for the outfit I'll throw on upon arrival. I think the invasion of Iraq may have been planned with less fanfare and concern.

A short woman with a long, gray braid and enormous glasses beckons me over to a small tent and hands me two gigantic glass jugs of orange juice. She has the bored, efficient look of someone who has probably been doing this job since the Carter administration. "Go around the tables and ask if people want more orange juice," she instructs me, to which I want to reply in my best flaky voice, "Orange juice? I thought these jugs were full of wallpaper paste!" But I don't and instead start to weave my way through the tables, cursing the weight of the jugs. Although I suppose I should give thanks that at least I'm not carrying something hot. It's positively sultry this morning, and the guys hefting the silver trays of steaming omelets are covered in sweat, grimacing as they set down the brunch fare and try to delicately mop their brows.

The next two hours find me carrying out glass bowls filled to the brim with pieces of fragrant, exotic-looking fruits, offering replacements for dropped flatware and napkins (the grass beneath the tables looks much tidier than my kitchen floor, I muse to myself, when a tan, sinewy woman in a flowery sundress becomes hysterical at the prospect of using a fork that touched the ground), and trying desperately to avoid tripping over chairs that have been carelessly left out by guests who decided to wander over to another table and didn't deem it necessary to push them back in. Harvard, what a place.

When the last of the coffee and tea have been poured, I

check my watch. It's five after twelve, and I unbutton the top button on my sweat-soaked shirt and stride over to the gray braid woman, who is furiously writing on papers attached to a brown clipboard.

"Well, I'm going to leave now," I say, reaching into the pile of purses and backpacks beneath a small table under the tent. I find my messenger bag and see her looking at me with a quizzical, angry expression. She is using facial muscles that I didn't even know humans had, and it's a look that I won't soon forget.

"You're here until one," she says. "For clean-up. Didn't the temp agency tell you?"

"No, they said noon," I answer quickly. "I have to go. I have another job."

"Look, if they told you the wrong time, that's their problem, not mine," she brays, tossing her braid over her shoulder. It comes to rest precariously close to a bowl of sour cream. "You need to stay for the whole time, otherwise we don't count you on the payroll."

I fold my arms for a few seconds, wondering what to say. What I'm really thinking is, how did I let myself stray so far from what I really wanted to do in life—what I once believed I really *needed* to do in life—and end up standing here weighing the benefits of staying for another hour and removing dirty linens, just so I could get my measly check from the temp agency for this inane job? When I realize that the answers are too complicated and numerous to consider, it makes my heart sink. "Do you have a cell phone?" I ask crisply. "I need to call my other employer."

She snickers. "You don't have your own cell phone? Who doesn't have a cell phone?"

I don't answer and instead walk over to a friendly guy who helped me dish colorful fruit into the bowls earlier. "Hey, do you have a cell phone I can use for a local call? Mine's dead," I lie. He nods and pulls it out of his pocket, and I walk over to the edge of the tent and call William.

"Hiya," I say into his voice mail. "Look, I don't think I'm going to have time to go home and change or anything, I have to stay here in Harvard Square later than I thought. So I guess you can just pick me up at one o'clock by the Out of Town News, all right?" I pause before hanging up, unsure if I should say, "Looking forward to seeing you," or "I can't wait to tell you what I've been through this morning," or something similar, a sign-off that implies a personal connection. I'm leery after Vegas, and choose to say nothing more.

I spend the next hour cleaning up, and at one o'clock I defiantly throw my ball of dirty napkins on the ground near the braid woman. She doesn't even notice; she's now engrossed in an argument with a silver-haired man wearing a Harvard crimson-hued sport coat. I unlock my bike, pedal as hard as I can across Harvard Square, and am just lighting a cigarette when William pulls up. He takes one look at me in my catering ensemble and laughs.

"You poor thing!" he says, running his hand through my sweaty hair.

"I can't believe I'm going to a wedding like this," I complain. There is a bit of egg on the waistband of my skirt, and my neck is itchy with sweat. "It's so hot!" I shout, angry at everything, sneering at a blissful, young couple crossing against the light.

"Why don't you close your eyes and relax for a few minutes?" William suggests. "You seem really tired and stressed-out, Iley." He says this with such tenderness in his voice that I'm caught off guard. Is this the same man who was lashing into me about the phone calls?

I close my eyes and plunk my head against the Volvo's headrest. "William, I feel like I've forgotten something," I say as we pull onto the highway.

"Back at the catering thing?" he asks, lighting a cigarette.

"No, I mean something else, something at home, or someone I was supposed to call or see. Something like that," I say limply. I would worry more, but I'm too tired. Tired from catering. Tired from this constant push-pull with William.

"Well, can you call your roommate? Erin?"

"No, she's away visiting her brother this weekend," I say. Sailing and snorting.

"I'm sure whatever it is, it will be all right," he says reassuringly, and I close my eyes for the rest of the ride. We pull into the parking lot of the Topsfield Hilton, and I wearily pull everything from the trunk with William, who *tsks* me when I lift the heavier tripods and wrests them from my hands. We go inside and are immediately chastised by the mother of the bride for not arriving sooner; didn't we know that Lisa had decided to get ready earlier than planned? Well, uh, no we didn't. So we rush to the bride's room and hurriedly begin shooting the bride and her four bridesmaids readying, tubes of mascara and pots of lipgloss and hair-straightening irons and bottles of nail polish in every shot. There is a room service tray on the bed, with leftover runny eggs and bits of cantaloupe rind on a big plate, and I yearn to sarcastically ask if they want a shot of that, but decide not to, in case they actually do.

By the time the bride walks down the aisle, all smiles and girly giggles in spite of the fact that she screamed at her sister-in-law only moments before, I'm ready to call it a day. I'm sick of these weddings, I decide as I take four quick shots of the couple kissing. The groom's skin has a slight greenish cast as they lock lips, and I swear I saw him in a pre-fainting sway more than once as she walked down the aisle. I'm sick of this thing with William, where I don't know where we stand from one day to the next, and he claims never to know what's going to happen with Kendra. I'm sick of not believing in myself, of having lost my motivation to take and develop photos, of feeling confused and adrift.

When the guests take their seats and the first of the bumbling toasts begins, I ask William if he can handle it for a few minutes, and head to the bathroom. I splash water on my face and take a seat on a tired wicker sofa adjacent to the wall of sinks. A wedding guest flushes and emerges from one of the stalls; she is a tall woman with an outdated, feathered hairdo, and a tight, pinched face. She washes her hands, holds them for a few cursory seconds under the dryer, and fumbles in her purse for a minute. She puts fifty cents in a small basket next to the sink, and says to me, "Thank you." She pushes the door open and I am left totally perplexed, until I look down at my outfit and realize she thinks I'm the bathroom attendant. I stand up and sigh. "Well, I don't see how this day could possibly get worse now," I announce to myself in the mirror, hiking up my black skirt and giving myself a giant, insincere smile.

Five hours later, we are at William's studio, dropping off the film. Other than the fateful afternoon I came here for my interview, I've only been here two other times. Normally, William goes home after dropping me off, preferring to leave all the cameras and tripods and flashes in the trunk for the next day's wedding, and brings the precious film into his house for safekeeping. But tonight is special: the bride's family requested that proofs be turned around with lightning speed so the couple can take them on their honeymoon and show them to some nana in a far-off country. William explained that a rush job like this would cost them dearly, and they said fine, anything for Nana. So the rolls and rolls of film will await William's darkroom assistant Arvin, who will come in tomorrow at the crack of dawn and get busy.

William is showing me around the back portion of the studio, and I'm utterly consumed by how much I just want to go home and figure out what I've forgotten. We get to the small, humid bathroom, and I flip on the light. "Very nice," I muse, looking at the ugly linoleum floor and pink toilet seat. "I like what you've done here." He gently pushes me against the vanity so I'm facing the mirror and starts kissing me on the neck.

"Aw, come on, William. I don't want to do this anymore," I say weakly. I'm sweltering and uncomfortable and have perspired through this catering outfit many times over. Yet none of this seems to deter him. He reaches around and unbuttons my shirt, cupping my damp breasts with both hands and breathing hard. I'm too beaten down to whip around and ask what the hell Kendra would think of all this. I'm too overheated and weary to say no and have this turn into a confrontation. So I continue to stand there as he pulls down his pants and boxers, hikes up my skirt, and slips down my underwear. I lean over as he slides inside me and study myself in the mirror. My mascara is smudged, and my stick-straight hair is drooping around my face in oily sheets. My eyes look dull and detached, like the girls on the cover sleeves for porno movies, and there are tiny beads of sweat decorating my upper lip. And suddenly and involuntarily, I do what Thomas suggested the night I ran from his apartment, when he said a person should step outside of herself and think about what she sees. And what I see is a girl who is not at all happy. A girl who is not enjoying this one bit. A girl who is in much too deep. I glance up at the ceiling as William lets out a low moan and decide I'll keep my eyes trained on a water stain up there until he comes. Because I don't want to look at the girl in the mirror anymore.

"Hello?" a woman's voice asks from several rooms away. William abruptly pulls back, making a sick squishing sound as his thighs move away from mine.

"Hello?" the voice says again, this time much closer.

William looks at me, wild-eyed. He yanks up his pants and hurriedly fastens his belt. "Kendra," he mouths, swiping the back of his wrist against his wet forehead. The heat suddenly feels even more oppressive in here than it did before, and I swallow hard. He opens the door to a small, dark closet and points inside. My mouth drops open and I lift one eyebrow at him.

"What are you doing here, honey?" he asks in an unnatural, quivery voice as he locks the bathroom door. He is so pale that it looks as though he might pass out. "I thought you were coming in tomorrow night." He gestures again to the closet, which has two shallow shelves filled with toilet paper and cleaning supplies, and a tiny nook down below.

"Well, I finished up some work early, so I took the train back tonight. You weren't home, so I figured I'd find you here." She's outside the door now, and I gesture for William to flush. He does, and then runs both taps for good measure.

"One minute, Kendra," he says. "Get in there," he whispers in my ear, and in one fluid motion, I bend and insert myself into the nook. It's stuffy and mildewy in here, and a sharp paint chip sticks to my calf. He pulls a set of two keys from his pocket and grips them together tightly to prevent any jingling. "Just stay in here until I'm gone, then lock up, all right?" he begs quickly, his face contorted into an expression of complete panic. "I'll be right out," he yells.

"You jackass," I hiss at him, "it reeks of sex in here." I nod toward a can of Glade on top of the toilet tank, and William grabs it and holds the nozzle down. Then without another word, he shuts the door to the closet. Except that there is a tiny crack where the swollen door doesn't fit properly in the jamb, so I can see a thin strip of the ugly bathroom. I shift my weight, trying to ignore the itchiness in the crook of my knees, all that sweat trapped between my flesh as I huddle into a ball.

"Hey, there," he says uneasily after opening the bathroom door. "I'm so surprised you got home early and came here to find me! Let's go home."

"I just have to go to the bathroom," she says, and there is a split second where I think I can almost hear William piss his pants.

"Are you sure you wouldn't rather go at home?" he asks, and just as the words leave his mouth, my eye falls on the empty toilet paper holder next to the toilet. There is no toilet paper. Which means that when it's time to wipe, Kendra will undoubtedly reach for the handy rolls stored on the shelf in the closet. "It's kind of gross in there—not very clean, plus I was just in there for a little while, if you know what I mean," he urges. And after one more back and forth about the relative merits of holding it versus going now, I realize that she's not going to back down. I hold my breath, reach blindly above my head, and wince when my damp fingers land on a toilet paper roll and make its paper wrapper crinkle a bit. My heart is racing a mile a minute and I think I may vomit as I open the door and send the toilet paper rolling across the floor.

I pull the closet door closed, and the toilet paper stops rolling just as she enters the bathroom. "Whew! It stinks in here!" she shouts, and I hear the sound of pants unzipping, her butt landing on the toilet seat, and a strong stream of piss hitting the water. Well, she really did have to go, at least. "Why'd you spray so much of this air freshener garbage? You must have really had a problem," she chuckles, as I try to ignore a droplet of sweat that's just trickled past my eyebrow and into my eye. It hurts like hell, a few strands of my hair are caught in the bristles of a dirty toilet brush, and my bra and shirt are still draped limply around my clammy shoulders. She rinses her hands and there is a very long pause, during which I hold my breath and count backwards from one hundred. When I reach ninety-two, the bathroom light goes off and I hear low murmurs as they make their way toward the back door. I wait a good fifteen minutes before emerging, and when I do, my legs are wobbly and barely carry me to the door. I feel as though my body is made of foam rubber, limp and weak, and I'm so light-headed from heat and anxiety that it frightens me.

I re-hook my bra and button my shirt as I race out the front door, dry-mouthed and gasping. My feet pound the hot pavement hard and somehow know precisely which direction will lead me home, without my having to think about it. I reach the T station and buy a token from a guy sitting in a Plexiglas booth and silently mouthing the words to Sinead O'Connor's version of "Nothing Compares 2 U," which is blaring from a radio in his little prison. I've never liked her whiny rendition, instead preferring Prince's original, sultry arrangement, but watching this lonely man doing mute karaoke to it makes me break down, and I weep all the way back to Harvard Square. Once there, I unlock my bike and begin the ride home, knowing I'll suffer from blurry vision the whole time.

When I arrive home, it reeks in the stuffy apartment. Stinky, awful, diarrhea smell permeating the whole place, and all of a sudden I know what's going on. I race to the kitchen. No Gary, but a big, brown, fetid mess right by the refrigerator. I run to the bedrooms, neither of which contain Gary (nor any diarrhea, which is a plus). Then I run into the bathroom, where Gary is lying on the floor motionless, his eyes rolled back. There is another slick pool of diarrhea near his back legs. I look at the toilet lid. Closed. No way for him to get water there. And I could look at his water dish next, but I don't have to. Because I now know that I forgot to fill his water dish before leaving this morning. Because I was so concerned about my catering job, so I could make some easy money and not have to deal with the shame of trying to shop my sub-par photos around anymore, and then spend the evening fucking my married boss. And now my dog has heat stroke. I stand still for nearly a moment, stunned into inertia by my own selfishness and sheer stupidity.

"Oh, my God," I finally gasp, lifting him and putting him into the tub, a wide stripe of diarrhea branding my forearm. "I am the worst person in the world," I tell Gary, and I see one of his eyes turn toward me. He looks as though he agrees, and would agree more heartily if he had the energy.

I run the cold water and rub it all over his body, but his coat is so thick that it will be a long while before it can really penetrate his fur and cool his skin. He is panting lightly, taking tiny, labored breaths, and I fight back tears as I wonder how I will tell Erin if he ends up at Angell Memorial Animal Hospital. I grab our bath towels (swag from a shampoo trade show Erin went to a few years back, in plush, red terry with the words "Get More Body!" splashed across each one in large yellow type) and soak them with cold water, then race to the freezer and wrestle with a half-dozen ice cube trays, my hands shaking uncontrollably. I plunk as many ice cubes as I can onto the towels, then lay them on top of Gary. I bring him a small bowl of water and place it right near his mouth, but he doesn't respond. Now I am starting to get hysterical, and I beg him to drink.

"Come on, boy," I whimper, choking on my plea as I bend over him and rub his muzzle. "How about I give it to you instead?" I cup my hand and hold it beneath the tap for a few seconds, then present him with the cold water in my palm. He sticks his tongue out and takes a few weak licks, but the water is slipping between my fingers. "Yay for you!" I applaud him, and fill my hand again. We do this for a few more minutes as I wrack my brain for a more efficient way to hydrate him. I yank open the medicine chest, discover an eyedropper among all the cold and flu remedies and combs and clips and Tylenol PM, and fill it with cold water. I kneel next to the tub and attempt to speak in soothing tones as I slide it in between Gary's gums and drip the water into his parched mouth. We stay like this for the better part of a half hour as I take deep breaths and attempt to calm myself. Finally, Gary's head makes a move toward the water dish, and before long, he's lapping at it.

I heave a sigh of relief as he uncertainly rights himself in the tub, and I sit on the closed toilet lid with my head between my legs for a few minutes. Then I yank the giant fan from the window in Erin's room and bring it to the bathroom, where I plug it in and aim it right at Gary. He's far from looking like his vivacious self, but he's at least sitting up and drinking, and that's something. I go to the kitchen and mop up the diarrhea, the activity making me drool and gag in the stifling heat. I smoke a much-needed cigarette. When I return to the bathroom, Gary has gotten out of the tub and is now sitting on the bathroom floor. One of the towels is still draped over his back, and he looks thoroughly nonplussed.

"Hey, look at you," I say as I remove the towel and clean up his backside. I mop the diarrhea in the bathroom, and order Gary to stay. Then I take off my shirt and skirt, throw them in the trash with the diarrhea-soaked paper towels, and step into the shower. Despite feeling like I could shower until my next birthday and still not feel clean, I make it short, because I don't want any steam to heat Gary up. I step out and run the cold water for a few moments, then gesture for Gary to get in the tub, because it's the coolest place in the house. I grab a fresh towel and a big T-shirt out of my room, fill three more water dishes, and place them in the tub near Gary. I unfurl the towel next to the tub, lie down on the floor, and try not to cry; it upsets Gary so, and he certainly doesn't need any more stress tonight.

I manage to stay dry-eyed until about three in the morning, at which point I can't hold it in any longer. I spend a good, long time in the kitchen, weeping quietly, my mind playing the View-Master game with me again, this new reel entitled, "What If You'd Been Gone Just an Hour or Two Longer?" It features Gary dead, his eyes lifeless as he sprawls in his own waste on the bathroom floor; Erin weeping hysterically at the loss of her beloved pet; our friendship dissolved, a guilt from which I'd never recover. I see William and Kendra go by, side by side in the tiny square; then a few blank, white squares near the end. Finally, the reel reaches its last click, and I'm pictured all alone.

Seventeen

At nine o'clock, the phone rings, and I drag myself from my towel to answer it. I was awake anyway, so it's not as though the loud jangle interrupted any quality REM cycles or pleasant dreams. Between repeatedly checking on Gary and replaying my moments spent in the bathroom closet last night, I think I've slept a grand total of forty minutes. I awkwardly rise from the bathroom floor and stumble to the phone. "Hello?" I croak.

"Hello, Iley!" William says brightly. His voice is tight and cheery yet officious; Kendra must be near. "Listen, is there any way you can get to the wedding in Watertown yourself this morning?"

I swallow and close my eyes. "What?" Gary bounds into the room on steady legs, and I give him a wave. At least one of us is having a good start to the day.

"The Corey wedding in Watertown, at the Commander's Mansion," he replies, all politeness. "We've got an eleven o'clock start time."

OK, not only is Kendra near, she doesn't know that William picks me up. Picks me up, drives us around, drives us to motels, spreads my legs in that car. "Yeah, whatever," I say sourly.

There is a long pause, a weighty few seconds of silence during which I can hear William's thoughts coursing through the line. *I can't talk to you about this now, please give me a break. We'll talk later.* "Great!" he says, his bubbly tone annoying. "See you at eleven!"

I light a cigarette, reheat some old coffee, and sit on the sofa for the next half-hour, completely numb. Gary, ever the trooper, nuzzles my legs and tries to comfort me in spite of his own brush with death less than twelve hours earlier. "Today is my last wedding," I inform him in a loud voice, and he looks as though he approves. And having made that momentous decision and shared it with one of my life partners, I stand, stretch, and ready for my final set of shots of lisping flower girls and teary bridesmaids.

The first people I see at the Commander's Mansion are two florists, who look at me askance as I ride up on my bike and nearly hit a tree. I'm so thoroughly exhausted I can barely see straight, my head buzzing and my eyes blood-shot. "Can I help you?" asks one snippily as he hefts a large, lilac-filled centerpiece from the back of a red van.

"Photographer," I mutter, and the guy shoots a "What's up with her?" look at his partner, a short, muscular man gripping a block of green floral foam. I trudge around to the back of the giant mansion, where a beautiful trellis has been decorated with lilacs and lilies. The heat wave miraculously ended at daybreak (I placed six oversized bowls of water around the apartment for Gary nonetheless), and there is even a slight breeze. In a little less than an hour, a couple will take their vows beneath this trellis and kiss and weep, while I try my hardest not to fall asleep or sob. I scan the yard for William, and do a double take when I see that someone is with him. A woman wearing a short-sleeved, button-down shirt and blue rayon skirt. A woman who is most definitely wearing the same footwear I spied from my cramped spot in the bathroom closet last night. A woman who must be Kendra. William spots me shielding my eyes with my hand and studying her and jogs over to me.

"Nice to see your business is a family affair now," I say, my voice flat. This was my second choice of accusatory phrases; the initial one that instinctively leaped to mind was, "What is *she* doing here?" But in my head, it sounded so trite, so hopelessly soap opera and clichéd that I was forced to abandon it.

"She wanted to come with me today and help out. I don't know why; I don't know why she came home early, or why she came to the studio last night. I'm so sorry, Iley," he says wearily, his eyes darting all over the yard. Watching. Waiting for her to walk over so he can change the subject to something innocuous.

"Save it," I spit, and walk over to the trellis, where William has our tripods set up. He trots along next to me and gives Kendra a happy shout.

"Honey!" he shouts awkwardly. "This is Iley, my assistant," he says, and she walks over to shake my hand. She has wispy red hair, thin, nibbly lips, and bright blue eyes, and she's not wearing an ounce of makeup. Her handshake is very limp, and I can swear she winces when I grab her fingers with my standard firm grasp.

"It's nice to meet you," she says. "I understand you help William quite a bit," she smiles.

"Oh, yes, that's true," I nod, looking directly at William, who has suddenly become very interested in what might be at the bottom of an empty film canister in his right hand. I am suddenly unable to suppress a yawn, and after daintily covering my mouth, I explain, "I'm sorry. I had a very rough night, so I'm pretty tired." William looks as though he might collapse, and I give Kendra a big, disingenuous smile before beginning to load my camera with film.

The guests arrive and slowly take their seats—smiling, happy friends and relatives who probably didn't spend the evening crouching in a closet half-naked and then sleeping next to a terrier in a bathroom that smelled of dog diarrhea. I study them one by one, hating each of them immensely, hating this day, this job, myself, and I gasp aloud when I recognize one of them. It's the dress I notice first: a yellow, frilly, off-the-shoulder frock that reminds me of the slutty girl I kept seeing over and over and outed at one of the last proms. And hovering above the dress, on top of overly tanned shoulders, is the face of that very girl. Her hair is pulled back tightly into an uncomfortable-looking bun, and she's wearing too much glittery eye shadow and hot pink, wet-look lipstick. She narrows her eyes and pouts as she follows a similar-looking, forty-something woman to her seat, painted in the same garish shades of makeup and wearing her own, more mature version of a prom gown, a cheap, off-the-shoulder sea foam green dress that is ill-fitting and unflattering.

By the time the gorgeous bride walks down the aisle, flanked by two beaming parents, I am checked out, mindlessly snapping pictures and counting the minutes until this afternoon is over. In truth, this is one of the loveliest weddings I've attended yet, with the tasteful lilacs and breezy cotton dresses on the bridesmaids and the harpist playing quietly in the side garden. But I can't appreciate a single moment of it. Every time I see Kendra needlessly hand William a different camera or a new roll of film, my face burns so hot that I wish I had my own sopping wet "Get More Body!" towel to throw over my head.

The ceremony finally ends, and the grinning guests file inside to the mansion, which consists of a labyrinth of tiny connecting rooms on multiple floors, each with its own collection of four tables that seat six, and lilac swags over the mantels. The bountiful buffet and bar are on the first floor, and it's as I'm standing and shooting the bride talking animatedly with her sister on the second-floor landing that I realize I'm being watched. And I know that William and Kendra are readying for the toast in the far corner of the house, so it can only be one person. I breathe in, turn slightly, and see my prom nemesis, her eyes narrowed into malevolent slits and her mouth set into a high-gloss line. My tired eyes meet hers for a few seconds, and I make a mental note to check the place card table so I can avoid the room that contains her table.

The rest of the reception is tailor-made for an eager wedding photographer, with potential candids of the bride and groom's grandmothers laughing over a private joke, the best man walking around with the ring bearer on his shoulders, and a once-in-a-lifetime shot of two giggling bridesmaids lifting up the bride's train as she awkwardly tries to enter the ladies' room. It's too bad there aren't any eager wedding photographers here, though—between William anxiously looking at Kendra every thirty seconds and my feeling drained to the point of near-fainting, I worry that the Corey party may not be fully satisfied with their proofs. Still, I press on, studiously trying to avoid my prom pal. It's hard to do in this setting, because if a guest wants food or booze, it requires a trip through the whole house, and the lobby area is choked with people waiting for their omelets and Bloody Marys. Each time she passes me, she fixes me with that same hideous stare, and my stomach drops when she throws her head over her shoulder to look at William and then whips back around to give me a creepy smile.

By the time brunch is over, she's looking a little looped—a look I remember well from her prom days last spring. And what goes better with drinking than driving? As I'm standing next to the guest book, I spy her asking the similarly made-up older woman (her mom, I presume?) for something, and the woman extracts a set of keys from her pink vinyl purse and hands them over. She hooks her own vinyl bag over her shoulder, flounces past me and out of the mansion, and I heave a sigh of relief. Thank goodness for the impatience and insouciance of teenagers, I think. Let her go home and smoke weed or play video games or whatever the hell she wants to do.

After about another half hour, I get the high sign from William that we've got about five minutes until cake-cutting time, and I make a quick trip to the bathroom. I sit on the toilet and exhale deeply; it's the first time in several hours that I can relax a tiny bit. When I finish, I wash my hands, dry them quickly on a scratchy paper towel, open the door, and find that the next person in line is Kendra.

"Oh!" I gasp, my face reddening. What is it with me and this woman and bathrooms? "I didn't know you were next in line."

"It's me, all right," she says in a kicky tone. "How do you like the wedding photography business? William says you've really taken to it."

"It's OK!" I say too quickly, gulping hard. "I mean, it's been quite an experience." A barely perceptible flash of suspicion crosses her face; her woman's intuition is telling her there's something fishy here. Or am I just out of my mind with paranoia, the lack of sleep and guilt conspiring to drive me insane? "Anyway," I add, "I should probably get ready to get pictures of the cake." I slink past her and practically run to the cake, which has been wheeled to the center of the dance floor. It's multi-tiered, with white gooey frosting and fresh lilies, and for me it represents the end. Because after the cake is cut, everybody always starts saying their good-byes. It's the end of the wedding day, the end of all the hoopla for the bride and groom and the families and the caterers and florists and deejays and photographers. And it will be the end for me, as I decided this morning. I heave a sigh of relief as the bride takes hold of a giant knife, knowing there are just a few more shots left. No more weddings, no more William.

And that's when I see my prom friend, who has returned and is now standing very close to William and

Kendra, right next to the cake. The bride and groom are chattering and laughing, and as the wedding guests press in closer to watch them cut the cake, I study the girl through my camera lens. She looks at me, licks her lips, and brings something small up near her face. It's a black and white photograph, and she gives me a look of smug satisfaction as I drop the camera from my face and my mouth falls open. Now the bride and groom are feeding each other the cake, getting the sticky icing all over one another's faces as though they are the first couple in the world to think of such hilarious shenanigans, and the prom girl is stepping closer to William and Kendra.

The tired caterers in their white shirts and black aprons push through the crowd of guests to take the cake away, and I begin to stride over to the prom girl, but it's too late. She has flung the photo onto the floor in front of Kendra, and as she bends to pick it up, I see William's face fall. With once glance, he knows what it is, and he takes a large step back from his wife. I reach them and quickly scramble to take the photo from Kendra, and we get into a frenzied shoving match that is unseemly at best and hideously unprofessional at worst. William is standing limply next to us, the color drained from his face, and the guests begin to murmur about the two photographers scrapping on the dance floor. After cursing and fighting valiantly, I lose the battle, and Kendra looks at the photo as time stops. Suddenly I'm not breathing, not moving, not hearing anything around me.

She looks from me to William and opens her mouth, but nothing comes out. I am sweating profusely now, and I know it's either fight or flight, so I impulsively choose flight. I turn on my heels and race toward the lobby, smacking directly into the wedding cake as it's being wheeled toward the kitchen. A collective gasp goes up from the crowd as three of the tiers squish and fall down the side of the cart, and I can hear the anguished cries of the bridesmaids as I race down the front steps and run toward my bike.

I stay in my room for the next two days, leaving only to use the bathroom and refill my glass of water. I barely sleep and hardly eat; I just spend my time smoking and brooding. I hear Erin come and go from the apartment, and she occasionally shouts out, "Hey, do you want me to come in?" I reply no each time, and she leaves me alone, just the way she knows she should. Gary periodically lopes in and out, but quickly grows bored of watching someone lying stock-still on her bed for hours at a time, and heads for more stimulating environs. The phone rings twice the first day and once the second day; each time I think I hear William's voice, strained and pained on the machine. I don't answer.

On the morning of the third day, the front door opens unexpectedly and I hear Erin come into the apartment, sniffling. This is most unusual for two reasons: one, Erin normally works all day on Wednesdays, and two, Erin doesn't suffer from allergies, and she weeps with such rarity that I can't think of the last time I heard her crying. Gary rouses from my bedroom floor; he is undoubtedly grateful to be able to abandon this moribund patient in bed one, and move on to someone more responsive in bed two.

"Erin?" I ask, clearing my throat. I've spoken no more

than one or two words during the past couple of days, and my voice is thin and scratchy.

"Yeah," she replies sullenly.

"What's up?" I ask, sitting up on my bed. I look around the room and shudder. It's a mess in here, with my clothes from Sunday night strewn on the floor and dirty ashtrays overflowing with cigarette butts everywhere.

She peeks into the room, and I can see her face is tear-stained, even though the blinds are drawn and it's dim in here. "Come in," I say. Gary stands at attention, and she wearily enters the room. She scrunches her nose immediately.

"What's that sugary smell?" she asks, her voice thick.

"It's frosting all over my clothes," I sigh as I point to the pile on the floor and lie back down. "I'm surprised you can smell it through the cigarette smoke."

"I can smell it, just barely. It has a really sickly sweet odor," she explains as she lies down next to me and takes a deep breath. "Why do you have frosting on your clothes?"

"You first," I say, looking at the ceiling and lacing my fingers together over my chest.

There is a long pause and when she finally speaks, her voice is choked with tears. "I got busted at the salon."

At first, I don't comprehend. "What?" I ask, still looking at the ceiling.

"I was working on a client's hair—a modified shag. It was really, really nice," she muses, sniffling again. "And out of the corner of my eye, I saw my great-aunt walking into the salon. She was over by the reception area, plain as day, with her gray bob." She puts both hands over her face.

"I thought your family doesn't go in for those kinds of places," I say, still confused. "What was she doing there?" Gary leaps up and tries to wedge himself between us, and Erin shoos him away. He settles with sitting perpendicular to us at the foot of the bed, and I use him as an impromptu ottoman.

"How the hell should I know?" she asks with exasperation. "All these years doing this, and no one knows what I'm up to. And then stupid Helen must be visiting Boston and decides it's time to trim that hideous helmet of hair," she spits. "She was walking into the salon and was going to pass right by my chair. So I had to create a diversion, and before I even knew what I was doing, I threw the jar of combs on the floor. It was a huge, fucking mess," she says sadly. "Clients were jumping out of their chairs and screaming. Glass and Barbicide everywhere."

"Is it really that electric blue color when you see it on the floor?" I ask, suddenly grateful for this nutty, distracting story. "Or is it just when it's in the glass jar that it looks so vibrant?"

"I don't know, Iley," she answers wearily. "I ran to the bathroom and locked myself in, then Furious George thought I'd gone crazy or something, so he called the cops. This is easily the most stupid thing I've done in my life," she wails. "I made a mess at the salon, upset clients, and made Furious George even more furious than usual. And the worst part?"

I don't answer, knowing that this is a rhetorical question, and Gary and I both breathlessly await the worst part.

"The worst part is that I'm pretty sure that Helen saw me anyway. So I'm probably going to be out a job, *and* have to explain to my parents what I've been doing all these years." She says it with a tone of dread that someone might use when thinking about telling her parents she is a crack addict or harbors a lifelong dream of becoming an exotic dancer.

"That sucks," I say sympathetically. It's a bit halfhearted, mainly because I'm still too burdened by my own misery to truly comfort Erin. She hears this in my voice and is ready for her own diversion.

"So why do you have frosting on your clothes? Does it have to do with why you've been in here for two days?"

"Uch," I answer, propping myself up on my elbows. "Did I ever tell you that I took a photo of me and William in bed, and then I lost track of it back in the spring at a prom?"

She sits up and fixes me with a stare, her eyes wide. "No," she says nervously.

"Well, to make a long, stupid story short, it turns out that horrible girl from the proms must have made off with it. Remember, I told you about her at Charlie's Kitchen that time?" She nods. "She, um, sort of had a grudge against me," I add, a bit embarrassed. "I called her a slut one night at one of the proms."

"Ohhhhkaaaay," says Erin slowly as she lies back down and lights a cigarette. "Go on."

"Anyway, she was at this wedding on Sunday. She was just a regular wedding guest, like everyone else. And William's wife was there that day, too."

"Wait, his wife was a guest at the wedding?" Erin asks in a confused but happier voice, her mood lightening as she undoubtedly realizes that her tale of hurled Barbicide can't possibly hold a candle to this one.

"No, no, she was there with William. She came home for a visit," I explain, choosing to keep the bathroom chapter of the story to myself for now. There is only so much shame I can handle in one sitting, even when talking with a best friend. "So this prom girl goes home, I guess, and gets this really dirty picture of us fucking in a motel room, and basically flings it down in front of William's wife, right at the reception." I finish and wait for a response, but there is none yet. "I tried to get the photo away from her but I couldn't. So I ran and smacked headlong into the cake." I point to my icing-encrusted shirt and skirt on the floor.

"Hold on. Why on earth did she keep the picture of you guys?" she asks.

"Who knows? Maybe she liked it, or maybe she was just hoping that something like this would happen someday. Although that seems like a lot of advance planning for her, frankly," I say. "It was crazy, Erin. Really awful. I'll never, ever forget the look on William's wife's face." A big sob catches in my throat, and Erin turns on her side to face me.

"I can't believe what a mess I've made of everything," she says quietly after a minute.

"Me too," I whimper.

"I don't know why I thought I could be so deceptive and have it all work out just the way I wanted," she continues as she sits up and strokes Gary's head.

"Me too," I say.

"I really, really need a drink," she declares.

"Me too. But I need to go and do something first," I decide aloud.

Eighteen

I lock up my bike outside the New England School of Photography and shield my eyes as I look up at its dated, brushed aluminum sign. After being shuttered inside for nearly thirty-six hours during the dog days of August, I feel like a mole in the bright sun now, squinting and scurrying to the shade of the building's awning.

Once inside, I breeze past Therese, who doesn't so much as move a muscle when she sees me. She'll be the worst one to contend with today, I decide. She's going to make something that's already difficult that much more unpleasant. But that's OK; I've resolved to do it anyway. When I'm sure she's not going to deign to turn around, I grab a giant, black plastic trashcan on wheels and roll it into my darkroom space. It's already nearly full of other people's photographic detritus: dozens of crinkly contact sheets, dead rolls of underdeveloped negatives, a small mountain of chemical-soaked paper towels, loads of soggy prints.

I get to work, yanking all of my photo drawers open and angrily hurling everything into the trashcan. Bye-bye, sleeves of negatives. Thanks for nothing, dodge and burn experiments. See you in hell, photographic tints that I never had the patience to learn to use properly. And finally, all the prints that have been sitting in these drawers for so long, unworthy of portfolio placement. I toss dozens of shots taken while biking all over Boston and don't grow the slightest bit maudlin. I violently smash down a pile of prints that I'd planned to do something with months ago, a series of grafittied walls on Washington Street, with elderly Chinese ladies ambling in front of the spiky colorful script that spells out words like DAWG and NUMBAH 1.

I grab an unused box of photo paper and throw it to the side; I certainly won't need it anymore, but it will come in handy for Rithy. I open the bottom drawer and excavate a small pile of prom prints, developed just for fun whenever I needed a break, and hurl them on top of the pile. I heave an exhausted sigh and stare down at the open drawers for a long minute. Then I stand with my back against the sink, extend my leg, and try to push the bottom drawer closed with my foot. The wood is swollen and the drawer sticks, so I give it a sharp kick and curse at it for good measure. Ten seconds later, there is a knock on the wall.

"Iley?" Rithy's voice asks excitedly. "Is that you?"

"Yeah," I answer. "Listen, come over here, I want to talk to you." A split second passes, and Rithy comes into the darkroom, doing a double take when he realizes he's been able to navigate the entryway perfectly because it's not at all dark in here.

"Why are the lights on?" he asks, sounding suspicious.

Before I can answer, he breaks into a wide grin. "Hey, Iley, I have great news! I wish I could have told you sooner, but I haven't seen you in a long time. I got a grant, so I can keep using the darkroom for a little while! I got a letter from a man named Mr. Meany," he says, his eyes shining.

"That's wonderful," I say ruefully. "I'm happy for you. You're so talented that I'm not surprised. But listen," I say, changing the tone of my voice, "I think I'm going to be throwing in the towel on the photography thing."

He looks at me with his brow furrowed and crosses his arms in front of his gray T-shirt. "What?"

"Oh, sorry. It's an expression. It means to give something up or stop doing something," I apologize.

He scoffs. "I *know* what 'throw in the towel' means," he says angrily. "I said 'what' because I don't know why you would do that." He frowns and peers at all the empty drawers.

"I just don't know if I'm meant to be a photographer. I'm sick of trying so hard and . . . and some other things have happened lately that made me want to stop trying," I explain lamely. "I think this is the right thing to do," I add, not sure who I'm trying to sway. "Look, when your, um, grant runs out, you can use my darkroom space here as much as you want. I've got a year pre-paid, so it's all yours." I gesture around the place and meet his eyes. He looks away from me and starts pawing through the trashcan. "Don't do that—it's all junk," I implore him.

"What are these?" he asks, pulling a photo of drunk promgoers from the pile. "Who are these people?"

"Oh, just some jerks that I photographed outside of schools and catering places, drunk high school kids acting stupid at the prom," I explain. I assume Rithy will laugh and nod knowingly at this, because never once did he suffer his foolish classmates gladly in high school, but he is silently absorbed in another photo. This one is from the Boston Performing Arts Academy and features a girl in a velvet dress getting a piggyback from a guy also outfitted in a velvet dress. He pulls out another, and then another, and looks me square in the eye.

"Iley, these are very interesting," he decides. "You were going to throw these away? You should develop more of these." He gently places the small pile of crinkled prints next to the enlarger.

"I don't think so, OK?" I ask in an annoyed tone. I am starting to get a bit hysterical. The plan was to come here, clean out the darkroom, turn my back on my art and this phase of my life, and never look back. And I don't need some plucky Thai teenager to tell me to do otherwise. "I just don't want to do this anymore."

"Oh, but you have to!" he implores. "Just do some more of these. I'm sure you have more negatives, right?" I nod and roll my eyes. "Sometimes you never know what might happen, Iley. I thought I never use my darkroom again, and then I get a grant that I didn't even know I could get." He looks quite pleased at this analogy he's created, and I have to suppress a smile when he speaks of this magical grant. He continues to stand and look at me, boring holes into me with his big eyes as I decide what to do.

"All right, I'll do a few," I concede, sighing. "Just four or five, for you. These photos are really like nothing I work on normally," I say a bit snobbishly. "I have no idea what I would even do with them."

"So what?" Rithy asks as he removes the rest of my work from the trashcan. I can't believe I succumbed to this little pipsqueak with the mystery grant and the job waiting tables. On the plus side, I won't have to roll a trashcan overflowing with my work past Therese, which I had been dreading since I mounted my bike to ride here.

I spend the next few days making Rithy proud, and then some. To my surprise, I find that hunching over the enlarger and swishing the photos in the chemicals keeps my mind off William almost entirely, even in spite of the pictures' subjects. At the end of the fourth day, I have a dozen near-perfect-quality prints, and I have thoroughly confused Don, who through all his heavy-lidded confusion has noticed that I've been here more in the past week than I have in the entire month preceding.

"What's goin' on in there?" he asks when I step outside for a smoke break. "You're sure busy with something."

I hand him a cigarette and light it for him and notice the patch of gray stubble on his chin and the split in his lower lip. It's deeply cracked, with dried blood caked around the fissure, and I wonder how it got there. "I don't know what the hell I'm doing in there," I admit. "Just trying to keep my mind off some bad times."

"I hear what you're saying," he says, searching the street for the methadone clinic. "Gotta keep busy." I smile at this and finish my cigarette, then head back inside to develop a few more pictures. I'm still unsure about what to do with these images, the ones of girls vomiting in the bushes and guys with their thick necks oozing over the tops of their satin bow ties, but I keep at it nonetheless. On my way out,

I spy a discarded *Boston Herald* in a garbage can near the school's entrance and flip to the police blotter. The stories are the standard inane fare, but one in particular catches my eye and makes me laugh aloud. I tear the page from the paper and stuff it into my messenger bag.

When I arrive home, Erin is sitting cross-legged on the sofa, frowning and clutching an enormous pair of shears. I'm not at all worried about a possible suicide attempt, but it does cross my mind that it would be an extraordinarily funny way for a stylist to go.

"How was work today?" I ask, putting my bag on the floor and dropping down next to her on the sofa. It was her first day back, after a short break imposed by Furious George.

"Terrible," she says sullenly. "Everyone treated me like some kind of mental patient," she frowns. "Plus my confidence is really shaken, Iley." She looks extremely worried as she admits this, and she sets the shears down on the sofa, then removes them just as quickly when Gary begins curiously sniffing them. "I gave someone a bad cut today."

"No, you didn't," I say immediately.

"Yes, I did," she retorts. "I know I did, because she complained. No one has ever complained about my cuts before." She bites her lip and lowers her chin to her chest. We sit in silence for a minute. "If I can't cut hair anymore, I don't know what I'll do," she adds quietly, and I know she is sadly envisioning herself in one of her mother's fantasies for her, either outfitted in a prim, Brooks Brothers suit at the type of job she purports to have, or poolside at the club, lolling with other ladies of leisure. She picks up the shears. "Will you let me cut your hair?"

"Ohhh, I get it now," I say knowingly. "Well," I add a little bit uncertainly as I ruffle the side of my hair, "why not? It's been a long time since you've given me a cut." I flash back to me sitting in Erin's room this spring as my damp, black locks fell to the floor, while I silently prayed that this new hairdo would positively sizzle for William. The memory of it turns my stomach. "I'd like something very different," I say firmly.

"Well, that's good, because that's what I was hoping to give you," she says, brightening a little bit. "I just want to see if I've still got it."

We stand up and make our way to Erin's room. On the way, I take notice of my bag on the floor and ask, "Hey, did you see the police blotter recently?"

"I'm off that now," she replies briskly. "I spent too much time at the salon looking for those stupid things; now I've got to focus on hair." She gives me a slightly haughty look, complete with the Brooks family's firmly set jaw. I shrug and sit down as she drapes the too-tight cape around my shoulders.

"Well, suit yourself," I say, smiling. She goes into the bathroom to fill a spray bottle, then returns and douses my hair with water. Gary watches from the doorway as Erin takes a slow, deep breath, lifts the scissors to my head, and begins tentatively snipping.

Another day, another dollar. Or, to put it a different way, I've quickly realized that without the weddings, I need a new way to bring in those dollars, and I've begun to step up my temping schedule. Today I am working at a candle cart in Faneuil Hall, watching as tourists and suburbanites stumble over the cobblestones and study their Freedom Trail maps with quizzical expressions. The candles I am hawking seem to be nothing more than your standard wax-and-wick deal, but the way the manager of the cart has been blathering on about them, you would think they are the height of sophisticated illumination.

"See, what's wonderful is that the color goes all the way through," she says, pointing into the well of a pre-burned candle. We can't light any by order of the city, so the company packs up and sends some artfully burned candles, their cores neatly hollowed and soot-free. "That's unusual in a candle, so be sure to point that out."

"You bet," I say, as I tighten the strings on my green, folksy apron. It's embroidered with the name of the candle company in yellow thread and is positively hideous. It could provide the underpinnings of a fabulous Halloween costume, and I wonder if there might be a way to make off with it at the end of my shift.

"Also, if they buy three candles today, they get this decorative snuffer for $1.95," she continues, flashing a toothy grin at two elderly women who smell a watermelon-scented candle on the end of the cart. "See?" she asks, holding the piece of metal up for me to examine.

"All right," I reply calmly, picking up a candle that is billed as the cure for stress and anxiety. I take a sniff and give a mirthless laugh when I realize that the prescription for stress and anxiety smells an awful lot like honeydew melon.

"That one is for stress and anxiety," the manager explains,

as though the psychological symptoms in question weren't printed in faux Victorian script on the candle's pink wrapper. She abruptly yanks her long, dyed-blond hair into a makeshift ponytail and tosses it over her right shoulder. "Also, we have candles for PMS, depression, asthma troubles, and constipation," she adds, pointing to the squat candles that surround the honeydew stress-and-anxiety treatment.

"OK," I sigh as I give the asthma candle a sniff and try to imagine how the cloying odor of ersatz apple pie might help with respiratory illness. A sweaty, frizzy-haired woman in a "Cheers" T-shirt walks over to me, bearing a coffee-scented candle in one meaty hand and a cinnamon-scented one in the other.

"Do you think if I burn these at the same time, it will smell like a cinnamon latte?" she asks brightly.

I take a deep breath. "Lady, I'm a photographer," I reply, crossing my arms in front of my apron. "This isn't what I do for a living." Her mouth drops open, and the manager quickly swoops in, assuring her in syrupy tones that of *course* her home will smell of cinnamon latte with the simultaneous burning of the candles. After making the sale, she turns to me.

"What the hell was that?" she asks angrily.

"Sorry," I say, grinning. I'm clearly not sorry at all, and this makes her face grow as red as the pomegranate candle on a nearby shelf. I untie my apron and hand it back to her; so much for my Halloween costume this fall. "I gotta go," I say and shrug apologetically, as though this wasn't my decision. And in a way, I realize as I pedal away on my bike, it wasn't. When you need to be in the darkroom, you need to be in the darkroom. You can't fight it when the urge to develop photos returns to you, and I'm so relieved that it has that I would gladly forsake a thousand dollars' worth of PMS candle sales for it.

And so once again I immerse myself in the darkroom, developing photo after photo of blitzed prom queens, bleary-eyed boys, and girls clustered around the mirror in the ladies' rooms, brandishing goopy mascara wands and eyeliner pencils and stubby joints. The pressure is low but the payoff is high, and this inverse proportion keeps me motivated and happy. Because I think of these photos merely as a vehicle to placate Rithy, keep myself out of trouble with William, and definitely not art in any conventional sense, I breeze through them with hardly a care. As each image magically appears on the paper floating in the developer tray, I smile when I note how perfect the contrast and composition are. Who cares if the subjects are ridiculous?

I'm nearly finished for the day when one develops that takes away my smile; it's an image I shot outside of the gym at St. Albans, of a girl whispering in another's ear at the end of a long hallway. I remember being captivated by what gossip might have been shared—is someone pregnant? about to drop from alcohol poisoning? wearing the most hideous gown of the night?—and didn't even realize that Thomas was standing in the foreground, off to the side and leaning against a locker. I shot this before he introduced himself that night, and in the image, his eyes are turned toward me in a furtive and curious way.

I sigh deeply as I study his face, and my own face burns as I remember how despicably I treated him the night of our last date. I finish developing the photo and slowly clean up, filled with a palpable dread that consumes me as I slowly pedal my way home. When I arrive at the apartment, I take off my bag and drink a glass of water, and position myself next to the phone before I can change my mind. My hand hovers over the TV remote, then I quickly draw it back and reach for the phone instead. He picks up on the third ring.

"Hello?" It's that slow drawl, that soft voice. I gulp.

"Hi, Thomas. It's Iley." Silence. "Iley, from earlier in the summer," I say. There is a long pause, and I can hear him breathing.

"What's up?" he asks, his voice crisp. It's clear he's not going to give me an inch, and who could blame him?

"Well, what's up with you?" I reply, vainly attempting to keep my tone upbeat as I try to figure out why I felt so compelled to do this. I don't wait for his answer. "Look, Thomas," I explain, sighing deeply, "I feel really bad about what happened this summer."

"I called you, like, four times," he says angrily. "I left messages."

"I know," I admit quietly. "I know you did, and I'm sorry I didn't call you back. Listen, I was in a really messed-up situation, but I'm not anymore, and—"

He cuts me off. "Yeah, you mentioned that before," he says unsympathetically.

"Well, I just wanted to apologize and find out . . . well, maybe I could see you again. To explain myself and apologize in person." I sit quietly and blink back tears and listen to him breathe.

"I'll have to think about it, Iley," he says, his voice flat.

"OK," I say. I sit and stare straight ahead for a few seconds, pressing the phone so tightly to my ear that my earlobe grows hot and uncomfortable. I sniff and continue to listen to the silence on the other end.

"No, I mean I'll have to think about it and get back to you," he says in a voice that is struggling to remain impassive and angry. "I'm not going to think about it right now," he explains, and I can almost hear him smiling as he says this.

"Oh!" I say. "I misunderstood. Well, whenever you decide, whatever you decide, is fine," I say encouragingly, inhaling and exhaling properly for the first time since I picked up the phone. Three hours later, at ten o'clock, he calls back. The news is good.

Nineteen

Now that Labor Day is nearly upon us, Gary has a spring in his step, a rejuvenated bounce that comes from the lack of humidity and the hint that crisp, fall air is ever so slowly arriving. We've just finished a nearly mile-long walk all over the neighborhood, during which he periodically would look up as though to say, "Hey, check me out! I'm taking a long walk and don't need to stop for water every few minutes—and I bet I won't have diarrhea later either!"

When we get home, I hang up his leash and am about to sit down when there is a knock at the front door. I open it, and standing in front of me is William. He looks very tired, a quiet sort of exhaustion that brings out the blue in his eyes and the deep circles beneath them. He's got a shadow of dark stubble, and his glossy hair has grown out a bit. These things make him even sexier than I remember, and it takes my breath away. And despite everything that's happened, I realize with a certain sense of disquiet that a part of me really missed him.

"Hey, your hair!" is the first thing he says, and even he seems surprised to hear himself exclaim this way.

"Oh, yeah," I say, remembering that I've now got a short hairdo, a groovy variation on a pixie cut that bolstered Erin's confidence and translated into a whole new look for me. "I got a haircut," I explain.

"I can see that," he says, smiling. "Can I come in?"

I waver for a moment and then step out of the way so he can come into the apartment. He scans the room, taking in the sagging sofa and overflowing ashtrays and hairstyling magazines, and I realize that never once has he seen where I live from the inside. The concept of my own personal décor must be non-existent when he thinks of me, limited to lumpy, polyfil bedspreads, fake mahogany nightstands, and trial-sized bars of soap. He looks at the sofa as though he'd like us to sit, but right now I think it's safer to remain standing.

"So," I say, crossing my arms in front of my chest. Upon realizing that no one is laying claim to the sofa, Gary leaps onto it and spreads out to watch the show.

"I tried calling here a few times after the Corey wedding," he says, locking eyes with me. "I never got hold of you."

I shudder at the memory of the reception and wonder if perhaps when I'm eighty, I'll finally forget it. "I know, William," I say. "I know you called."

"Well, I wanted to tell you that, well, Kendra and I are separating," he says, frowning and studying the scuffed hardwood floor. There is a large piece of clear packing tape covering one of the rougher slats; Gary kept catching his paw on it, and it was easier than sanding it down.

"Separating?" I gulp. "Really?" Months ago, when fantasizing about him making this announcement, I imagined myself nothing short of ecstatic. Now I just feel sick. "Well, in a way, you were sort of separated before, with her traveling all the time, William," I reason, trying to make myself feel better.

"Yeah," he agrees wearily. "I know. I guess now it's just that we're technically saying that we're probably headed for . . . you know. Divorce." He swallows this last word as he says it, and peers up at me through a tangle of hair. Newly freed of commitment, he takes one step toward me with his arm extended. I look down at the packing tape on the floor and close my eyes.

"Oh, William," I whisper as he reaches for my shoulder. I can feel my skin start to tighten and my heartbeat quicken. I open my eyes and he licks his lips, and I think, oh, this would feel *so* good right now. He kisses me hard and I ask myself, *What could it hurt?* Maybe it's just the first step toward something wonderful, a reconciliation that could lead to a life together. We take two steps backwards in unison and he pulls me closer, and I decide that because I can't answer the question, it must mean that this is OK.

Then as he reaches for the first button on my shirt, I realize that I can't answer the question because it's the wrong question. The question is not *what* could it hurt, but *who.* And once I reframe the question, it's remarkably easy to answer. And the answers are: William, who should not be rekindling an extramarital affair; Kendra, who might be able to forgive him during their separation and want to make a go at their relationship again; Thomas, who has generously agreed to have coffee with me next week; and of course, myself. After instantaneously answering the correct question to my satisfaction, I pull away from William.

"What?" he asks, confused. He's clearly aroused and ready to go—I guess I've still got it, even with the short hair.

"I can't, William," I say, breathing deeply and trying to will the heat away from my crotch. "I just can't."

He looks crestfallen. "But—"

"But what?" I ask, starting to get angry. "But you thought I'd just be sitting here waiting for you, now that Kendra is nearly out of the way?" I put my hands on my hips and whirl around, catching sight of my face in a mirror that Erin had propped up on the table last week to trim her bangs. My eyes are fiery and my jaw is set hard; I'm the very picture of *sisu*, the Finnish word that is an approximate but imperfect translation of strength or determination. "No," I say, shaking my head, deciding that not only can I handle a life without William, I *should* have a life without William in order to make things right. Or if not right, then at least something closer to what will make me happy. "No," I repeat firmly. The word makes me feel formidable, and I nearly say it again.

He starts to open his mouth, and his eyes well with tears. I drop my arms to my sides and sigh. "William, you need to—" I stop mid-sentence and we both snap our heads up as Erin walks in the front door, a bag from Lord & Taylor tucked under her arm. She looks from me to William and instantly knows what's going on.

"Excuse me," she says awkwardly, stepping around us and making her way to her bedroom.

"It's all right, William was just going," I say. I primly re-button my shirt, and we walk out onto the front steps.

"I'm sorry I came here today," he says remorsefully as we watch two school-age kids in the street playing with a plush, Patriots mini football that I think was a McDonald's giveaway last winter. Dirt and mud have stuck to the low-pile acrylic, and the thing is soiled and deeply depressing.

"Yeah," I agree. He wraps his arms around me and buries his head on my shoulder, seeking the comfort that he used to claim my long, soft hair gave him when we were in bed together after the proms and weddings. Now it's just my concave neck in that space, taut and a bit sweaty, no doubt providing very little solace.

Erin has emerged from her room, outfitted in a blue pleated skirt and short-sleeve Oxford shirt. "I look terrible," she announces as a preemptive fashion statement. "I know." She looks around the living room and peers out onto the front steps, as though William might be lurking out there. "So that was William."

I nod and light a cigarette. "So it was."

"If I had come home only five minutes later, would I have caught you guys . . ." she trails off, lighting up her own cigarette.

"No," I say firmly. "I had already decided to ask him to go. Your arrival just sealed the deal. So, thank you." I give her a gracious curtsey and plop down on the sofa next to Gary. "Why are you dressed like that? Someone coming to town?"

"Uh-huh," she answers nervously. "Bitsy. She never

comes into Boston, or if she does, it's rarely to have dinner with me. I'm guessing she has spoken to my great-aunt Helen." She chews her left thumbnail. "We're eating at Number Nine Park," she adds, invoking the name of a famous downtown restaurant that garners such gushing reviews that I often imagine the restaurant critics climaxing under the table as they attempt to take notes about the Chilean sea bass or raspberry chocolate torte.

"Too bad you won't be able to appreciate it," I say, studying her outfit critically once again. "You really do look terrible."

"Thanks," she says wearily. "Hey, wish me luck, all right? I'm pretty nervous." Her face looks like she's been suffering from a year's worth of constipation. She is also wringing her hands, an unheard-of activity for Erin, if ever there was one. She smoothes the pleats on her skirt and takes a deep breath. "Well, here goes. If nothing else, even if I'm disowned, my last meal will be a delicious one."

"Order the most expensive thing on the menu," I shout after her as she clomps down the front steps in unfamiliar, low-heeled pumps.

After she's gone, I turn to Gary and ask him what I had really wanted to ask Erin, before I realized that she needed a pre-Bitsy pep talk and couldn't really be bothered with my own story at that moment. "Aren't you proud of me for getting rid of that guy?" I ask him as he nuzzles his head in my lap. He doesn't answer, but I'm sure I know what he's thinking. "Me, too," I say quietly.

And so, emboldened by my total lack of worry about how my prom photos might be received and my smug satisfaction about having successfully rebuffed William, I make an appointment with Peter Spring of Spring Gallery on Newbury Street. I had shown him my work a few years back, and he'd sniffed and suggested I try some different directions. Well, I can't think of a more different direction than this, and after vaguely describing what I planned to show him, he agreed to spend thirty minutes with me today. I even have abandoned my standard portfolio review uniform of black pants and a black top, and have recklessly chosen to wear colors: dark blue jeans and an orange and pale blue striped shirt.

I step into the gallery and study the photos lining the walls, a collection of weary-looking little boys and girls, sitting on planters in malls, limply holding the hands of parents in line at the RMV, picking their noses at the airport. They are very peculiar and arresting, but I have a sneaking suspicion that I've got these beat.

Peter steps out from behind a large, gleaming white desk and glides across the gallery. He is preternaturally tall, with white-blond hair and a nose that's too small for his big, square face. We shake hands and get down to business, sitting at a low table in the far corner. He slowly turns the pages, and his face remains impassive. Normally, by this time I would be feeling the tension starting to bubble and boil beneath my skin, but today it remains at bay.

"These . . . are," he says slowly, glancing at a picture of my prom slut nemesis getting felt up behind the school at one of the very first proms, ". . . very . . . very . . .good."

"I'm glad you like them," I say calmly, despite the fact that I want to shout, "WHAAAA?"

"Yes, they are quite fascinating, a real inside look at

what teens in America are like today," he muses as he pushes his sleek, frameless glasses up his nose. I have to resist the urge to point out that I think teens have been engaging in these sorts of shenanigans since the dawn of time, but I control myself. He licks his lips and points to the one of the deaf teens signing as they dance. "This one is stunning," he says.

"Oh, thanks," I say, smiling broadly as I remember the screaming pain in my eardrums that night. "You know what?" I offer. "At that prom, they had the music turned up so loud that my ears rang for three days afterward. It was for the benefit of any kids who might be able to hear even a little." I realize I am actually starting to enjoy talking about my portfolio with Peter Spring, and I uncross my legs and lean back in my molded plastic Philippe Starke chair.

"Huh," he says, intrigued. He's clearly engaged now and keeps studying a few photos in particular, the ones that would be my favorites as well, I realize, if I'd cared enough to prioritize them in any way before coming here today. "Look, I think I could mount a small show," he says to me thoughtfully. I don't respond. I've never heard such a thing before from a proper gallery owner—I understand each word individually, of course, but strung together, the sentence is foreign. "Of *your work*," he adds forcefully. I still don't respond, so he opens his eyes wide and points at the portfolio. He does everything short of knocking on my head in *Back to the Future* style and braying "McFly!" as though I'm Crispin Glover playing the hapless, obtuse father.

"Oh!" I exclaim. And then I blush, which embarrasses us

both. I want to hug this man, shower his minuscule nose with sweet kisses. "When?"

"Well, I need to check the schedule. I'm thinking soon I'll have some space in here. Say, on that far wall?" he asks, pointing to a short wall near the window. "Seems like we could show about ten or twelve of them there." He studies the wall for a few seconds. "All right?"

"Yes, of course," I smile, trying to summon an ounce of professionalism here. "So I'll wait for you to call? Or should I call you?"

"I'll call you," he says, reaching for a leather-bound pad of paper and beginning to scribble. "How do you spell your name?"

"Oh, I'll write it," I offer. "It's easier that way." I write my name and phone number, and he closes up my portfolio with a hearty *zzzzip*.

"You'll need to get these framed, of course," he says. "That takes some money, as you know. But hopefully you'll make it back when we make some sales," he says, smiling for the first time, undoubtedly at the word "sales." "I can hook you up with some framers if you like. You might be able to get a little discount." We both stand up, my head reeling from the thought of someone actually paying money for one of these photos.

"Oh, that's OK, I know where to go," I say confidently.

"Hey, pick up after the third ring, OK?" Erin shouts from the living room.

"Are you sure?" I shout back from the kitchen.

"Yes," she says firmly as the phone trills for the second

time. "I really need you with me for this one." The phone rings for the third time, and I hold my breath as I pick up the receiver in the kitchen. It's eight o'clock on Tuesday, precisely when Bitsy informed Erin she would be calling her as they parted ways after their dinner at Number 9 Park. The dinner wasn't as bad as Erin expected, she'd admitted when she returned that night and stripped off her preppy costume. After being confronted by Bitsy, Erin confessed everything: her fake position at the Harvard Business School, her love of all things tonsorial, her long and illustrious styling career. Bitsy's face remained impassive the entire time, leaving Erin completely unable to judge her reaction to her outré career but relieved that her mother wasn't making a scene. As Erin worked her way through her cheese plate and oysters and chicken with mushroom fricassee, Bitsy sat and studied her daughter, silently taking her in and speaking only to order fresh scotch.

"Hello, dear," Bitsy says after Erin and I pick up the phone. I swear I can hear Bitsy sucking her teeth and Erin sweating.

"Hi," Erin says in a tight voice, as I shoo Gary away from the kitchen. He's chosen this moment to tuck into his dinner, and is gnashing his kibble at top volume.

"Well, Erin, your news has really made quite a splash around here," she sighs. The far-off sound of a vacuum cleaner hums in the background. "I must say that your father and I weren't quite as surprised as you might think, though." She pauses. "That is, we suspected that something wasn't quite right, but we assumed that you might have an issue like Scott's," she explains, neatly avoiding any direct mention of his cocaine problem. "Or we thought perhaps you were in a . . . romantic relationship with your roommate Iley." Erin screeches with laughter and races into the kitchen with the portable phone, and I accidentally drop my receiver to the floor as I look at her and try to contain my hysteria.

"What's going on there?" Bitsy asks tersely, after I've picked up my receiver and Erin has retreated to the living room.

"Sorry, Gary was just jumping around and knocked into the phone," she explains.

"You know, I'll still never understand why you wouldn't let me breed that animal," she replies airily. "Such good stock, such a waste," she adds, and I quietly hand Gary a Nutter Butter just to spite her. "In any case, Erin, your father and I have decided that it's quite stupid to spend your life cutting hair—"

I can hear Erin's heart break, I swear it. I listen to her inhale sharply, readying for the fight, and then Bitsy finishes her thought.

"—if you're going to work for someone else and have that person—what would it be, a salon owner?—taking so much of your profits. You know how Daddy and I feel about that, Erin," she lectures. "You want to maximize your money, dear, that's the most important thing in business. So as long as you're going to be doing this, you may as well have your own . . . salon," she says, audibly gulping at the end of the sentence.

There are a few beats of silence, and Gary looks up at me with a bit of peanut butter filling stuck to his muzzle. I pluck it off and he licks it from my finger. "What?" asks Erin.

"I'm saying that we would like to fund you, so you can rent space and start your own business," Bitsy says impatiently. This is clearly uncomfortable for her, and she's looking to wrap things up. Still, in the course of the last two minutes, she has redeemed herself ten thousand-fold in my eyes.

"Um . . . all right," says Erin, mystified. "Wow. I don't know what to say." I poke my head out of the kitchen and she is wearing a look commonly associated with the people visited by Ed McMahon and his giant novelty check.

"Well, we want you to be happy," Bitsy replies in a quiet tone that suggests that it might actually be true. "Even if you're not at Harvard." Erin doesn't say anything, so Bitsy gets down to business. "You should get in touch with Mark, our financial advisor. You remember him?"

Erin nods. "Yup."

"Talk to him about what you hope to do, where you'd like to get space, what you would need in terms of financing, that sort of thing. Then he'll take care of accessing what you'll need."

"All right," says Erin, still stupefied. "Thanks so much, I just can't believe it."

"You can thank me by cutting my hair when you see me next, dear. If only I had known, I would have asked you long ago." She pauses and breathes in, as though readying for a revelation or an admission. "I've had this same horrendous style for years, but it is such a bore, finding new people, you know," she explains.

"It's a deal," Erin says. "Anything you want." She says good-bye and we both hang up our phones, then proceed to jump up and down and scream ourselves hoarse for the next thirty minutes. Gary barks and leaps around like a lunatic, unaware of the reason for the celebration but enjoying the spoils of the party nonetheless and eating an additional four Nutter Butters before the evening is out.

I pat down the pockets of my denim jacket as I search for the slip; even though it's only the start of September, the cool air has arrived quickly, leaving me to ransack my closet this morning in search of weather-appropriate clothing. I fish the pink scrap of paper out of my left breast pocket and plunk it on the counter at The Framery. The frame shop of my past, where I'd hoped I'd be able to wow my former knucklehead of a manager last week, when I proudly sauntered in requesting frames for my upcoming Newbury Street photo exhibition. He wasn't there that day, and I was instead attended to by a dour older woman whom I didn't recognize from my frame shop tenure and who grunted loudly every time I asked her to pull down a new frame sample. Today neither she nor my old manager are present; instead, I'm helped by a young guy with tiny silver-rimmed glasses, dyed yellow hair, and a small silver spike emerging from beneath his lower lip.

"Pickup?" he asks dully, glancing at the slip on the countertop and listlessly walking to the back of the store, where all of the orders sit sheathed in plastic. I'd spent many an hour rifling through piles of framed images in this very spot, ugly baby photographs and lame reprints of Degas ballerinas from the Museum of Fine Arts gift shop, and I feel sorry for him as he rustles around back there.

"Yeah," I call over to him. "Iley Gilbert." The rustling stops for a moment, and he walks back over to me.

"Didn't you used to work here?" he asks, his head cocked. "Your name sounds familiar." Before I can answer, his face registers recognition, and he puts his hand on the front of his Misfits T-shirt. "Hold on. Didn't you throw something at Andrew?" he asks, squinting at me.

"Yeah, that was me," I admit. "Not my proudest moment. Although in my defense, I wasn't exactly throwing something *at* him," I explain.

"You're . . . like . . . a legend around here," he says slowly and respectfully. "We all totally hate that guy. That musta been *so awesome*," he decides, shaking his head and looking around the place, as though trying to imagine a frame sample hurtling through the store. "Anyway, I'll get your stuff," he sighs, and returns a moment later with my framed prints. I peel the plastic back from each and check them over, as my new friend hovers at an uncomfortably close distance.

"These yours?" he asks.

"Yeah, someone on Newbury Street is going to give me a little show. You know, just one wall, but it's a great gallery," I reply.

"Awesome," he says again. "That's what I wanna do. I'm into printmaking, you know, mostly linoleum block, but I also like lithography."

"Well, if I can get out of this place, anyone can," I say encouragingly, as I wave my arms around the store. He smiles broadly, exposing a tongue with two oversized silver studs. "I think I owe you the other half," I say, turning the slip around and trying to make out the scrawl of the dour saleswoman. "I paid a fifty percent deposit when I dropped them off." I open my messenger bag.

He looks at the slip and quickly crumples it up and shoves it in the pocket of his black jeans. "It's OK, don't worry about it."

"What?" I ask, confused.

"You're cool, you shouldn't have to pay so much. Shit, you know how little these frames are really worth, right?" he laughs. "Andrew's such a douche, we're always doing stuff to fuck up the store and the register, and then we make him think he's crazy," he boasts.

"Well, won't you get in trouble?" I ask, a bit worried. My mind flashes to this kid temping like I did, suffering through catering gigs and mind-numbing office jobs.

"Nah, fuck it. It's cool," he assures me, and I'm flabbergasted at the amount of money I'll be saving for having flung around a frame sample nearly six months ago. "You got anything else that needs framing? Now I really feel like messing with his head."

I laugh and look up at the ceiling for a moment. A woman comes in the door, bearing a large Picasso reproduction, and my sales boy rolls his eyes at me. "I do have one thing," I tell him, and fish a tiny piece of paper from my bag. He takes it from me and looks it over.

"It's really small," he says. "You want a big mat around it, or just keep the whole thing small?"

"A big mat," I decide. "I want it to have some presence."

"OK," he says, ignoring the Picasso lady, who is drumming her fingers on the countertop adjacent to us. "You want to pick out the mat color and the frame?"

"Nah, I trust you to pick everything out," I say earnestly. "I mean, you are an artist, after all." I give him a smile and am rewarded with another flash of shiny silver. I step outside with my photos, hail a cab downtown, and drop off my work with Peter Spring, still unable to believe that this is actually happening.

Twenty

I breeze into the coffee shop on Commonwealth Avenue, three minutes early and congratulating myself on my punctuality. Thomas, however, has beaten me here, and is sitting in a far corner, poring over a spiral-bound notebook and drinking an iced coffee. The summer has agreed with him; his hair has turned a burnished blond and his skin is in the final stages of a sun-kissed glow. He looks up as I pull out a chair and gives me a small, perfunctory smile.

"Hi," I say awkwardly as I sit down. I rest my elbows on the table and put my chin in my hand. He does not follow suit with his body language, preferring to lean back and grip his chair instead. "So, um, planning stuff for school already?" I ask, pointing at the notebook.

"Well, it starts next week, so I guess I'd better be," he shrugs. "I'm just making notes about things to talk about on the first day, things that can get the class thinking about history." He picks up the iced coffee and takes a sip. "Are you going to get something?" he asks, nodding in the direction of the counter.

"No," I say. "So what are you going to talk about the first day?" I prod, desperate to keep this conversation moving forward.

"I think we're going to talk about Iraq," he says, tracing his notes with his finger. The ink is thick and smeary on the page, and he ends up with a little smudge of blue on his fingertip. "About how the issues of the past keep returning, about how history is destined to repeat itself again and again if people don't learn from their mistakes." He leans back and looks up at the ceiling.

I sigh. "Well, I guess that's as a good a segue as any, Thomas." I give him a wry smile. "You know, learning from mistakes?" I eye his iced coffee. "I *am* thirsty," I decide. I reach into my messenger bag for my wallet and he pushes the iced coffee across the tabletop at me, the cup's condensation leaving a slick trail on the Formica.

"You can drink this for now," he says. "Go on." He gives me a look of encouragement, so I take a big swallow from the oversized yellow straw and continue.

"This summer, I was in a really messed-up relationship with someone I should *not* have been involved with. The guy who I took the pictures with at the proms. It was . . . awful of me, and I don't know what possessed me to do it," I say quickly. "He was married, and I would wake up in motel rooms and not even know where I was half the time, and—"

"OK, that's enough detail for now, Iley," he says forcefully. "You can be honest, but you don't have to tell me everything." He looks quite discomfited, as though he would pull his collar from his neck if he were wearing something with a collar, and not a retro Allman Brothers T-shirt.

"Yeah," I agree. "Sorry. Anyway, then I met you and I just . . . you're so kind, and I didn't want to pull you into the middle of my mess. And I know," I say, breathing fast and getting flustered, "I *know* I should have called you back. But I didn't. I didn't do a lot of things I should have done. And I did a lot of things I shouldn't have done." I fold my hands in my lap and hunch over the table. "I even nearly killed Gary from dehydration during the heat wave because I was so selfish," I whisper, keeping my eyes on the gray and blue flecks of the Formica and biting my lip. I feel certain that Thomas is going to call Animal Cops on me as soon as he leaves here, and I look up at him guiltily, imagining them leading Gary away from our dirty apartment as I wail inconsolably off-camera.

"How is he now?" he asks in a low voice.

"He's fine," I assure him. "I had to give him water through an eyedropper to bring him back." He looks less disgusted than I expected, and I start to breathe more slowly. "How is Guy?" I venture.

"Good," he says. "A bad case of fleas in August, but that's nothing unusual." We sit and look at one another for a few seconds, and I nervously trail my finger through the water on the tabletop. "I like your hair," he decides, tilting his head and studying me. "It's very flattering."

"Thanks," I reply, and another silence falls over the table. "So look, Thomas, did I totally blow this?" I blurt out, flopping back in my chair. "Do you still like me even a little bit, or did I make an irredeemable mess of everything?"

He smiles against his will, his lips curling up at the corners. "Of course I still like you a little," he admits. "You did make a mess, but maybe it's not the irredeemable type. I'm still trying to decide."

"Oh," I whisper, suddenly exhausted. I look up at the wall and study a crooked row of small paintings, an exhibit hung by a young artist undoubtedly elated at landing exhibit space in a coffee shop. I recall those days all too well, and the memory of them and the current wrenching conversation with Thomas conspire to put a firm lump in my throat. I swallow hard and nod up at one of the paintings, a gooey rendering of the BU Bridge stretching over a murky Charles River. "I have a little show at a gallery on Newbury Street," I tell him. "Just a few photos, but it's a wonderful, well-known gallery. It's been up for about a week. They are actually candids from the proms, if you can believe that." I take another sip of his iced coffee.

"Really?" he asks. "That's interesting, Iley. You must be very proud."

"I . . . am!" I say slowly, as though it's a revelation. "So *that's* what that feeling of self-esteem about my art must be."

He laughs at this and I relax completely, then chuckle my way through telling the story of my meeting with Peter Spring, when I nearly required treatment for shock upon being told he'd like to display my work. When I look at my watch, an hour has passed, and I think I may be able to get him back.

* * *

Erin flops onto the sofa, looking over the little notepad with the glittery heart on the cover. I sit next to her, and we both studiously avoid meeting eyes with Gary, for whom "people arriving home" invariably translates to "Gary going out," even if said people left the apartment only two hours earlier.

"I'm not taking him o-u-t," Erin complains as he stands impatiently next to his leash. "He can't possibly have to go again so soon." She flips a few pages in the pad and looks at her notes critically. "The second one was awful. But I really liked the fourth one."

I close my eyes and try to picture them; all the spaces are starting to meld together in my mind. Was the fourth one where Erin said it would be great to have a row of sinks beneath the windows? Or was it the place with the tiny, dank room in back, where she complained that she would need to ventilate it better if people were to be mixing color back there?

"It was the one with the skylights," she explains, reading the poorly concealed confusion on my face. "And the tiny entryway with the exposed brick that I said would make a great reception area, remember?"

I nod vigorously. "That's right," I say. "Now I remember. That exposed brick was awesome. When do we go shopping for salon chairs and tiny pieces of tin foil?" I ask eagerly.

"Not for a while," she says, laughing. Gary gives a canine *harrumph* when he finally realizes that no one is leaping off the sofa to take him for a walk, and lopes into the kitchen, where he drowns his sorrows in his water dish. "I need to talk to Mark about so many things first—leasing the space, insurance, all that stuff." She smiles at me. "Hey, if you like that exposed brick so much, maybe you could be my receptionist," she jokes as she lights a cigarette. Except that it doesn't sound entirely like a joke, which immediately makes both of us uncomfortable.

"I hope I'm destined for something better than that," I say, feeling uneasy.

"Of course you are; I'm just screwing around, Iley. Come on," she says guiltily, trying to wave away my anxiety. I sigh and realize I'm extraordinarily thirsty, and as I pass the phone on the way to the refrigerator, I see the red light blinking on the machine.

"Message," I call into the living room. "Probably a telemarketer." I press the play button, and Peter Spring's voice fills the kitchen.

"Hello, this is Peter Spring calling for Iley. Give me a call at the gallery when you get this. 617-555-4144. Thanks." His voice is completely void of emotion, and I replay it three times, searching for nuance in the cadence and breathing. After the third time, Erin picks up the receiver and wordlessly hands it to me. I take a deep breath and dial; he answers on the third ring.

"Peter Spring Gallery. Peter Spring speaking." That same inscrutable tone that makes me want to scream. If you want me to take down my photos, why couldn't you just be a man and say it on the machine, you pompous jackass?

"It's Iley," I bray defiantly. "You called?" Erin gives me a wide-eyed look that says, *Chill. Back off.*

"Yes, I have some exciting news for you. Oh, hold on a minute," he says. "Just leave that there . . . no, not there, by the door . . . no, on the other side. OK, right there is fine." I hear a creaky door close and he gives an impatient sniff. "I had someone in today from a publishing company, and she was very interested in your work. She left me her card, and said you should get in touch with her as soon as possible."

"OK," I say slowly, looking at Erin with my brow furrowed. "But . . . what . . . I mean, what does she want?"

"Well, I don't know, but my guess is that since she's in publishing, she'd want to create some sort of book. It wouldn't be the first time that Peter Spring launched a publishing career for a young photographer," he says, irritatingly referring to himself in the third person. "Although you'd be the first to have it happen so fast," he adds charitably. He reads me her name and number, and I write them on Erin's glitter heart pad, which she's shoved under my nose. I dutifully read him back the contact information and underline it twice, right above Erin's "Sunny, but idiotic location" and "Where to put big mirror?" notes. "I'd recommend you call her soon," he urges. "You've got to strike while the iron is hot with these creative types," he says critically, as though he and I work in an accounting firm.

"All right, I will," I say, and hang up the phone, stupefied. Then I pick it up again and dial the number with the 212 area code, whispering to Erin as the phone rings. "Someone from a publishing company in New . . . hello!" I say, caught off guard when a pleasant female voice greets me. "This is Iley Gilbert. My work is in the Peter Spring Gallery." Erin gives me a dramatic, "Aren't we impressed?" look, and I have to stifle a laugh. "My work." How I hate that expression, but what else should I have said?

"Yes, yes, yes," the woman says. "My name is Anna Infeld, and I'm an editor here at Merrywood Publishers. I was in Boston for a one-day meeting and stopped into Peter's gallery literally for a *minute* to see what was new. And I *love* your photographs," she coos. "Just *love* them. Such a good eye, and *what* a subject matter you've chosen! Peter told me you have many others beyond the ones hanging in the gallery; is that so?"

"I do," I say, sitting down in a kitchen chair. I fear I might faint if I don't get off my feet.

"Well, I'd love the opportunity to see them. Basically, my idea here is that I'd like to create a beautifully produced volume of your photos around the theme of the secret life of teens. That's really hot right now," she informs me briskly, and I smile as I think about these pimply kids, falling down on the parking lot and brawling with one another and getting to third base in the back of the limo, blissfully unaware of how "hot" they are right now. "If this all comes together, I'd ask you to write a short introduction, then perhaps some commentary on each photo. One I loved at the gallery was taken at the school for the blind," she says dreamily. "Peter explained the image to me."

"Deaf," I correct her. "They were deaf."

"Oh, right. Anyway, can you FedEx me the other pictures from this series, so I can get this moving on my end? I'm thinking if this all works out, I'd like this to release during prom season next year, which is . . ." She pauses and I hear the sound of papers shuffling. "Not very far off, really, in terms of how our production schedules work. Oh, and Iley?" she asks.

"Yes?" I say, frozen in place, my back rigid against the chair.

"We can't do a *thing* with this book if you can't get photo permissions. That means that anyone who is pictured needs to sign a release form. And if anyone pictured is under eighteen, a parent or guardian needs to sign for him or her. *Very* important," she intones. "So put that at the top of your list, after you send me the rest of the photographs. I'll get some paperwork started for you, as far as what needs to be on the release form. But I expect you might have to do quite a bit of legwork now. I'll bet this is all quite a surprise, no?" she asks brightly. It sounds as though asking this question of unsuspecting artists is one of the great joys of her job.

"I can't begin to explain it. My palms are sweating," I admit, as I wipe my right hand across the edge of the kitchen table.

"Well, keep those sweaty hands off the prints," she says in a serious voice. She gives me her mailing address and tells me to select the fastest delivery option, then to go out and have a stiff celebratory drink. We don't even wait to go to the bar, instead breaking out the bottle of VSOP sent to Erin last week by her parents. The brandy came accompanied by a card that simply read, "Congratulations!" and we'd decided that the message must have been this pithy only because the shipper claimed not to have room to write, "Congratulations! We're so happy you're only into cutting hair, and not a cokehead or lesbian!" It was delicious, and fully blotted out the nagging worry in the back of my head about one of the photo permissions.

The next day, when I emerge from thc darkroom hung over, bleary-eyed, and exhausted—yet more ecstatic than I've been in months—I find myself face-to-face with Therese. I'm shocked; I had no idea she was even capable of dragging herself this far from behind her metal desk. I suppose I imagined that they stored her in a nearby closet at night, and yet, here she is at the entrance to my darkroom space, nearly twenty-five feet away from her protective metal shroud.

"You need to go upstairs right now," she says, nodding north as though she's willing me to heaven. "Mr. Meany needs to talk to you, and he leaves at five."

I look at my watch; it's 4:55. "Well, I guess I do, then," I say, giving her a wide grin. She looks disappointed at my acceptance of this activity that came with so little notice, and I stride over to the elevator, humming. When I reach the fourth floor office, Mr. Meany is already wearing his jacket, a green tweed garment with outdated, razor-thin lapels. He looks more than a touch angry.

"I have to leave promptly at five. Why did you wait so long to come up to see me?" he barks. "I asked Therese this morning to let you know as soon as she saw you come in." He fishes around in a small drawer for a set of keys and opens a battleship gray lock box as I stand there with my mouth open, stalling for time. I close my mouth, then open it again, and think about Therese. How miserable she is, how this is all she has. How I can't imagine anyone else employing her, ever. How it's very possible that someday I might be able to create my very own darkroom in a stylish studio downtown and never have to see her jaded face again. And so I cover for her.

"You know, she did tell me, and I just got very distracted," I say calmly.

"Well, we have some money here for you," he says, pulling a pale green check from a business-sized envelope and handing it to me. "Joey Suchinda has paid his darkroom fees for the next six months, so he won't need the last two months of your 'grant.' "

"Really?" I ask, surprised. "Where'd he get the money?"

"I don't know," he replies impatiently. "You'll have to ask him. I need to leave now," he says, bending his arm and glancing at his watch. He dashes over to the stairs and looks at me for a few seconds. "I hope your work in the darkroom is going well," he shouts over his shoulder, running down the steps. I push the button for the elevator and say to no one, "I'm going to have a book of my prom pictures released." I say it again, and again once more in the elevator on my way down to the basement.

"Are you sure we don't need to wear black?" Erin asks as she swigs from a can of Red Bull. It's eleven-thirty at night on a Wednesday, and we've got a long evening ahead of us. "It seems like it would be more dramatic that way."

"Well, you can if you want," I laugh. "I figure the cover of darkness is enough, but if you can dig out a black turtleneck in the next few minutes, you're welcome to." I reach into the pocket of my jeans for the thirtieth time this evening, to make sure the keys are still there. The very keys that William shoved at me as I hunched in his bathroom closet in August.

An hour later, Erin and I are at the back door of William's studio space, and as I nose the key into the lock, Erin keeps watch outside. The street is empty at this hour, yet my heart races anyway. We tiptoe inside and I turn on a few lights, trying not to feel sick as we walk past the bathroom and into the back room, where the thousands of negatives and proofs are stored. We stand at a workbench and I push a pile of papers to the side, swallowing hard when I think I recognize William's handwriting.

"All right," I announce. "Here's the deal. All of these kids need to be identified," I explain, opening up an envelope and laying out a copy of each of my prom photos in front of us. "I wrote the name of the school on the back of each one." I flip over a picture of a dimwitted-looking kid wearing a tuxedo T-shirt under his tuxedo jacket, and show her the "Melrose High" written in china marker on the back. "We need to look through all of William's files for the prom proofs, *and* the forms the kids filled out with their names and addresses." I gesture to a wall of gray filing cabinets as Erin's brow furrows. "They are all catalogued by school, I think. William sort of showed me once," I bluff. "So we need to match *his* pictures of the kids to *my* pictures, so we can get all the names and addresses and phone numbers. The worst one is going to be this," I say with distaste, holding up a picture of my nemesis. Her eyes are rolled back in her head as she sits next to a shrub, one of her high-heeled, dyed-to-match shoes off, and her purse sitting limply in her lap.

"Ew, who's that?" Erin asks, and I raise an eyebrow in response. "Oh. Why will she be the worst?"

"Because she was always the date from another school,

the guys never wrote her name down. I doubt if the guys even ended up ordering photos," I say.

"That's sort of sad," she replies as she picks up the photo. "This girl is really depressing."

"But I think her name must be somewhere," I say hopefully, walking over to the wall of filing cabinets. I scan the room once more and my chest tightens unexpectedly. "And you have one more job, Erin." She looks at me with a serious expression. "If for whatever reason William shows up here, you are not to leave. You are to stay here and make sure I keep my legs closed, no matter what."

"A human chastity belt. I like it," she grins. We settle into our sleuthing, and the night passes quickly as we piece together the information. The kid with the tuxedo T-shirt is Artie Edson. The skinny, longhaired girl from the deaf school is Linda Calabresi. The boy from the arts high school with the curvy upper lip and lush blond hair is Auden McKenna. The girls who ogled William at the very first prom I attended are Marisa Richard, Nina Maggiani, and Lucy Miller. And so on, until four-thirty in the morning, when Erin's Red Bull buzz has worn off entirely and we've yet to find the name of my prom girl. William's assistant Arvin will be here in just a few hours, and we've got quite a cleanup ahead of us, with proofs and sheets of negatives and papers strewn everywhere. I rest my head in my hands and massage the spot between my eyebrows as Erin sleepily pokes around in the files. The room falls silent and I nearly drift off to sleep, and then Erin suddenly trills with joy.

"Tina Kempczynski," she says triumphantly.

"What?"

"Tina Kempczynski," she repeats. "I have your girl." She holds out a sheet from a prom in Revere, and on the upper portion, in messy handwriting, it says, "TOM CABOT, 18 Chestnut Drive, Revere, MA." And beneath that, in the same scrawl, it says, "TINA KEMPCZYNSKI." with two squiggly horizontal lines running through it. Clearly someone thought better of adding her to the sheet—Tina? Tom?—but did a sub-par job of getting rid of the evidence. The letters are legible through the halfhearted squiggles, and I do a little dance in the middle of the floor.

"It doesn't have her phone number or address, though," Erin says, sounding worried. "What will you do?"

"Oh, I'm sure I can convince Tom Cabot to help me," I say confidently, and Erin joins me in my jig as the sun starts to come up.

Twenty-one

And so I spend the next month running to and from the darkroom, churning out photos as fast as Anna Infeld requests them, and truly losing myself in my work for the first time in many, many months. Every time I study a prom photo emerging in the developer tray, I think of William less and less, until one crisp fall day when I realize that the pictures create no sting at all. My memories of the entire experience have given way to pure excitement about my book, which Anna trills about on a weekly basis, telling me that it's going to be like nothing else out there.

At home, I plow my way through the information that Erin and I stole, making calls and quickly learning which kids have gone to UMass, which are in the armed forces, which are still living at home. I talk to confused parents who can't understand why someone is calling about prom pictures this long after graduation, and listless siblings who take messages and promise that they'll pass them on.

When I reach the kids on the phone, a handful are mortified and want nothing to do with me once I've explained the project, but the bulk are eager to be included. It seems that their desire to be famous far outweighs the potential embarrassment of having one's family see photographic evidence of having been dragged across a catering hall parking lot while swathed in yellow taffeta. Or, as one Lynette Madsen of Milton High spat, "That'll show the people who didn't give me a callback for "American Idol." Whatever it took, whatever their motivation, I begged and wheedled and cajoled, and one by one, they returned their signed photo permission forms in the self-addressed, stamped envelopes I'd mailed to them. I collect them in a folder that I've borrowed from Erin, a somber, slate blue number given to her by her parents' financial planner.

The folder grows fatter each day with permissions, yet I still can't bring myself to track down the worst one. So I throw myself even more deeply into my work, creating print after print and starting to draft the written portions for the book. I distract myself with errands, take Gary on long walks, have a few friendly phone conversations with Thomas. I tour more potential salons with Erin, and write up needlessly elaborate recap notes for her afterward. I ride my bike around town until my legs are sore. Yet at the end of each day, I go to sleep knowing that there is no getting around Tina Kempczynski.

"Well, well, well," I murmur as I hold the glossy pages of the magazine open on my enlarger. "Look, that's your place!" I add, pointing to a photo of the tangerine-colored wall of the restaurant.

"I know!" exclaims Rithy. "We got this review last month in *Bon Appetít*, and now the restaurant's full all the time." The Gallic pronunciation is too much for him, and he mistakenly refers to the culinary monthly as "bone appetite," shrugging when I smile involuntarily at this. No matter what it's called; Thai Palace finally got its due, thanks to its fine service and superior pad thai dishes. The hordes of curious, hungry tourists have led to a perpetually ringing register, meaning that Rithy is back in the darkroom for good, doing what he loves and no longer dependent on the faceless benefactor actually standing opposite him. "You come in with your editor woman from New York, OK?" he urges me as he tips an empty box of photo paper on its corner and gives it a spin.

"Yeah, maybe sometime," I say, scratching my head. "But I doubt it. She seems very busy, very New York, know what I mean?"

"No," he admits, then turns and studies all the photos drying on a far table. "I am so happy for you, Iley," he says earnestly.

"Well, I have you to thank, right?" I ask as I hand him the magazine back. I sigh and put my hands on my hips, looking at two pictures that feature my prom girl. "I have one more thing I have to do to make this book happen," I say nervously. "I'm dreading it."

He rolls up the magazine and sticks it under his armpit, then looks at me. "You'll do it," he says. His tone is classic Rithy, unassuming with neither a trace of force nor pretense. I decide to take it as an order, figuring that he hasn't steered me wrong yet.

* * *

I smoke two cigarettes, one right after another, until Gary dashes into the kitchen to escape the carbon monoxide cloud. I tuck my feet underneath me on the sofa, and gingerly reach for the phone. I dial Tom Cabot's number and look at the clock: 6:18 p.m., the time during which people who work are home from work, people who go to community college are back from class. I've got a hunch that Tom Cabot falls into one of these categories, but I'm so nervous that I momentarily pray for him to prove me wrong. "Yale?" I imagine myself saying to his mother. "You must be very proud."

After two more rings, someone lifts the receiver and says a garbled hello. It's a man, and he's clearly eating something. The food sounds crunchy—pretzels, perhaps? A cable news channel is blaring in the background, the earsplitting sound effects trumpeting another bit of bad news.

"Hi, I am looking for Tom Cabot, please," I say loudly.

"Speaking." More crunching.

"I need to get in touch with Tina Kempczynski," I say evenly and hold my breath. I hear an unctuous reporter in the background yelling about a recent car bombing.

He gives a little snort. "Why?"

"She won some money. A lot of money, actually. And I need to make sure it gets to her," I lie.

"Really?" he asks, his tone changing. Then there is a long pause. "Where'd she win the money?"

"It looks like she entered a raffle. I just work for the company that handles tracking down the winners. We work with a lot of different places, so I don't know where she won it. Anyway, if you could help me, I can tell her I got her name from you, if you like. A lot of times these winners end up giving a little bit of the money to people who help my company out," I say confidently. "You know, like a reward to you, for helping me find her."

"Yeah, fat chance with that bitch," he spits. I hear the rustle of a foil-lined bag. More snacks? You're going to ruin your appetite for dinner, Tom Cabot. Unless, of course, this *is* dinner. "Well, what the hell?" he asks. "Why not?" He gives me her phone number, and I repeat back the seven digits slowly, making sure I got them right. I thank him and hold down the button on the receiver, letting it up again slowly and preparing for the next call.

The phone rings twice at the Kempczynski house, and a woman answers. Her voice is deep and scratchy, as though I interrupted a gravel-gargling ritual.

"Hello, I am looking for Tina," I say pleasantly, inhaling as I ready to explain the raffle.

"She's at the pizza place," she says heavily. "At work."

"Oh, you mean Miele's?" I ask, thinking fast and conjuring the name of my favorite childhood pizza joint. My heart starts to race, and I long for another cigarette. The craving is immediately made worse when I swear I hear a match striking against a matchbook, and the woman taking a slow, deep breath.

"No, Conti's," she answers in an irritated voice that suggests that I'm the most moronic person to ever grace her telephone line. So I go with it.

"Oh, stupid me!" I laugh. "Conti's, yeah. She there tomorrow?"

"I don't know her schedule," she says, puffing and letting out a wet cough that turns my stomach. "Maybe."

"All right, I'll catch up with her there," I say, speaking

quickly before she can ask who this is. Although she hasn't seemed particularly concerned yet. "Thanks."

"Congratulations, Miss Brooks," I say, toasting Erin with my bottle of water from where I'm sitting at the kitchen table. Mark the financial consultant has just left the apartment with all of the appropriate signatures, and Erin is alternately beaming and looking nauseated. She is standing near the sink, twisting the corner of her T-shirt and shaking her left leg as though she has to pee.

"Yeah, I can't believe it's going to be mine," she says, amazed and more than a little nervous. "Well, not mine, it's really Dad and Bitsy's," she corrects herself.

"Ah, that's just semantics," I say, grinning. "People who come in will think of it as *your* salon!" I exclaim. She grins back. "What will you call it?"

"I don't even know," she admits. "I've been thinking about it, but I don't have anything I really like yet." Gary comes into the kitchen, and she feeds him a small handful of celebratory Snausages.

"I'll ask Thomas if he has any ideas," I say. "I bet he's really good with stuff like that," I add confidently, and then smile a tiny bit when I think of him. Last night we spoke on the phone for nearly forty-five minutes about the insanity of the SATs. One of his students told him that she was so worried about the impending test (which is still nearly five months off) that she has diarrhea every time she thinks about it. Especially the math portion, she explained. I suggested to him that she stock up on Immodium for the big day and added boastfully, "Tell her that I barely broke a thousand on the SATs, and look at me." Thomas laughed and said, "Yeah, just look at you," in a mock-wry tone that was all admiration and bashful affection.

"Now I get to live the American dream," Erin says, wiggling her fingers and walking around the kitchen. "I can go and give my notice to Furious George. 'Take these shears and shove them.' "

"Ouch," I say, grimacing and rubbing my butt.

"Also I've got to poach my best clients, then start pricing the lighting and the furniture . . . there is really just so much to do," she says, jittery and elated.

"Well, now you know why Furious George is so furious all the time. A salon is a lot of work, right? Just don't become Furious Erin on me, OK?" I ask, smiling.

"Of course not," she promises. She takes a deep breath and looks around the kitchen, as though she might discover appropriate salon lighting tucked in between the old newspapers and catalogs. "I have to meet an electrician at the new place this afternoon. I can't wait to see it again."

"That reminds me," I say, getting up from my chair. "I have something for your salon."

Erin looks shocked. "You do?"

"I do. I got it made when it looked like this might really happen for you. And I know it will look great in that exposed brick foyer," I call over my shoulder as I go into my room and dig the plastic-sheathed piece out of my closet. I carry it into the kitchen and lay it on the table. "Go ahead," I urge, nodding at it.

"All right," she says, looking perplexed. She peels away the clear tape and slowly unwraps the milky plastic wrapping, exposing a beautifully matted and framed image. My pal at The Framery chose a deep matte silver frame and a slate blue, beveled mat, and in the center is a two-inch square of newsprint, clipped from the *Boston Herald* police blotter. It reads:

Now That's What We Call a Bad Hair Day!

Police responded to a call last Thursday at George Salon on Newbury Street, where stylist Erin Brooks, age 32, was seen throwing salon supplies and terrorizing customers. The harried hairstylist locked herself in the bathroom while order was restored at the salon. "I just wanted to curl up and die," said one frightened customer who was getting highlights at the time. Or was it curl up and DYE?

"Oh, my God," Erin says slowly, her eyes growing huge and her face reddening perceptibly. "Where . . . on earth . . . did you get this?"

"Where do you think?" I ask, laughing. "The *Herald*. I found it almost by accident after you gave up reading the police blotter, and I've been saving it this whole time. Isn't it great?" She doesn't reply for a few seconds, and I get a sick feeling in the pit of my stomach.

"I can't believe it. This is so . . . embarrassing . . . and . . . *I love it*!" she crows, throwing her arms around me. "I'm in the police blotter!" she shouts twice, and Gary starts barking. "This is going right up on the wall before I do anything else in there. Oh, Iley, thank you so much!" She holds it out in front of her and beams, then rewraps it neatly in the plastic. "If this doesn't make this salon a success, I don't know what will," she says earnestly, hugging me again.

* * *

I hold my breath as the phone rings twice, and a young male voice answers. "Conti's. What can I getcha?"

"Hey, is Tina there today?" I ask in a gruff voice, as I hear the sound of clattering dishes in the background.

"Yeah," he answers after a few seconds.

"Well, you know when she goes on break?" I press on, continuing to match his bored tone.

"I think she goes on break at . . . well, wait, who is this?" he asks, potentially destroying my plans with spontaneous shreds of curiosity and good judgment.

"It's just a friend. I have something I need to drop off for her," I say, lowering my voice and hoping that kids in mind-numbing food service jobs entertain themselves in the same way I did at that tender age. At the wing take-out place where I worked during my freshman year of college, my co-worker Casey's pal would visit twice a week with a generous stash of weed, and we'd spend our shifts blissed out while packing up the orders of wings. Being deferential to Casey on the days of the deliveries would only increase said bliss, and I pray that this same protocol is in place at Conti's.

"She's off at one-thirty for lunch and then again at six," he answers pleasantly, and I smile.

"Thanks very much," I say. I hang up the phone and race out of the house, speeding away in Erin's old Saab. In my hysteria, I reach Conti's in Revere well before one-thirty, and I sit in the car, drumming my fingers, smoking, and looking at salon chair catalogs. God, these things are expensive, I think to myself, when I suddenly realize it's one twenty-five. I leap from the car, give the taupe door a hard slam, and stride into Conti's, where I immediately spy Tina. She looks tired and worn, her hair overgrown and fried on the ends from summer sun and a bad dye job. She's dressed in a black T-shirt and unflattering, twill black pants, and I notice how scrawny she is. Swathed in all the layers of her gowns, it had been impossible to see her whole shape, but in her drab, cotton-poly Conti's uniform, her unhealthy-looking physique is in full view, and I immediately pity her. It's the look of a girl who smokes too much and eats and sleeps too little—much like how I spent my days in my room after my last interaction with Tina herself.

I watch her carefully place four red plastic glasses of cola on one of the tables and give the patrons a weak smile, and she suddenly snaps her head up and sees me in the doorway. Even with my new haircut she remembers me instantly, and she scowls and hustles back to the kitchen as I approach the counter and consider what to do next. Without warning, the double doors to the kitchen swing open, and Tina rushes through the restaurant, her black vinyl purse swinging behind her. I turn tail and chase her out the door, where I catch up with her in front of a dingy-looking dry cleaner's.

"Get the fuck away from me!" she screams, sending a woman with an armload of dry cleaning and two small children into a panic, racing away from us. "Leave me alone!"

"Tina, please," I say, panting. "Please, just listen to what I have to say." Now we're in front of a wholesale beauty outlet, its windows filled with professional-size tubs of hair goo, and I think about whether or not to get the name of the place for Erin before I realize I'd better focus solely on the task at hand here.

"How do you know my name?" she shouts, her face reddening. "I *hate* you! You ruined my life!" I start to shout back that she ruined *my* life, so now we're even, except that isn't really true. She actually saved my life, by bringing my affair with William into the light. And now I'm starting to worry that there may be no way to get what I want here.

"Come on. Come on, please. Let's just stop for a minute and have a smoke. You can't spend your whole break running around the parking lot," I reason, lighting a cigarette. "You want to sit in my car for a minute, and just hear me out?"

"I'm not going anywhere with you!" she shrieks, but with a bit less intensity. It's the power of the cigarette, I know it, and sure enough, she sighs and drops her hands to her sides before rooting through her bag for a pack of Virginia Slims. She puts one in her mouth and tries to light it, but her lighter is dead. I listen to the *shhhhck, shhhhck, shhhhck, shhhhck* of the useless lighter and watch her thumb futilely work the metal roller for a few seconds before throwing her my lighter. She gives me a look of defeat and angrily lights her cigarette, then folds her skinny arms hard over her chest.

"You just have to listen to me," I say. "You don't even have to talk, all right?" She juts out her jaw and starts tapping her foot, and I inhale deeply. "When I . . . said what I said about you at the prom, it was totally out of line. I feel really, really terrible about it. It's your business if you want to go to different proms. I don't know what the fuck my problem was," I explain apologetically. Except that I do know what my problem was, and I impulsively decide to tell her. "The thing is, I was going through something sort of similar at the time."

"Yeah, I guessed that from the photo," she sneers. These are the first words I've heard from her that haven't been hurled in a scream or shriek, and I'm surprised by how high-pitched and squeaky her voice is. It takes the sting out of her comment completely, and I have to suppress a smile. "So if you tell people I'm a slut, it makes you feel better, is what you're saying?" she brays, exhaling a mouthful of smoke at me.

"I don't know what I'm saying, I'm just here to tell you that I'm very sorry for what I did. And I—well, I might be able to make it up to you." Two men emerge from the beauty supply store, each bearing large, overfilled shopping bags, and a little plastic container of purple hair clips falls from one of the bags and onto the sidewalk next to me. I hand the container back and receive an annoyed grunt in reply.

"Oh, yeah? How is that?" she asks, tilting her head and putting her hands on her hips. "You gonna get Rory back for me? 'Cause he was the one I liked." Her voice softens during this last sentence, barely perceptibly, but just enough to break my heart.

"Well, no," I say quietly. "But—" Before I can finish my thought, a short woman wearing a bad perm emerges from the beauty supply store with a frown.

"No smoking," she says, sniffing and coughing. "Get away from my store with that smoke."

"We're *outside*," Tina and I say nearly in unison, and then look at one another.

"I don't care," the woman says. "I don't want you in front of my store."

I roll my eyes; this tête-à-tête with Tina is getting worse and worse. "Can we go back to Conti's, just for a minute?" I ask her. "I promise I won't take too much more of your time." She nods and we walk in silence back to the restaurant, where we slide into a small booth by the window. The seats and table have been covered in a red melamine that's faded in the sun and chipped at the corners. Tina flops back in her half of the booth, now looking more bored than angry by this whole thing.

"Here's the deal," I begin. "Some of the pictures I took outside the proms caught the attention of someone who wants to make them into a book. But I need to get people's permission to put their pictures in the book, and you're in a bunch of the pictures. So if you say it's OK for me to do that, I can—"

"What?" She laughs, astounded. "You want me to help *you* with something? Why would I do that?" She laughs again, this time cruelly.

"Look, this might be hard for you to understand, but you have your whole life ahead of you to do stuff," I say quietly, squishing a ketchup packet between my left thumb and forefinger. "I'm thirty-one, and this might be one of my last chances to pull it together." I look up at her and her face is impassive, her arms still shielding her chest. "I mean to say that I know I've made some shitty decisions, but I'm trying to turn things around, and if I could have your help, I'd be very happy to—"

She interrupts me by laying her hands flat on the table, her gold filigree rings clicking against the melamine. "*Any-*

one knows that doing what you did with that guy is a shitty decision," she tells me snidely. "You don't have to be thirty-one to figure that out."

I nod and put my chin in my hand. How to explain to her that it wasn't just that decision; rather, that life is made up of each day's infinitesimal decisions, decisions that don't seem weighty at the time, but slowly accrue to shape you into the person you become? The decision not to write down the phone number of the woman from the adoption agency who promised that I'd be able to be a part of Matt and my baby's life. The decision to surf to the temp agency's Web site for the very first time. The decision to work with William, even though he had looked at me like a wolf while scratching his face with his left hand during my interview, his wedding band in full view like a warning beacon.

"You're right," I say sadly. "You don't have to be thirty-one to figure that out." I gulp hard; flipping through my mental catalog of decisions has left me feeling emotional, and Tina responds by softening the muscles in her face ever so slightly. "Anyway, I am basically begging you, Tina," I implore her. "If you let me use these pictures, I'll buy you whatever you want. I mean, not like a car or anything, but I really want to do something for you. I didn't do that for anyone else who gave me permission, but I really feel like I owe you." A waiter emerges from the men's room, drying his hands on his little red apron, and he casts a suspicious glance at us as he passes by the booth.

"You OK, Tina?" he asks Tina.

"Yeah," she replies quietly, scratching her head and

pursing her lips. She looks at me. "Are there gonna be pictures of me with guys?"

I look up at the stained drop ceiling as I try to imagine which images I had planned on using, and sure enough, two or three of them feature her in rather compromising positions. I look back at her and decide there's no way I can do that to her. "No," I tell her. "I won't do that."

"Hmm," she says. "It would be cool to be in a book," she admits. We sit in silence for a few long seconds, and we both watch as a Conti's delivery guy dashes out to a blue Honda Civic with a stack of puffy, red, insulated pizza bags. "What do I get?"

"Well, I don't know what you like," I say, trying to conceal my joy at her coming around. "You want a gift certificate to the mall? Or a PSP? Jewelry?" I suggest, peering at her rings, bracelet, and dangly heart earrings. "I want it to be something that would make you happy," I add earnestly, wondering if such a tender statement will queer the deal with this tough cookie.

"I want . . ." she says slowly, her eyes darting around the place as though she might choose a jar of oregano or a stack of paper napkins, "I want that." She points across the booth and into my messenger bag, which I'd opened to furtively remove a folded-up photo permission form. Sitting in the bag is my camera, on its yellow strap.

"You want my camera?" I laugh. "You can't have my camera."

"Not *your* camera," she snaps. "*A* camera."

I look at her, dumbfounded. "You want a camera?"

"Yeah, what's so stupid about that?" she asks, getting irritated.

"It's not stupid at all," I say carefully. "I'm just surprised, that's all. You don't want a DVD player or an iPod or something?"

She shakes her head. "Naw. All that shit is boring. When we were playing with the camera at the prom, out in the parking lot, it looked like fun. So that's what I want," she finishes, jutting out her lower lip.

"Well, you probably mean you want a *digital* camera," I reason. "That's what most people have nowadays."

"No, I want one like that, the kind you have," she insists, crossing her legs and thumping back in the booth.

"OK, OK," I say quickly. "I'll pick one out for you and buy you all the stuff you need. You're *sure*?"

She tilts her head at me. "I make bad decisions too, but this isn't one of them," she says, giving me a sassy, closed-mouth smile.

Twenty-two

I wake slowly to the aroma of strong coffee, and when my arm lands on a warm body lying next to me in the sheets, I panic in my half-awake haze and instinctively search for the strip of light beneath the door. I locate it against the far wall, leaking in a thick line beneath an ecru-colored door that doesn't quite close properly, and then sigh with relief as I simultaneously realize that the warm body is covered in soft brown fur and has a wet nose to boot.

I give Guy a few quick rubs behind his ears, and he and I stretch and yawn in unison. I swing my legs over the edge of the bed and study all of the books on the floor, the piles of papers on a nearby chair, an oversized, framed crucifix never removed from a Lucite box. After talking and drinking wine until nearly two in the morning, Thomas and I decided that I should just crash at his place, and we maturely opted to have me bunk in the living room for the night. Once left alone, however, I found I couldn't sleep on his couch, the same one where I treated him so deplorably during the summer. So I crept into his bed, where I learned that he'd been wide awake, as well. We continued the night in the same mature fashion, keeping things decidedly PG-rated in his cozy bed. It felt like high school again, and somehow, just right.

An hour later, after two jitter-inducing cups of chicory coffee, Thomas walks me to the front door and I give him a kiss good-bye. I'm dying for a cigarette after all that coffee, but for now, the kiss is pretty good at providing a distinctly similar rush. "Sorry I have to go," I say.

"That's all right," he says in a mock dejected tone. "No, seriously, I know you have stuff to do for the book," he adds. "I have papers to grade today, anyway. Fifty-six of them, to be exact." He shudders at the impending work.

"Yeah, I saw them in your room," I say, smiling.

He gives me a quizzical look. "Oh, no, those are examples of really awful papers I've graded over the years; ones where the students didn't even want them back. I took them out because I was looking for a book report to show you. It was the one where the kid kept writing, *The Boy with the Red Bandage*, and it wasn't until I got to the end that I realized he had been talking about *The Red Badge of Courage*."

I burst out laughing. "Oh, Thomas, you know me so well already," I applaud him.

"That's the plan," he says, his eyes twinkling. "So you're going to the darkroom?"

"Yeah. Then I'm going over to Cambridge to buy Tina her camera," I say, shaking my head in disbelief.

"You think she's really going to use it?" he asks skeptically as Guy steps between us in the doorway, sniffing at my green and yellow sneakers.

"Who knows?" I reply, shrugging. "I hope so. I'm going to put my phone number in there with all of the equipment, in case she needs help. We'll have to see, I guess." Guy loses interest in my sneakers and goes back into the apartment, and I hook my messenger bag over my shoulder and cast a glance at the stairwell. "I think I should probably go."

"So I'll give you a call tomorrow?" he asks hopefully, leaning in for a quick kiss.

"Of course," I reply.

Because I took the T from Thomas's neighborhood and am not engaging in my standard bike-locking ritual this morning, it takes Don about ten long, slow blinks to piece together who I am. "Hey," he says gruffly after a minute, clutching a plastic bottle of Nestlé Quik that is half-filled with something other than chocolate milk. The orange fluid sloshes in the bottle as he swings it from side to side, looking past me and down the alleyway.

"Hey yourself," I reply cheerily as I study his torn pants. He's got a frayed Red Sox schedule stuck to the space between his cuff and his gray sneaker, detritus from last night's game no doubt, the tiny fold-out brochure with its neat red and white grid resting on the spot where a sock should be. Despite my recent joy about Thomas and my photography book, I am suddenly overwhelmed with sadness for Don. "Don," I say, turning to him, "I have to tell you something. It's important."

"Huh?" he asks. I'm unsure if this means he didn't hear

me or he's ready for me to continue, but I press on anyway, hoping that this is the way to help.

"The methadone clinic is never coming back," I say firmly as I point down the alleyway. "Never." Our eyes meet, and I study his eyebrows. Despite his age, he's started to go gray, with several unruly eyebrow hairs sticking up onto his forehead. There is a long silence, with only the light, Saturday morning traffic providing low level, ambient city noise. He licks his lips and takes a long swig from his Nestlé Quik bottle.

"I know," he says, sounding defeated yet relieved. He nods, a quick little nod that would barely be visible if I weren't studying him so closely. "I know it's not."

"OK," I breathe quietly. We trade a small smile and I turn to go. "I have to develop a lot of pictures today, but maybe I'll see you later," I tell him.

"You better be developing into something nice, too," he says, shifting his gaze from the alley to the window of the tiny art store two doors down from the photography school. The window is filled with supplies, brightly colored displays of photographic tints, and crisp boxes of photo paper for young photographers full of promise.

"Don't you worry," I say as I open the door to the school. "I think I am."

Want More?

Turn the page to enter Avon's Little Black Book —

the dish, the scoop and the cherry on top from

EUGÉNIE OLSON

My Prom Night With Homer

The year was 1987. I had been preparing for my senior prom for ages, securing everything I would need for the big night.

First, the date. I was to be escorted by my boyfriend, a Scandinavian exchange student who lived a few towns away. Neither especially striking nor hideous, I felt certain he'd make the right impression at my school.

Next, the dress. It was a Laura Ashley number, with pink and white vertical stripes, a nipped-in waist, a hemline that grazed the ankles, and a square neckline. In retrospect, this garment was something that Holly Hobbie probably would have regarded as too saccharine for words. Then there were the shoes, pumps gleaming in white satin; and the jewelry, the memory of which escapes me. My hair was cut in a stylish, asymmetrical bob, and the Sun-In applied religiously during my family's February vacation to Florida made my highlighted strands glow in a surreal shade of yellow.

About two weeks before the prom, I started to feel weary. I got a sore throat that wouldn't go away. I didn't want to run track, my 100- and 200-meter dashes seeming too daunting. While driving to visit relatives one Sunday, I slumped in the backseat of my parents' car and peered at my face in the vanity mirror when my mom pulled it down to inspect her lipstick. What I saw wasn't pretty: ghastly pale face, circles the color of eggplant under my eyes. A week later, after getting much weaker, I was diagnosed with a scorching case of mono. That meant complete bed rest until I was better. No school. No activities with friends or boyfriend. No Senior Shore Trip. And no prom.

The dress went back in the closet, and the limo was cancelled. I can't remember if the cost of my prom tickets to the Richfield Regency was refunded. I think I would have been more miserable about the situation if I hadn't been so ill, hallucinating and sweating as I lay in my childhood bed with the pink and green patchwork quilt.

My siblings and I were never allowed TV in our rooms, but in light of my condition, my dad rolled in a thirteen-inch black and white set and put it at the foot of my bed. While I convalesced, I watched soaps, cartoons, "The Golden Girls." When prom night rolled around, my boyfriend visited briefly, fleeing quickly from the stuffiness of the room and the sights and smells of my dirty hair and unbrushed teeth, no doubt. My grandma called to say hi and tell me to hang in there.

I sighed and sat back in my nightie, turning on the TV. I flipped around until I found a kooky program on FOX called "The Tracey Ullman Show." Tracey Ullman made me smile with her skits, but it was the crudely drawn, four-fingered, yellow people that made me laugh, probably for the first time in weeks. It was "The Simpsons," making their debut in bumper format on the show, and I loved it.

The little snippets couldn't have been longer than thirty seconds apiece, but they made an unmistakable impression. From that moment on, I became a lifelong "Simpsons" fan. My then-boyfriend went back to his home country and things ended shortly afterward. Since that time, there were countless more dates and several long-term relationships, but none as lengthy and unwavering as my one with Homer, which is going on nineteen years and strong. Whenever I tell people about this novel, many adults strain to remember the details of their prom. But I will always remember my prom night with Homer J. Simpson.

From the Desk of Reggie Meany

Iley,

I was on Newbury Street with my wife last week and saw your photos at the Peter Spring Gallery. I had no idea that you were doing so well with your work! I ask Therese to keep me updated on anything new that's going on down there in the basement, but she never has much to report. Congrats on your success. I know you will be an inspiration to many of our students here.

Reggie Meany

Rockin' with Iley and Friends

Some of the songs playing in heavy rotation while I was working on *Love in the Time of Taffeta* (I thought about listening to songs that were popular when I was of prom-going age, but wisely refrained in the end):

Interpol—"NARC"
The Replacements—"I Don't Know"
Dinosaur Jr.—"Little Fury Things"
Beastie Boys—"Shadrach"
Finley Quaye—"Sunday Shining"

Green Day—"Whatsername"
Michael Nesmith—"Different Drum"
Rupert Holmes—("Escape") "The Piña Colada Song"
Oojami—"Fantasy"
Figurine—"New Mate"

The Upper Crust—"Minuet"
The Beach Boys—"Hang on to Your Ego"
David Bowie—"Queen Bitch"
The New Pornographers—"Chump Change"
Television—"See No Evil"

Supergrass—"Moving"
Devo—"Gut Feeling"
Ben Folds—"Landed"
John Mayer—"Something's Missing"
Billy Strange—"The Rockford Files"

EUGÉNIE OLSON

David Olson

EUGÉNIE OLSON lives in Somerville, Massachusetts, with her husband, David, their two cats, Loki and Kiddun, and their fish, Lulu. Her interests include belly dancing, low rider and hot rod cars, and make-up. This is her third book.